Gringos

BOOKS BY CHARLES PORTIS

GRINGOS

CHARLES PORTIS

A Novel

THE OVERLOOK PRESS
New York

First published in the United States in 2000 by
The Overlook Press, Peter Mayer Publishers, Inc.
141 Wooster Street
New York, NY 10012
www.overlookpress.com

For bulk and special sales, please contact sales@overlookny.com

Library of Congress Cataloging-in-Publication Data

Portis, Charles.
Gringos / Charles Portis.
p. cm.
1. Americans—Mexico—Fiction. 2. Mexico—Fiction. I. Title.
PS3566.O663 G7 2000 813'.53—dc21 00-055752

Manufactured in the United States of America
ISBN 978-1-58567-093-2
3 5 7 9 8 6 4 2

GRINGOS

CHRISTMAS AGAIN in Yucatán. Another year gone and I was still scratching around on this limestone peninsula. I woke at eight, late for me, wondering where I might find something to eat. Once again there had been no scramble among the hostesses of Mérida to see who could get me for Christmas dinner. Would the Astro Café be open? The Cocina Económica? The Express? I couldn't remember from one holiday to the next about these things. A wasp, I saw, was building a nest under my window sill. It was a gray blossom on a stem. Go off for a few days and nature starts creeping back into your little clearing.

I bathed and dressed and went downstairs to the lobby. Frau Kobold hadn't opened her door yet. She had a room on the ground floor and by this time she was usually sitting in her doorway. She parked there in her high-back wickerwork wheelchair and read paperback mysteries and watched the comings and goings. Fausto himself was at the desk. Beatriz, poor girl, finally had a day off. Fausto saw me but kept his head down, pretending to be absorbed in some billing calculation.

"Well, Fausto, I'm back. *Feliz Navidad.*"

". . . *días,*" he muttered. He was annoyed with me because I had paid him two months rent some weeks back. Now he had spent the money, and I was staying free in his hotel, or so he viewed it. He disliked these *anticipo* payments. Much better that I should get behind in the rent, like everybody else, and be beholden to him. I had arrived in the night, too late to check my mail, and he handed me a letter and a long note, in a flash of fingernails. Not otherwise odd in appearance, Fausto made a show of his high-gloss nails. They were painted with clear lacquer, to indicate, I think, that he was of that class of men who did not have to grub in the earth with their hands.

"*Gracias.*"

"Joor welcome."

The letter was from my unknown enemy who signed himself "Ah Kin" this time. He also called himself "Mr. Rose" and "Alvarado." Or was it a woman? The letter was postmarked here in Mérida, and it read, without date or salutation, "Well, Mr. Jimmy Burns, I saw your foolish red face in the market again today. Why don't you go back where you belong and stay there?" Ah Kin (He of the Sun) used a Spanish typewriter, with all the tildes and accent marks, but I had the feeling he was a gringo. The note was a long telephone message, taken down by Beatriz. A hauling job in Chiapas.

I went outside and smoked a cigarette, looking this way and that, the very picture of an American idler in

Mexico, right down to the grass-green golfing trousers. They had looked all right on the old man from Dallas but they made me feel like a clown. They were hot and sticky, too, made of some petroleum-based fiber, with hardly any cotton content. The town was quiet, no street cries, very little traffic. Christmas is subdued in Mérida. Easter is the big festival. Holy Week, when all the fasting and penitence is coming to an end, I could sense nothing in the air. Art and Mike had told me that something was stirring. What? Just something—coming. They couldn't say what. We would see. It was old President Díaz who said that nothing ever happens in Mexico until it happens. Things rock along from day to day, and then all at once you are caught up in a rush of unforeseen events.

The street frontage of the Posada Fausto was not very wide. There was a single doorway at sidewalk level, and beside it a small display window, like a jeweler's window, backed by a velvet curtain. A blue placard behind the glass read SE VENDE. Strangers paused to look but found nothing on display other than dead beetles. What was for sale? The nearsighted drew closer. Finally they realized it was the hotel itself that was being offered. Fausto's hope was that one day some strolling investor or whimsical rich man would stop dead in his tracks there and throw up his hands and cry out, "Just the thing! A narrow hotel on Calle 55! Between El Globo Shoe Repairs and a dark little bodega!" The sign had been there for years, along with the same bugs.

My truck was parked across the street in an enclosed lot. The watchman, old Paco, was asleep in his sentry box, and the wooden gates were secured in exaggerated fashion, like some Houdini contraption, with great looping chains and huge flat padlocks shaped like hearts, and long-loop bicycle locks. It was all a bluff, and if you knew where to look there was a snap link that undid the whole business. There it was in the corner, my white Chevrolet with a camper shell. The old truck was sagging a bit, getting a bit nose-heavy with age. A film of red dust had settled over it. The engine fired up first shot.

I had decided to drive over to one of the tourist hotels on the Paseo Montejo. Their dining rooms would be open. A big gringo breakfast there would be expensive but would hold me for the rest of the day, what with a few supplementary rolls stuffed in my pockets. Then I would go out to the zoo for a few minutes and look over the fine new jaguar.

Paco jumped up in his box and waved me on through, as though he had been on top of things all along. As I was going around the *zócalo,* the central plaza, a girl flagged me down and jumped in beside me without invitation. It was Louise Kurle, the ninety-pound woman, in her tennis cap with the long visor, with her mesh bag and her tape recorder.

She said, "Say, where have you been anyway?"

"Dallas."

"I've been looking for you. I need a ride. Can you take me out to Emmett's place? You need some white shoes and a white belt to go with those pants."

"Where's your car? Where's your strange husband?"

"He's out of town."

"Where?"

"I'm not supposed to say."

"Ah."

"You know how Rudy is."

"I do, yes."

"But first I want to go to church. Come and go with me."

"All right."

"Look what I've got."

She had a package of Fud bacon, a good brand, already limp from the heat, and a small bottle of imitation maple flavoring. She and Emmett were to have a bacon and pancake feed. I was invited.

She wanted to go to the cathedral, but I thought that was too grand for us and I drove instead to a lesser church beside a small park. Everyone was moving inside at that Indio quickstep, the men doffing their straw hats and the women pulling up their rebozos over their heads. Louise and I composed ourselves for public worship and entered the dark vault. Not being a Roman Catholic, I took up the position of respectful observer, at the very back, from which point I could just make out flickering candles and the movement of a young priest in white. I sat alone in a pew and recited the Lord's Prayer, the King James version from Matthew, asking forgiveness of debts instead of trespasses. I carried on my business largely in Spanish but I still prayed in English. Louise had to be in the thick of things. She wasn't a *católica* either but she went all the way up front to get in on the ceremony and the wafers. I could see her white cap bobbing up and down, all bill. What was she doing now? Recording people at prayer?

Children stopped to stare at my green trousers, better suited for the links. Off to my left in an alcove there was a gray marble figure, a barefooted man, some medieval figure in short belted coat and flat Columbus hat, shedding two marble tears. He was about three-quarters life size, standing on a pedestal, the whole thing fenced off with a low wooden rail. There was a gate and a contribution box, with people standing in line, each waiting his turn to approach the statue and give thanks or ask for something. Surely that was a graven image. It always took me by surprise to find these secondary activities going on during a mass. I knew the woman at the end of the line. Lucia something. She worked at a juice bar, cashier now, up from squeezer. Then I saw Doc Flandin holding the marble feet. He had a fierce grip on them with both hands and he appeared to be demanding something, not begging, though it's hard to tell with that kind of anguish. I hadn't seen him since his wife died.

The people behind him had begun to stir. Doc was taking more than his allotted time. Or maybe they didn't like his belligerent manner in the face of this mystery. Suddenly he dropped his hands. He was done. He had finished his pleading and was off like a shot, scuffling along, head down, for the door. A strange scene. I had never known Doc to take more than a scholar's formal interest in the church.

Louise had two more stops to make. She took a jar of something that looked like pickled beets to some Indian friends who lived north of town off the Progreso highway. It was a Christmas present. The Mayan family gathered in puzzlement around the jar of red matter. Then she delivered another gift, a Spanish songbook, to an older woman who lived nearby. I watched her standing in the doorway of the hut, trying to explain to the old woman what it was, singing a little. Louise was a good girl. Some days she went out into the countryside plucking bits of blowing plastic from bushes so the goats could get at the leaves. She truly wished everyone well, reminding me of my grandfather, a Methodist preacher, who included the Dionne quintuplets and the Postmaster General in his long, itemized prayers. Louise and Rudy were graduates of some college in Pennsylvania and had come down here to investigate flying saucer landings. Her degree was in Human Dynamics. Rudy had one, a dual degree, he said, in City Planning and Mass Communications. First he would build the city and then he would tell everybody about it in the approved way.

Emmett lived in a trailer park out by the airport. I took a back road and ran over a dead snake on the way. Louise turned on me. "You just drove right over that snake."

"That was an old broken fan belt."

"It was white on the bottom. Do you think I don't know a snake when I see one?"

I told her he was already dead and that women were easily taken in by serpents. Yes, she said, but even running over a dead one in that heedless way showed a lack of delicacy. I had to concede the point. Little Louise was pitching in to help with my program of moral improvement if no one else was.

Three hippies were trudging along the back street in single file. One wore a comic Veracruz hat, a big straw sombrero with a high conical crown that came to a point. Louise waved to them. "A lot of New Age people passing through town." That was her term for hippies.

"What's the occasion?"

"I don't know. They all seem to be going to Progreso."

We had difficulty raising Emmett. He lived in a sturdy trailer, the Mobile Star by name, all burnished aluminum, very sleek, but no longer mobile, at the rear of the park. The wheels were gone, and it rested on concrete blocks. He had bought it here, *in situ,* some years ago, from another American. This was his home now. He didn't like hotel rooms and he didn't like the feudal bother of maintaining a house in Mexico, with servants running underfoot and a parade of vendors coming to the door. This way he could live in an exotic land and at the same time withdraw into his own little American box.

We knocked and called his name. No answer. I knew he must be on the grounds because his air conditioner was humming, or rather his evaporative cooler, which didn't pull as many amps as a real air conditioner, with a compressor. It didn't cool as well either if the air was at all humid.

We set off to look for him, and then he opened the door. "All right. I'm here. I heard you. You have to give people time to get to the door. I can't be at the door one second after you knock." You would think we had caught him upstairs in the tub. He was touchy about his poor hearing. He had heart problems, too, and the worst kind of diabetes, where they cut your legs off and you go blind. His sixth or seventh wife, a local woman, had recently left him.

I said, "How's the single life, Emmett?"

"It's killing me."

Louise presented him with his Christmas gift, a clip-on bow tie, and then apologized several times because she had nothing for me. She and Emmett prepared the food. He liked his bacon burnt. I stirred the maple flavoring into a can of corn syrup. It turned out well enough though I believe I could have gotten a more uniform blend if I had first heated the syrup. The dinner was good—salty and sweet and puffy and greasy all at once. A few pancakes were left over, but nobody ever leaves strips of crisp bacon lying around, nobody I know.

We sat back and Emmett poured us each a *copita* of brandy. He talked about his new medicine and how effective it was. Soon, to my alarm, our chat drifted into a confessional.

Louise said, "I've really found myself here. I could be happy here keeping a herd of milk goats. Rudy hasn't quite found himself yet."

Emmett said, "My life is over, for all practical purposes. I no longer have enough money to keep a woman." He looked back on his long bright empty days in Mexico and said he had lost his honor over the years. He hadn't noticed it going. Small rodents had come in the night and carried it away bit by bit on tiny padded feet. The best I could do in this line, the most I was willing to do, was to say that I hoped to be more considerate of other people in the coming year. Louise gave me a cold look.

Being a facetious person I got no credit for any depth of feeling.

She kissed Emmett on top of his bald head and popped his suspenders and went out for a swim in the pool. This trailer park had all the amenities. There was a lull. She had a way of leaving people speechless in her wake. We had already gone over my trip to Texas. A retired couple had come down here to spend the winter touring the ruins in their motor home, a huge thing, of the *Yamato* class, with about ten feet of overhang behind the rear wheels. After a week or two of it, they longed for home but had no stomach for driving the thing back. I was hired for the job. They insisted on taking the coastal route, which they thought would be a straight and simple shot, but the road was all broken up from the pounding of oil rigs and sugar-cane trucks and farm combines. At Tampico there was a storm, and we had to wait five hours for the Pánuco ferry. Water was running a foot deep in the city streets. The *Yamato* plowed right through it. We had to stop every few hours and let the fat spaniel do his business on the roadside. Or not do it, as the whim took him. He wouldn't be coaxed or hurried.

But they were nice people and paid me well and even gave me some clothes, this green resort attire. In Dallas I bought an old Chevrolet Impala and drove it down to Belize and sold it. You can always unload a big four-door Chevrolet or Ford there, for service as a taxicab. They know what they want. You can't force a sale. Then I came back to Mérida by bus.

Emmett pulled the curtains and began moving about in a stealthy way. I knew more or less what was coming.

He brought out a shoebox, inside of which, wrapped in a towel, was a Jaina figurine.

"What do you think?"

I looked it over. "It's a nice piece."

"Nice? It's mint. What do you think it would bring in New Orleans?"

"I couldn't even make a guess, Emmett. I'm out of touch. You know I'm out of the business now."

He smiled. I was riding the bus these days and living at the Posada Fausto and wearing castoff clothing and still no one believed me.

"You might ask Eli."

"I bought it from Eli."

"Well, whatever you do, I don't want to know about it. I really am out of the game. You might pass that word around."

"I was just curious about the current value. I wanted you to see it. You're not the only one around here with an eye for these things. I don't plan to sell it right away. It's a wonderful investment."

It was an investment worth about $35 and there was no telling what he had paid Eli Withering for it. The piece was six or seven inches high, a terra cotta figure of a haughty Maya woman, seated tailor-fashion, with earlobe plugs, bead necklace and upswept hairdo. She held a fan or rattle across her body. There was a piece just like this under glass in a Mexico City museum, dated 800 A.D., and it too was a fake, or a fine copy, as we say.

This one was in mint condition all right. An old grave-looter named Pastor had minted it very recently in his shop at Campeche. It wasn't worth much, unless you could find another gullible buyer, but in a sense it wasn't altogether a fake. Pastor had come by a genuine Maya mold from the island of Jaina and he used it to press out and bake a few of these things now and then. Maybe more than a few. He was getting careless. He had left a sharp ridge on this one, untrimmed, where the base of the mold had pressed against the excess clay. The ridge was much too sharp and fresh. Along the back he had beveled off the clay with his thumb, the way you do with putty on a window pane.

Things had turned around, and now it was the palefaces who were being taken in with beads and trinkets. Emmett carefully wrapped it again and put it away in a drawer. I dozed. I had work to do, bills to pay, an overdue delivery job in Chiapas, but not today. Emmett read a detective novel. He and Frau Kobold read them day in and day out, preferably English ones and none written after about 1960. He said the later ones were no good. The books started going wrong about that time, along with other things. I put the watershed at 1964, the last year of silver coinage. For McNeese it was when they took the lead out of house paint and ruined the paint. I forget the year, when they debased the paint.

Poor Emmett. He had been here more than thirty years, perhaps the only person ever to come to Mexico seeking relief from intestinal cramps, and still he thought he could beat a *zopilote* like Eli Withering, a hard-trading buzzard, at his own game. Emmett came from Denver and went first to Tehuacán for the mineral water treatment, then drifted on to Mazatlán, San Cristóbal, Oaxaca, Guanajuato, Cuernavaca, Mérida, in that order. It wasn't a natural progression or one easy to understand. Along the way he had been married and divorced many times. He could still call all the wives by name. Now his money was gone, from the family-owned chain of movie theaters in Colorado, or almost gone.

I said nothing about the anonymous letter. It was unlikely that Emmett would write such things, but then sometimes he was out of his head, from all that medication.

Later that evening Louise came by the hotel and gave me some green figs and a handmade card for Christmas. She had tried to give Frau Kobold a little knitted belt of some kind, only to be turned away at the door.

"What's wrong with that old woman?"

"She won't accept charity from strangers. I've told you that, Louise."

"A Christmas gift is not charity."

"No, but that's her way. I wouldn't worry about it. Just leave her alone."

She walked around inspecting my room. She pulled the curtain and looked into the closet, which was so shallow that the coat hangers hung at a slant. She asked if she could use my bathroom. When she came out she said, "I didn't really have to go but I wanted to see how you had organized your bathroom. I wanted to check out your shaving things and your medicine cabinet."

"Well? What did you think?"

"I knew you wouldn't have much stuff. I knew it would be neat and noncommittal. Where are all your Mayan things?"

"I don't have any."

"You must have one or two things. Some keepsakes."

"No, I'm not a collector."

"You just dig things up and sell them."

"I used to. A little recovery work, that's all. People make too much of it."

"Rudy says you're not really a college-trained archaeologist."

"Well, he's right about that. All I know is that the older stuff is usually at the bottom."

"You know, I was looking at you today in the truck and you look better at a distance than you do up close. I mean most people do but in your case the difference is striking."

"I'm sorry to let you down."

"That's all right. Can you see anything out of this window?"

"Not much. Just a wall back there and a little courtyard below. A pile of sand and a broken wheelbarrow."

"If I lived here I would have a room with some kind of view."

"I did have one, up front, but I had to move out. I couldn't get any sleep. The women wouldn't leave me alone. They were out there at all hours of the night throwing pebbles against my window."

"Uh huh. Don't you wish."

"You say that but here you are."

"Not for long. I'm way behind on Rudy's tapes. I've still got a lot of typing to do tonight."

YOU PUT things off and then one morning you wake up and say—today I will change the oil in my truck. On the way out I looked in on Frau Kobold. I threaded a needle for her. She was no seamstress but she did do a little mending. "You forgot my cakes," she said. I told her, once again, that when I was out of town she should get Agustín, the boy, to fetch her cakes. "Agustín doesn't show the proper respect," she said. We had been through this before. It was true, she and her husband had once been in Fox Movietone News, but how was the boy to know that? He was polite. What did she expect of him?

I stopped at the desk and gave Beatriz some money, and she promised to see that these confounded cakes were picked up and delivered. She and Fausto were listening to a soap opera on the radio. Fausto said they should put the story of his life on one of those shows and call it "Domestic Vexations" (*Vejaciones de la Casa*). He was suffering from a heaviness of spirit, an *opresión*, he said, because of troubles at home with his wife, all caused by her wicked sister, a *chismosa*, who had nothing better to do than spread poisonous tales.

I was feeling fine myself, back now in my honest khakis, all cotton, stiffly creased and starched hard as boards. I sent them out to a woman who knew just the way I liked them finished. West of town there was a clearing or series of clearings in the dense scrub thicket that covers Yucatán. It was a garbage dump where I changed my oil, adding my bit to the mess. Wisps of greasy smoke rose here and there from smoldering trash. Fumaroles from Hell. The air was so foul here that the rats couldn't take it. A city dump and not a rat to be seen. I parked on a sandy slope and while the oil was draining I shot grease into the fittings. Then I let the truck roll back, away from the oil puddle, so I could lie on my back in a relatively clean place and replace the drain plug and the filter. I poured oil into the filter before screwing it on, to prevent dry scuffing on start-up. It was a little trick I had picked up from a cab driver.

A car drove up. Doors slammed. I saw legs and heard American voices.

"What is this guy doing out here?"

"All by himself."

"Long-bed pickup with Louisiana plate. Some kind of sharecropper."

"With a stupid accent. Like Red."

"I've seen that truck before."

"Wait, don't tell me. I believe this guy is—*working on his car!*"

"That's all those cotton-choppers do. Day and night."

"They listen to car races on the radio."

I slid out from beneath the truck. A gang of hippies had piled out of an old Ford station wagon. They called themselves The Jumping Jacks, which name was stuck across the rear window, in letters made from strips of silver tape. The letters had an angular, runic look. The number of these clowns varied. I made them out to be seven this time, three males and four females, though they were hard to count, like the *chaneques* (chanekkies) in the woods. Anyway, a full load for the old Ford Country Squire.

Back in October at Tuxpan they had stolen three ignition wires from my truck. I saw them there on the waterfront as I was going into a café. When I came out they were gone and my wires were gone and a newsboy told me the gringo *tóxicos* in the Ford *guayin*, the station wagon, had been under my hood. I hadn't seen them since, but the car was unmistakable—cracked glass, no wheel covers, a red sock stuffed in the gas filler spout. Once black, the wagon was now streaked and blotched. They had painted it white with brushes, using some kind of water-based paint. A lot of it had peeled off in long curls. It was the only paint job I had ever seen blow away.

The leader was a big fellow with dirt necklaces in the fleshy creases of his neck, a fat man in his forties, with curly black beard, silver earrings, a fringed black vest with no shirt underneath, a rotting blue bandana on his head, and loose white *campesino* trousers. They were cinched up with a rope like pajamas, and the bottoms were stuffed into green canvas jungle boots. Big Dan looked like a wrestling act, beef gone to fat, but with his costume not quite worked out. It wasn't all of a piece yet. Maybe an old biker. Almost certainly an ex-convict. I could see the letters AB—for Aryan Brotherhood—tattooed under his left breast. It was a rough, homemade job done with a pin and spit and burnt match-heads.

He grinned at me, coming forward with a knobby walking stick, taking golf chops at cans and clods. The others hung back. The two boys were much younger than Dan. A pair of cueballs, these fellows, with shaved heads and vacant eyes. Much better than long hair. No hair at all meant you were at a more advanced stage of revolt. One of the girls, or a tall woman rather with lank brown hair, squatted where she stood and lifted her skirt and took a long noisy leak right there on the ground in front of everybody.

Dan called me Curtis. He said, "Merry Christmas to you, Curtis."

"You too."

"And *mucho* happiness for the new year."

The girls laughed. I had seen one of them before, and not, I thought, in connection with this crew. She was a little rabbit they called Red, standing about barefooted on the hot sand. She looked like a Dust Bowl child, a bony waif in a thin cotton dress that hung straight down to her knees. I had seen that face before but couldn't place it.

Dan said, "Well, did you get it fixed?"

"Just about."

"Curtis says he's just about got his truck fixed. What a relief that must be."

The girls laughed again.

"Hey, pal, just having a little fun. My name is Dan. These are my friends. We're The Jumping Jacks and we come from the Gulf of Molo."

"Where is that?"

"It's beyond your understanding, I'm afraid."

"Then why tell me at all?"

"Hey, don't come back at me so fast. We're getting off on the wrong foot here. I was hoping you might be able to help us. We lost all our things. We rely on charity, you see, for our daily needs."

"You came to a poor country to do your begging."

"Not just to beg."

The others chimed in.

"We came down here to clarify our thoughts."

"We have found the correct path."

"Big Dan, he is a lot of man. He is one set apart."

"We have fled the madness and found the gladness."

"People call us trash and throw turnips at us."

"Dan is more than our father."

"We're on our way to the Inaccessible City of Dawn."

"But *El Mago* didn't show up."

Dan spoke sharply to them. "Hey, none of that now. Didn't I tell you about that? Not another word on that." He turned back to me. "I can see you are not a person of wide sympathy, Curtis. Nothing escapes me. I can see right into your soul. Would you believe we have now made twenty-four enemies in the north and twenty-four enemies in the south? No lie. You are exactly the twenty-fourth person in Mexico to find us loathsome and undesirable."

"I would believe fifty-four, Dan."

"Hey! Would you listen to this guy! He keeps coming right back at me!"

He jabbered away, and I went on with my work, opening cans of oil. There was a rustling in the thicket. It was a browsing goat, a billy goat, shouldering his way through the brush. His coat was the color of wet sand.

Dan became agitated. "A goat! After him! An unblemished ram! Get the goat!"

The two boys went crashing into the thicket.

"You too, Red! Go, go! I want that animal! Get him! His name is Azazel! He's carrying off all the sins of the people! I must lay my hands on him and say some words!"

"And cut his throat!" said the tall woman.

Red dashed off to help. The other two girls took up the cry, facing each other and going into a hand-slapping game. "Get that goat and cut his throat! Get that goat and cut his throat! What does Dan say? Dan says get the goat. What does Beany say? Beany says cut his throat. . . ."

I finished with the oil and slammed the hood down. I had lost sight of Dan. He had wandered around to the back of the truck and was poking about inside with his stick. When I got there he was pulling the top off a can of my vienna sausages.

He raised the can to me and said, "Your good health," and drank off the juice. "Soup of the day. Do you have any bread?"

"No."

"I can eat these things plain but let me tell you— say, you didn't take us for vegetarians, did you? Wandering herbivores?"

"I hadn't thought about it."

"People get us all wrong. We gladly eat the flesh of animals. When we can get it. Why would God give us sharp teeth if not to rend and tear things with? Let me tell you how I usually go about this. There are seven of these little men to a can. I take three slices of bread and make three foldover sandwiches, with two sausages to each piece of bread, don't you see. Then I take the seventh one, the odd man, and just pop it into my mouth naked, like a grape. I've done it that way for years, and now you tell me you don't have no bread."

I said nothing. He shrugged and ate the sausages. "Do you have anything else to spare? I mean like sardines or beer or shoes or Mexico rum? Just anything in that line. I like your sleeping bag, all rolled up nice and tight like that. Your plastic lantern, too. I'll bet that thing comes in handy. Does it float or blink or have some special features I should know about? We could use a good light. The nights are long and we stumble in darkness. Maybe we could look through your stuff and just pick out what we want. I know you must set great store by all these material possessions but look here, my friend, it's the season for giving and you have so much."

More laughter from the girls. The tall woman said, "Or maybe he could just lend us a million pesos till payday."

"That's not a bad idea, Beany Girl. It works out well for him too. We get *mucho dinero* for our pressing needs, and he gets to keep all his much-prized possessions. But I don't know about this guy. You might think he would say, '*See see, Seenyore*, your house is my house and my house is your house,' but no, not this guy. Ask Curtis for bread and he don't even give you a stone."

His jocular manner had a dark edge to it that was meant to be unsettling, but it was a transparent act, a bit of old movie business, not well done. The two boys and little Red came back with no goat. A child can hem up a goat, but these three couldn't catch a goat. They talked about it. Beany Girl said that they hadn't really tried. There was a silence. Then, on what must have been a signal from Dan, all of them picked up rocks and looked at me. They stood perfectly still with their mouths gaping. They were a clan of early hunters in a museum diorama. And the rocks were big, not missiles but clubs.

I was wiping my hands on a rag and moving to the cab. I said, "Well, I guess I can spare a few beers. I keep some cans of Modelo in a cooler behind the seat here." I had rigged up a shallow storage compartment back there, really just a raised and squared-off cover made of sheet metal. It ran the width of the cab and appeared to be a structural part of the floor. I kept my double-barrel shotgun there, an ancient L. C. Smith 12-gauge with exposed hammers and double triggers. I had bought it from a hunting guide called Chombo. It was about sixty years old, and long too. I had sawed two inches off the barrels and the thing still looked like a goose gun.

I pulled it out and cocked both hammers and walked over to Dan and touched the muzzle lightly to his belly at the parting of his vest. His flesh jumped in a little spasm from the hot metal.

"No, I guess not. No beer today, Dan. This was all I could find."

"No need to get heavy, man. Have we offended you in some way?"

"Heavee," said Beany Girl.

I asked for some identification. Dan said he had none, that he never carried anything on his person.

"Maybe you ought to start. Where are your tourist papers?"

"Gone. Stolen. We got ripped off bad at the beach last night. We were supposed to meet someone at Progreso but he didn't show up. We had all our stuff in plastic bags. That's what we're doing here, man. I thought we could find some useful things here at the dump but this is the worst looking trash I ever saw."

I took his stick and pointed to a spot. "I want all of you to drop the rocks and sit on the ground, right there, back to back. No, better not say anything. Just do it."

Beany Girl had more spirit than Dan and she held back. She was just a little slow to comply, and I had to whack her across the neck with the knobby stick. The blow came as a surprise. It stung and was effective. She was lucky I didn't knock her brains out. A grown woman, squatting down like that in front of everybody. There was no *mingitorio* out here, naturally, but any decent woman would have gone behind a bush. Dan was picking and pulling at his beard. I had to pop him one, too, on the arm. "Get your hand down and keep it down. Nobody talks and nobody moves a finger unless I say so. You got that?"

When I had them all seated and arranged to suit me, I searched the car. There were no papers. I walked around the car breaking glass, punching at the cracked places with the stick. I smashed the headlights too. Then I propped one end of the stick against a wheel and broke it with my foot and flung the pieces away. Dan took that hardest of all. "My staff," he said. I raised the hood and ripped out all of the spark plug wires.

Something moved in the brush. I thought one of the hippies had slipped away. Even at rest these Jumping Jacks were hard to count. I wouldn't let them talk but I think they must have set up a high frequency hum to inter-fere with my head. When I reached the fourth or fifth one in my tally I became confused and had to start over again. But no, it was only the goat. He had come back, a curious fellow, bearing the load of sins well. He munched on a mouthful of briars and watched us with sleepy eyes.

I climbed into the truck with my shotgun and my handful of cables. Three of them were Packard-Delco wires that didn't belong on a Ford. I started the engine and almost at once the oil pressure needle moved. The pump had picked up the oil.

Dan said, "You got us wrong, man. No need for all this. You're not following the correct path."

Blood was roaring in my ears. I had to get away from these people before I did something. I could hardly trust myself to speak. "Don't let me catch you around this truck again," I said.

I still wasn't thinking straight. You let people annoy you and you forget your own best interests. It wasn't until late afternoon that I thought about checking to see if Dan were listed on one of Gilbert's Blue Sheets. I had missed a bet there. Gilbert ran a location service, nominally in El Paso but really out of an office in Mexico City, where these Blue Sheets come from, giving a rundown on Americans thought to be hiding in Mexico. I did a little work for him now and then, when I felt like it, just enough these days to get the monthly bulletins, blue paper stamped all over in red, CONFIDENTIAL, and AGENCY USE ONLY, and NOT FOR CIRCULATION IN U.S., and ALL RIGHTS RESERVED, GILBERT MOSS. Locate one of these fugitives for Gilbert and you were paid 40 percent of the posted fee. Bring the bird in yourself and you got 75 percent. Mostly they were runaway kids, alimony dodgers and the like, bond jumpers with a few tax evaders and swindlers and embezzlers, victims of surprise audits, and a very few violent criminals, but only those with substantial rewards on their heads. Gilbert was running a business and not a justice agency. The violent ones gave too much trouble.

I got my stack of Blue Sheets out of the closet and sat on the bed and went through them, starting with the latest ones. Dan may have been in there somewhere, but I lost interest in him when I came across a photograph of Little Red. I knew I had seen that face. Her name was LaJoye Mishell Teeter and she was from Perry, Florida. A runaway. The picture was a poor one, poorly Xeroxed from a poor reproduction of the missing persons column in *The War Cry*, the Salvation Army magazine. But there was no mistaking that rabbit face. The offered fee was $2,000, which meant $1,500 for me if and when I delivered her.

No time to lose. Back to the dump. I would bring Dan in and get the Judicial Police here, the federal police, to hold him on a turpitude charge, if not for kidnapping, while I checked him out with Gilbert by telephone. The girl was clearly under age.

I was too late. The Jumping Jacks were gone in their
Country Squire wagon, shattered windshield and all. They
were resourceful, I had to admit that. The two cueballs
must have stolen some more plug wires, eight of them this
time, plus a coil wire, and maybe a couple of headlights
too, or they would truly be stumbling in darkness tonight.
Dan had mentioned the beach. I drove to Progreso and
cruised up and down the beachfront. Nothing doing. I
should have burned that car up while I was at it.

ONE NIGHT in Shreveport I overhead a man trying to pick up a waitress in a bar. She asked him what he did for a living. He hesitated, then said, "I work out of my car." I thought he would have done better to lie, or even to confess to whatever it was he did out of his car, however awful, rather than to say that. I smiled over my drink in my superior way.

Now here I was years later, working out of my car, not smiling so much, and at a loss to say just what it was I did, out of my car. My truck rather. Light hauling, odd jobs. No more digging runs. I missed them too and I didn't think I would.

Two days after Christmas I was off for Chiapas with a load of mixed cargo. The long telephone message had come from the Bonar College people, who were camped out down there on a river bank, mapping a Mayan ruin called Ektún. Dr. Ritchie or one of his people had called my hotel from the Palenque bus station, the nearest telephone, and given Beatriz a shopping list of things they needed.

I had everything but the *embrague por la* Toyota—a Toyota clutch. That was the Spanish word for it all right, but in Mexico, where so many automotive terms had become Americanized, it was generally called a *cloche*. What kind of Toyota? Car? Truck? What year model? Did they want an entire clutch assembly? They didn't say or Beatriz didn't bother to take it down. Refugio and I had helped them carry their stuff in, and I couldn't remember seeing a Toyota.

Probably they had fried the disc pulling down trees and dragging blocks of stone around. But I wasn't going to buy one and then go through the agony of trying to return it. As a rule you get value for your money in Mexico, but it's hard to get any of it back, to get a deposit returned or any sort of refund. In their financial dealings with gringos, the Mexicans employ a ball-check valve that permits money to flow in only one direction. It can't back up. Buy the wrong one and I would have to eat that clutch, throwout bearing and all.

No *embrague* then, but I had everything else. Peanut butter they craved, and Ocosingo cheese and a sack of potatoes and flashlight batteries and two small hydraulic jacks and canned milk and pick handles and 35-millimeter color slides and bread and twenty-five gallons of gasoline and so on. I also had an old Servel gas refrigerator for Refugio. He had asked me to be on the lookout for one. It was too tall to transport upright—my camper shell was only cab high—so I stowed it sideways and hoped for the best.

Mérida, for all its associations with the Maya empire, is not really very close to any of the major ruins, except for

Uxmal and Kabah. Mayapán and Dzibilchaltún are nearby but they don't count for much, not as spectacles. I had a good 300-mile run ahead of me, south to Palenque on paved road, then another seventy miles or so of rough track through the woods. At Champotón on the coast I bought two buckets of fresh shrimp, one for Refugio and one for the college diggers. Refugio was crazy about shrimp.

I reached Palenque in the afternoon and worked the ruins there for an hour or so with my Polaroid camera, taking pictures of tourists at five dollars a shot. Hardly any business. The hippies, sunburnt and dazed, had no money, and the older gringos had their own cameras. I left the Mexican tourists alone, lest I be reported. As a foreigner I wasn't legally permitted to do this sort of thing.

Louise kept telling me the term "hippie" was out of date. She couldn't tell me why. These words come and go, but why had that one been pulled? The hippies hadn't gone away. There were even some beatniks still hanging around here and there in Mexico, men my age, still thumping away on bongos with their eyes closed, still lying around in their pads, waiting for poems to come into their heads, and sometimes not waiting long enough. I did perhaps use "hippie" too loosely, to cover all shaggy young Americano vagabonds. Refugio called the real hippies *aves sin nidos,* birds without nests, and *los tóxicos,* the dopers. These were the real hippies, the *viciosos,* the hardened bums, kids gone feral. I knew the difference between them and the ordinary youngsters knocking around on the cheap with their backpacks.

They came now the year 'round to Palenque, which is everyone's idea of a lost city in the jungle—real hippies, false hippies, pyramid power people, various cranks and mystics, hollow earth people, flower children and the von Däniken people—such as Rudy Kurle, with his space invader theories. At night they sat on top of the pyramids in the moonlight. They were right to come here, too, to see these amazing temples on a dark green jungle hillside. The scholars say that Uxmal has the finest architecture, and of course there is nothing to touch Tikal, for monumental ruins on the grand, Egyptian scale, but the hippies got it right instinctively. They knew Palenque was the jewel of Mayaland.

Between the ruins and the little town of Santo Domingo del Palenque there was a pasture where they camped out, these young travelers, with their vans and tents and ponchos. The rock music never let up. I stopped with my Blue Sheets to walk around the place and look them over. I took my flashlight and peered in tents and car windows. I put my light in their faces. What drove them to herd up like this in open fields? Even as a kid, and a foolish one, too, all too eager to please my pals, I couldn't see myself doing this.

It was getting dark. There was no one here I wanted. I gassed up at the intersection in town and headed inland, up the valley of the Usumacinta River. The road was paved for a mile or two then became washboard gravel. It was so rough that you could drive for miles on a flat tire and not know it. This was the dry season, so called, and the archaeologists were stirring again. In my experience it just rained a little less at this time. Damp season would be more like it. There was no moon. It wasn't a night for pyramid roosting.

When you see steel drums you're getting close to Refugio's trading post and salvage yard. He counted his wealth in fifty-five-gallon drums. They lay scattered along the road and in the woods all around his place, rusting away and more or less empty, but still holding the residue of various acids, solvents, herbicides, pesticides, explosives, corrosives, all manner of petro-chemical goo.

His people had heard me coming and were assembled outside to see who it was. The floodlight was on; dogs were barking. Small children jumped on my bumpers, front and back. A teenaged boy named Manolo was waving his arms. This was Refugio's son. He wigwagged me in around the old tires and plastic pipes to an aircraft carrier landing. The crowd parted to make way for Refugio—relatives, cronies, employees. He had the paunch of a *patrón* now but still he moved like a bowlegged and cocky little third baseman. The sleeves of his short-sleeve shirt hung well below his elbows. Around his thick neck he wore a Mayan necklace of tubular jade beads, with a heavy silver cross at the bottom.

"Jaime!"

"Refugio!"

We went into an *abrazo* there under the floodlight, with bugs swirling around us.

First I got the gifts out of the way. Some *futbol*, or soccer, magazines for Manolo, and a three-speed hair dryer for Refugio's wife, Sula, and a box of iodized salt. She was afraid of getting a goiter, like her mother. Refugio dredged up half the shrimp from the bucket with his hands and began shouting orders to Sula and the kitchen staff. This many *camarones* were to be boiled at once. Then peeled and chilled and served to him and him alone in a *coctel grande,* with *mayonesa* and green sauce. The rest could be fried with garlic and served up with a lot of rice. That would do for the rest of us.

He shooed everyone away, and we went to his office. It was like the waiting room of a cut-rate muffler shop, with an old brown plastic couch and some odd bits of automotive seating. Refugio sat at his desk, with Ramos at his feet, son of the late Chino, bravest dog in all Mexico. Refugio never would admit that old Chino tucked his tail when he heard thunder. I stretched out on the couch. Manolo brought me a cold bottle of Sidral, an apple-flavored drink, and a wet towel and a dry towel to refresh myself with. He showed me his Christmas present, which was a thirty-three-piece wrench set, all nicely chromed. Manolo had turned out to be a fine boy, from a brat. He was an only child, and Sula couldn't bear to wean him until he was four years old. He was a biter. He bit his playmates and threw rocks at strangers until he was twelve. Now here he was, a fine young man of sixteen.

Refugio turned on the air conditioner in my honor, though it wasn't very hot. The lights dimmed, as for an electrocution. It was only a small window unit but it put a strain on his generator.

"How is the bennee?" he asked me.

"Business is bad, Refugio. Life is hard for a gringo in the Republic these days. I'm selling hammocks on the street now."

"*¡No! Qué desgracia!*" He laughed and drummed his hands on the desk. "And the Doctor?"

This was Doc Flandin.

"I don't see him much anymore. He stays in his big house."

"His tobacco pipe is drawing well?"

"Oh yes."

Mexicans don't smoke pipes and they find them amusing.

"Still he throws his head back? So?"

"Not so much. He's not tossing his old white locks about these days."

"He works hard on his book, no?"

"So he says."

"It will be a hundred pages?"

"More like a thousand."

"No! This is one of your jokes!"

"I speak the truth. *Las mil y una.*"

He laughed and pounded the desk again. "No! What a miracle! So many leaves! Who could ever read them all?"

Not me. I went along with Refugio on that. Short was good in a book.

Then he became solemn and said, "My name is in this book, you know. Refugio Bautista Osorio. On many leaves."

"I know. Mine too. You and me and Chino. The doctor will make us all famous."

I told him about the Servel refrigerator and how the jet had been changed to use propane gas. I had found it in the port town of Sisal and cleaned it up. He summoned Manolo and another boy and told them to unload it and connect it to his gas bottle and light the burner.

"*¿Cuántos?*" he asked me.

I wrote "$150" on the palm of my hand and showed it to him.

"*Ni modo.*" No way. He made a quick slicing move on one index finger across the other. Too much. Cut your price in half. But he was only playing around. When a price really upset him, he called on St. James and the Virgin both in a whisper.

My pricing policy was simple. I doubled my money and then rounded that figure off in my favor. This refrigerator had cost me around $70, so my price was $150. My terms were cash on delivery, payment in full, *no acepto cheques.*

Refugio took a thermometer from the drawer and held it up. "I will place this in the box, and if the red line gets down to fifty in one hour, then we will talk about the value."

"There was no talk of fifty degrees before."

"Two hours. What can I do? You are my friend."

"All right. If you put that thing in the *congelador.*" The freezing compartment, that is.

"Gringos are so hard."

He wanted to barter and first he offered me an old hospital bed that cranked up and down. Then he dragged a wooden box across the floor, a hand grenade box with a rope loop at each end. It was there that he kept his *antigüedades*. He brought out a mirror, slightly concave, made of a wooden disk and shiny bits of hematite. Some Mayan queen had seen her face grow old in it.

"Worth more than two hundred."

"Yes, but not to me. I'm finished with that. No more relics. *Término*."

"That is what you say. Look. Fine orange ware." It was a ceramic cup.

"No, I'm serious."

Next a baroque pearl shaped something like a fish. Eyes and mouth and fins had been incised on it.

"No."

"And what do you say to this?"

At first I thought it was a piece of green obsidian and then I saw it was a carved lump of beautiful blue-green Olmec jade. The figure was a hunchbacked man with baby face and snarling jaguar mouth. Very old, even for Olmec. The nostril holes were conical. They had been drilled with wet sand and pointed stick, rather than with the later, bird-bone, tubular drill. I had no feel for Olmec art—more pathology than art—but I knew this weird little man was valuable. I knew a collector in St. Louis who would pay $7,500 for this thing, maybe $10,000. If a man wants something and you're any kind of salesman, you'll make him pay for it.

I knew that Refugio knew it, too, and would never trade it for an old icebox.

He said, "Green, see, the color of life. Dead rocks are brown."

"Where did you get this?"

"Who knows?"

"Tres Zapotes?"

"Who can say?"

"They make these things up at Taxco now, out of chrysolite and serpentine. On bench grinders."

"They don't make that one at Taxco. Look it over. *Impecable*. If you can scratch it with your knife, I give it to you."

"No, it's not bad. As a favor to a friend then. I'll trade you even."

"Ha! That is what you hope and pray to God for!"

What he wanted me to do was take a photograph of it and show the picture around in Mérida and New Orleans, put out some feelers. I had no intention of being a broker in the deal but I humored him and took a couple of shots with my 35-millimeter camera. He posed it beside the Sidral bottle to show the scale. The camera flash made him jump and laugh, as always.

Manolo reported that he couldn't get the Servel to do anything. I advised patience. The cooling to be gotten from a small flame and no moving parts was magical but slow. I reminded Refugio of his old kerosene refrigerator, which took three days to make mushy ice, if you didn't open the door. It was one of the earliest frost-free models.

"Turn it upside down for a bit, Manolo," I said. "Then try it again. Make sure it's level." I had heard somewhere that this headstand treatment did wonders for a balky gas refrigerator, though it seemed that any clots in the system would have been dislodged on the ride down.

Sula brought in the giant shrimp cocktail. The *camarones* were piled high in a soup bowl. Refugio squeezed limes over them and spooned mayonnaise and *salsa verde* on them. I asked him about the Ektún dig. What was all this about a Toyota clutch?

He threw up his hands. The subject disgusted him. He could no longer do business with those people. Dr. Ritchie was a good man, very amiable, but he was down with fever, and this new man, Skinner, who was running things now, was a person of no dignity, a monkey-head, a queer, and a rude animal, *una bestia brusca*. On and on he went. The woman who gave birth to Skinner was no woman at all but an old sow monkey, and his brother, if he had one, was worse than he was, certainly not a man of honor.

What Skinner had done, I gathered, was to insist that Refugio provide detailed price breakdowns on his goods and services, in such an offensive way as to suggest that Refugio was a crook. Nor would the man buy any steel drums or plastic pipe. And he had brought his own rope from the States! To Mexico, the home of rope!

"I can get his *cloche* in Villahermosa. One day and it's there. I can find anything he wants and Manolo can repair anything he can break but how can I do business with a monkey? No, I will never go back while that monkey-head is there."

And a good thing, said Sula, because Ektún was no place for people to linger around at night. For her part she was glad that he and Manolo had stopped going there. So many demons were lurking around those old *templos,* not to mention the *chaneques,* a race of evil dwarfs who lived in the deep *selva.* When you came upon these horrible little men in a clearing, they would point at you and jeer, making indecent noises, and they danced about all the time so you couldn't count them. They hated above all things to be counted. Sometimes they stole chickens.

Refugio was squeezing limes with both hands. "*¡Tu que sabes!*" he said to her. "What do you know? The *chaneques* don't really bother people very much, and as for the demons, all the world knows that they never show themselves in the light of day! At night, well, their powers are stronger, yes, in the hours of darkness they have certain powers, but not strong enough to interfere with a Christian! Not even with one of God's poorest servants! You know nothing of these things!"

All the same, she said, and be that as it may, Ektún was a place of evil gloom, and so was Yaxchilán, and Piedras Negras too, come to that, all those old abandoned cities of the *antiguos* along the river banks, and you couldn't pay her enough money to sleep for one night around those old stones.

Sula was Mayan herself, of the Chontal group, with heavy-lidded eyes and hook nose and receding chin. I had seen her face on a mossy stela at the Copán ruin, carved in stone a thousand years ago. She was one of the few Indians I had ever heard express strong feelings about such matters. The ones I knew—uprooted city dwellers for the most part, admittedly—showed little interest in the monuments of their ancestors. They neither feared nor venerated the *templos* of the old ones.

The Servel didn't make it to fifty at the given time, or even to fifty-five, but the door gasket was bad, I pointed out, and once Manolo had replaced it, the box would surely do the job. It would last for years too. Refugio wrote "$75" on his palm and showed it to me.

"That wouldn't even pay for my gasoline."

But I gave in and settled for a hundred. He agreed it was a good buy.

We stayed up late in the office talking about the old days, and one thing and another. Refugio fed tidbits to Ramos. He asked me to be on the lookout for a Tecumseh gasoline engine with a horizontal shaft, of about eight horsepower, and some of those little German cigarette-rolling machines that you used to be able to find in Veracruz. He asked me if I thought he needed one of those new water beds. "No." Motorized golf cart? "No." Food blender? "Yes, to make *licuados*. Milkshakes." Trash compactor? "No." It would take one the size of a house to compact his trash. He showed me an advertisement for elevator shoes in an American magazine. Could I get him a pair? One of the shoes was pictured, a brown loafer, which promised to give you an invisible three-inch lift above your fellow men.

"Three inches," he said. "How much?"

I showed him with thumb and finger. "Like that. About eight centimeters."

He studied the deceptive shoe with a dreamy smile. Three inches was a little more than he had thought.

I SLEPT ON the couch and was off early. I had breakfast as I drove. Sula had left me a sack of hard-boiled eggs, already peeled, and four buttered slices of Bimbo bread, some salt in a twist of paper, and a single *habanero* pepper pod, the world's hottest. Bimbo is like Wonder bread, or light bread, as we called it in Caddo Parish. I had told her many times that I preferred corn tortillas, but she took that to be a polite gesture or an affectation. She knew the *yanquis* likes their bread finely spun from bleached wheat flour. Sula felt sorry for me because I had no wife to look after me.

The washboard gravel ended just beyond Refugio's place. No more maintenance. From here on the road was just a rough slash across the hilly Chiapas rain forest. The drive had once been a shady one all the way, under the jungle canopy. Now there were cleared pastures with stumps where cattle ranchers had moved in. I met a log truck and saw a Pemex crew at work with their seismic gear, sounding the earth for pockets of oil. Here and there I passed a hut made of sticks and thatch, where a solitary farmer had squatted. This was his *finca*. It was more like camping out than farming.

The road, at this time, ended at the ruins of Bonampák, of the famous wall paintings, but I wasn't going that far. To reach Ektún and the Tabí River, you turned off to the left, or east, on a still more primitive track. I did so, and the trees closed in on me. Limbs whacked against my windows. I moved forward at a creep, but even so my poor truck was twisted and jolted about by rocks and bony roots. The glove compartment door flew open. Screws were backing out of their holes and nuts off their bolts. I had to hold my hand on the gearstick to keep it from popping out of gear. I saw a wild pig, a black squirrel as big as a house cat, darting green parrots. You don't expect parrots to be accomplished fliers, but they go like bullets.

I saw nothing human until I reached the fording place on the Tabí. There was a flash of yellow through the foliage. As I turned the bend, I made out a car stranded in midstream. It was a bright yellow Checker Marathon, towing a pop-top tent trailer. The trailer had been knocked sideways by the current.

Rudy Kurle. What was he doing out here? No use asking. How did he get this far in that rig? I honked my horn.

He was in the back seat, where he must have been asleep. He stuck his head out the window and shouted. "Hey, Burns! Great! This is great! Did you copy my Mayday?"

"What? No!" I could barely hear him over the rush of water.

"I need a jump start!"

He needed more than that.

He had been sitting there all night, dead in the water, trying to start the thing and calling for help on his CB radio, on one channel after another, until he had run his battery down. His DieHard had done died. I seldom turned on my own CB, and in any case there were no signals to pick up out here. The water was about knee deep, but with deeper potholes. He had dropped his right front wheel into one of these. I drove around him and positioned my truck on the hard ground of the opposite bank. I pieced together a chain, a nylon rope, and a nylon tow-strap.

Rudy wouldn't get out of the car to help. The water was too rough, or he didn't want to get his lace-up explorer boots wet, or something. Useless to ask why. Usually he wasn't such a delicate traveler. How long would he have sat there? The river was a tributary of the Usumacinta, tea-colored from dead leaves, only moderately swift at this time of year, and only about sixty feet wide at this ford. A bit more maybe. I'm a poor judge of distance over water.

I went out into the stream with my tow-line, jumping from rock to rock. Another of man's farcical attempts at flight. We keep trying but none of us, not even the high-jumper slithering backwards over his crossbar, ever gets very far off the earth. And yet we come down hard. My bad knee gave way on one of these landings, and I went head-first into the water and tumbled a ways downstream. I didn't matter, getting soaked, as I had to bob all the way under anyway to hook the strap to a frame member.

All the while Rudy was making suggestions. "No, no," I said. "Listen to me. Put it in neutral and just keep the wheels straight. Don't do anything else. Stay off the brakes. Stop talking."

First the chain came loose from my trailer ball, and then the nylon rope, twanging like a banjo string, snapped. The line parted, as the sailors say. Pound for pound stronger than steel! Such is the claim made for these wonder fibers, but I'll take steel. Third time lucky. I removed some rocks in front of his tires and then, in low-range four-wheel drive, in *doble tracción*, I yanked him loose and got him up on the bank, trailer and all, without stopping.

Rudy didn't thank me but he did offer me some food. He had brown cans of meat and crackers he had taken from his National Guard unit in Pennsylvania. All I wanted was a long pull on my water jug. I checked my tires for rock cuts. Wet rubber is easily sliced. Rudy showed me a nick in his bumper. "That's what your strap did." The bumper was decorated in the style of big Mexican trucks, with his road name, "The Special K," painted on it. That was his CB handle.

He said, "Wait a minute. Who told you I was going to Tumbalá anyway?"

"It was all over town when I left. There must have been something in the papers."

"Louise told you. Everybody wants to stick his nose into my business."

"Nobody told me. I'm not going to Tumbalá."

He thought that over as he spread meat paste on a survival cracker with his commando knife. "Well, it's funny, you coming along like this, right behind me."

"Yes, except I'm going to Ektún. This is not the road to Tumbalá."

"Your map says it is."

My map! He showed me. Yes, I remembered now. A month or so ago I had told him about this Tumbalá, a minor ruin on the Usumacinta, with curious miniature temples. They were small stone houses, built as though for people two or three feet high. Rudy was excited. This was his meat, tiny houses. Little rooms! An old logging road, no longer passable, even in four-wheel drive, led to the place, but you could follow it on foot easily enough. Quite a long hike, however. I had explained all this to him and sketched out a rough map.

"No, you came too far, Rudy. You didn't turn soon enough."

"Your map is not drawn to scale."

"Of course not. It's just a simple diagram. But it's easy enough to see where to turn off. You can't drive to Tumbalá anyway. I told you that."

"I was going as far as I could and then set up base camp."

He wore a bush hat with the brim turned up on one side, Australian fashion, and a belted safari jacket with epaulets, rings and pleated pockets, and he wanted to be known as "Rudy Kurle, author and lecturer." He and Louise were in Mexico to gather material for a book about some space dwarfs or "manikins" who came here many years ago from a faraway planet. There was no connection with the *chaneques*, as far as I knew. Their little men were benign, with superior skills and knowledge, and they had transformed a tribe of savages into the Mayan civilization. Not very flattering to the Indians, and it wasn't of course a new theory, except perhaps for the dwarf element. There had been recent landings as well.

As a geocentric I didn't find this stuff convincing. I knew the argument—all those galaxies!—a statistical argument, but in my cosmology men were here on earth and nowhere else, go as far as you like. There was us and the spirit world and that was it. It was a visceral belief or feeling so unshakable that I didn't even bother to defend it. When others laughed at me, I laughed with them. Still, the flying saucer books were fun to read and there weren't nearly enough of them to suit me. I liked the belligerent ones best, that took no crap off the science establishment.

Rudy was often gone on these mysterious field trips, to check out reports of ancient television receivers, pre-Columbian Oldsmobiles, stone carvings of barefooted astronauts strapped into their space ships. The ships were driven by "photon propulsion," although here in the jungle the manikins went about their errands in other, smaller, "slow aircraft." Rudy wouldn't describe the machines for me. He and Louise tried to draw people out without giving anything away themselves. There were thieves around who would steal your ideas and jump into print ahead of you. So much uncertainty in their work.

And so little fellowship among the writers. They shared a beleaguered faith and they stole freely from one another—the recycling of material was such that their books were all pretty much the same one now—but in private they seldom had a good word for their colleagues. There were usually a few of these people in temporary residence in Mérida. They exchanged stiff nods on the street. Rudy even expressed contempt for Erich von Däniken, his master, who had started the whole business, and for lesser writers too, for anyone whose level of credulity did not exactly match his own. A millimeter off, either way, and you were a fool. It was the scorn of one crank for another crank.

We dried off the contact points and the distributor cap and with a jump from my battery we got the Checker running again. The engine was a Chevrolet straight six, the old stovebolt six, very reliable but looking skinny and forlorn in that big engine bay. To help control this beast on the road, Rudy wore soft leather driving gloves perforated with many tiny holes. Inside the car there was a clutter of boxes, jugs, blankets, gourds, magazines, rocks, books— and a big scrapbook of newspaper clippings, telling of saucer landings in Russia and Brazil, near towns that could not be found in any atlas. The gas pedal was in the shape of a spreading human foot, with the toes all fanned out. It must have been on the car when Rudy bought it because he didn't go in for comic accessories. There was a press sticker on the windshield—PRENSA, in big red letters, courtesy of Professor Camacho Puut.

He followed me on to Ektún. Exploration by taxicab. He took that old Checker into places where few others would have ventured. Rudy was serious about his work. In the bars and cafés of Mérida I had heard anthropologists laughing at him, young hot shots who never left town themselves or who went out for a night or two and then scurried back.

We left the river for a bit and then came back to it downstream to the ruin site. Three pyramids of middling size, partly cleared, and a camp of red and blue tents. A canvas water bag hanging from a limb. A sagging grid of strings lay across the plaza. The Bonar College people stopped work and looked at us. No word of greeting. We came from the outer world bringing good things, and this was our welcome. No more joy here. The dig was falling apart. I had seen it all before.

Sula was right about the demons. The place was infested with them, many thousands of whom had taken the form of mosquitoes. They swarmed in my face as I got down from the truck and walked shin-deep in ground fog. It was cemetery fog from a vampire movie. A mockingbird perched on my bumper and pecked at the smashed bugs. Up high in the trees the howler monkeys were screaming. Our clattering arrival had set them off. It was like cries of agony from cats. You couldn't see them.

I took a bar of yellow laundry soap and went back into the river in my wet clothes. This was a little trick I had picked up years ago in Korea with the First Marine Division. You immerse yourself fully clad and have a bath and wash your clothes at the same time. Then you change into your dry dungarees, all rolled up and resting in your pack. Let dirty clothes rest for a while and they are almost as fresh as clean clothes. A bit stiffer, and the black glaze is still on the collar. There are tigers in Korea, but I never saw one. Nor had I ever caught a glimpse of a jaguar here in the Petén forest. Pumas, ocelots, margays, but not one *tigre*.

I went along to Dr. Henry Ritchie's tent and found him half asleep on a cot, behind a mosquito bar. His clothes were soaked with sweat. His breath came hard. A real gentleman, a good man, as Refugio said, and I always felt a little shame in his presence. Few *arqueos* had that effect on me. He knew my background but was always friendly. After all, as Doc Flandin said, permit or no permit, we all lived and worked by the same words, namely, *there is nothing hid but it shall be opened*.

In a minute or so he saw me sitting there on the stool. He gave me his trembling hand. It was cold. "Jimmy. You're here."

"Just now. I was out of town when your message came or I would have been here sooner. I hear you've been ailing."

"Oh, I've been through this before. Not quite so bad maybe. I can't keep anything down. Did you have a nice Christmas?"

"Very nice, thank you. I brought you some long cigars and a bucket of shrimp."

"Wonderful."

"Why don't I run you in to Villahermosa? I can have you there in the clinic tonight. That's where you belong. No use in punishing yourself."

"I don't know. Maybe tomorrow, if I'm no better. Can you stay over?"

"Sure. We can be off first thing in the morning. You can lie down in the back."

A man came barging through the flap and took off his dust mask.

"You're Burns?"

"Right."

"I'm Eugene Skinner. You should have reported to me first."

This was Skinner, the ape in a shirt. He was a nervous man, about my age, with kinky auburn hair, nappy hair, which must have suggested the monkey to Refugio. It reminded me more of a Duroc hog.

Then Rudy came in and wanted to know if he was at Tumbalá.

Skinner said, "No, my boy, this is Ektún. Which is to say, Dark Stone, or Black Stone. Who are you?"

I introduced him as a friend and a reporter.

Dr. Ritchie said, "Jimmy brought us some fresh shrimp, Gene."

"That's fine. How about the clutch?"

"I didn't bring one."

"They didn't have one in Mérida?"

"I don't know. You didn't tell me what model it was for."

"He doesn't know. We need a clutch, and he brings shrimp."

"What's it doing? Why don't we take a look at it?"

"It won't do any good to look at it."

He barged out again. I followed him and grabbed his arm. "Why haven't you taken Dr. Ritchie out of here? He's in bad shape."

"How? On a motorbike? If you and your pal Bautista had done your job, I would have some transportation here."

The expedition had begun with a respectable little motor pool, now reduced to a single motorcycle, owned by a young graduate student named Burt. The International

Travelall was down with a broken axle. The Nissan pickup was in a Villahermosa garage with a blown head gasket. Becker had returned to Chicago in his new Jeep Wagoneer, with a female student who had fallen ill. I was surprised to hear that Becker had bailed out. He who was so eager to get at it. He was a young rich man, a graduate of Bonar College (as was my friend Nardo, the Mérida lawyer) and a dabbler in archaeology. Becker was financing the dig. I think he must have seen himself as Schliemann at Hissarlik, or Lord Carnarvon at King Tut's tomb. Camp life didn't suit him, however, and when no treasures were turned up in a week's time, he went home, back to the trading pit of the Chicago commodities market, where things moved faster.

It might have been the digging itself. A man who has never dug a ditch or a well or a deep grave, as distinguished from the shallow grave of crime news, has no notion of the work required to move even a moderate amount of rocks and dirt about in an orderly way with hand tools. At this remote site there were no cheap labor gangs, only a few Lacondón Indians, and the professors and students had to do most of the work themselves. Becker must have looked at his little pile of dirt, his spoil, then saw how much remained to be removed before he could get down to work with the dental pick and the tweezers and the camel's hair brush. He despaired. It may have come to him in the night: *I am only Becker at Ektún.*

The Toyota pickup belonged to Skinner. He had driven down alone from Illinois, arriving a few days after the main party. The problem was that you couldn't disengage the clutch. Pressing the pedal did nothing. The flywheel of the engine was locked up to the driveline. I did what I called taking a look at it. Burt and I lay on our backs and examined the linkage and pooled our ignorance. It was alien to me. Some sort of Nipponese hydraulic booster up there, a slave cylinder. The only clutches I knew had a straight mechanical linkage. What I needed here was Manolo and his thirty-three wrenches. I was only a shade-tree mechanic, and an impatient one at that. Get a bigger hammer or put a bigger fuse in and see if anything smokes. That was my approach.

I decided on a show of violence. Burt and I got the truck going in the lowest forward gear, and I drove around and around the clearing, poking the gas pedal for a lurch effect, and pumping on the clutch pedal, hoping to pop something loose. It worked, to everyone's surprise. The clutch disc had stuck to the flywheel with rust or some fungoid rot and was now free again.

Skinner had been chasing after us, shouting and waving his arms. We were abusing his truck. Now he was doubly annoyed. All the to-do had ended with a quick fix, and he had made a spectacle of himself before his crew. He was a fat lady running after a bus.

Then he tried to beat me down on my prices. He went over the list, muttering, going into little fake body collapses. As the hated, profiteering middleman, I had seen this show before.

"You must think you've got a gold mine here, Burns."

"If it's such a gold mine then why can't you find anyone else to do it? What about the wear and tear on my truck? My prices are not out of line. I'm not even charging you for the clutch repair."

"Am I supposed to be grateful? It's not as though you actually did anything. I'm not even sure it's fixed. You and Bautista may be able to take advantage of Henry, but you're dealing with me now."

"You called me, I didn't call you."

"And this famous bucket of shrimp. I can't find the price listed. Where have you hidden it?"

"I was throwing it in free, as lagniappe, but now I want thirty dollars for it, and I want it now. I'm not going to stand here and haggle with you, Skinner. Pay me now or everything goes back. Nothing comes off that truck until I get my money."

A bearded engineer named Lund interceded. He took Skinner away to calm him down. In the end they paid. Lund paid me. It was all Becker's money anyway.

Some truckers refuse to lift things, but I wasn't proud in that way. We unloaded the goods and stowed them in the "secure room," which was a stone chamber in Structure II-A. Wonderful dead names these *arqueos* have for their pyramids. The entrance could be closed off with a ramshackle door made of poles and locked with a chain. Here the food was stored, and the more valuable pieces of equipment, and the finds, running largely to fragments of monochrome pottery. There were beads and other knickknacks sealed in clear plastic bags, and some chunks of organic matter—wood and charcoal—wrapped in aluminum foil, for carbon-14 dating. I saw nothing worth locking up. Pots put me to sleep. The romance of broken crockery was lost on me.

Great care would be taken here, every last pebble tagged. Then the loot would be sacked up and hauled away and dumped in the basement of some museum, where tons of the stuff already lay moldering. Buried again, so to speak, uncatalogued, soon forgotten, never again to see the light of day. But the great object would have been achieved, which was to keep these artworks out of the hands of people. Don't let them touch a thing! A sin! A crime against "the people!" By which they meant the state, or really, just themselves. At least Refugio and I had put these things back into the hands of people who took delight in them, if not "the people." We gave these pieces life again. Sometimes I thought there weren't enough of us doing this work. That was the way I put it to myself. I stole nothing. It was treasure trove, lost property, abandoned property, the true owners long dead, and the law out here was finders keepers. That was the best face I could put on it.

Rudy set up his tent camper, not bothering to ask permission. He sat on the black boulder, for which the place was named, and spoke into his tape recorder. "An extremely short astroport oriented from northeast to southwest," I heard him say. He stopped speaking as I approached but was in no way embarrassed.

"A word to the wise, Rudy."

"What?"

"Make yourself useful around camp and they may let you stay. They're short-handed. But don't make a lot of suggestions. Stay out of their hair."

"I know how to behave myself. How far is it to the big river?"

"Not far. Just remember, you're a guest here."

I walked out into the woods about a hundred yards, where there was an oblong structure standing alone, a *temescal*, a Mayan steam bath. Refugio and Flaco Peralta and I had punched a hole in the floor of this house years ago. We found nothing. Actually I lost something, my Zippo lighter, smoothest of artifacts, which rode a little heavy in the pocket. Some *arqueo* might turn it up in a hundred years, and with acid and a strong light bring up the inscription—CHAMPION SPARK PLUGS. I noticed that the carved panel above the door had been cut away with a chain saw. You could see the tooth marks in the stone. As soon as I got out of the business, people started buying everything. Slabs of stone.

There was a beating of wings. A flight of bats came pouring out of the doorway in panic, right into my face. No, they were birds. Swifts. Well named. They nested here but their life was in the air. They ate, drank, bathed, and even mated on the wing, if that can be believed. This aerial life was what the hippies were after. I had tried for it, too, perhaps, in my own way, but with me it was all a bust. I never got off the ground. I peered inside and saw that our pitiful hole was almost filled again with debris and guano. We had dug for treasure in a steam room, fools that we were. It took Doc Flandin and Eli to show us the ropes.

Back at the clearing Skinner was in another rage. "Who keeps moving this?" he said. It was a drafting table. No one confessed. I watched the excavation work at the base of Structure I. Burt was in charge of the job. His people had cut a ragged opening in the thing, such as I had never seen made by professionals. It was a bomb crater. They had broken through the limestone facing and were now into the rubble filler. They were going for the heart.

Mapping then, fine, and a certain amount of poking about and collecting of surface finds, nobody could object to that, certainly not me, but were they really authorized to make such a breach? I suspected them of exceeding the terms of their permit.

"Just a probe," Burt said. "We're going to put it back the way it was."

Some probe. I wondered if Dr. Ritchie knew about this. Well, it was no business of mine. I was in no position to object. Refugio and I would have used a backhoe if we could have gotten one into the woods. And they weren't going to find anything, just more rubble, perhaps the wall of a smaller, earlier pyramid. They had started too high above the base and they didn't have the labor or the equipment to do the job right.

The crew, a bedraggled lot, weren't even screening the spoil. They were two gringo boys, and two Lacondón Indians in long white cotton gowns, with bulging eyes and long black hair. These Lacondones were the last of the unassimilated lowland Maya. You didn't often find them working for hire. For what little cash they needed they sold souvenir bow-and-arrow sets for children that broke on the first pull, or the second. Only a handful of them were left, straggling about in the jungle, living in small clans. They burned copal gum as an aromatic offering to the old gods and kept to the old ways as best they could.

The younger one had some Spanish, and I asked if he knew a hunter named Acuatli who used to roam these parts with a 20-gauge shotgun slung across his back. He wore short rubber boots. Some years back this Acuatli had guided me and two Dutch photographers to Lake Perdido, over in Guatemala, where the Dutchmen took pictures of ducks and white egrets. We had no papers for Guatemala and no mule to carry our goods. We went up the San Pedro River and then followed an old *chiclero* trail overland. I made some money out of it but I wouldn't want to take that hike again. I learned, too, that slipping up on birds requires the patience of a saint.

The Lacondón said that Acuatli sounded like a Mexican name to him. By that he meant Nahuatl. He said in all his life he had never known a person named Acuatli. A few minutes later he told me that Acuatli was dead. It came to much the same thing. Sula had once told me that on the day the last Lacondón died, there would come a great earthquake, and a great wind that would blow all the monkeys out of the trees.

I bought a small bag of cacao beans from these two. Lund came by and wanted to know about Rudy. "Who is that guy? Can you vouch for him?" Lund was a surveyor who was plotting the site with his alidade and rod. He seemed to come third in command, after Skinner. A white towel was draped around his head and fashioned into a burnoose.

"Rudy's all right as long as you don't cross him," I said.

That night there was shrimp again, with onions and peppers and potatoes in a makeshift paella. It was good and there was plenty of it. The mess tent was a blue nylon canopy with mosquito netting hanging down on all sides. We sat on folding chairs and ate off card tables, or rather Carta Blanca beer tables made of sheet metal. There were two hanging lights, powered by a generator. A little cedar bush had been decorated as a Christmas tree. An electric bug killer hung on a pole outside. Bugs flew to the blue light and were sizzled on a grid.

A bath in the river and a good meal had perked up the diggers. Even Skinner was in a good mood. He held up a floppy tortilla and said that corn didn't have enough gluten in it to make a dough that would rise. Still, heavy or not, the flat bread it made was good, and yet nobody seemed to know it outside Latin America and the southern United States. Corn, potatoes, tomatoes, yams, chocolate, vanilla— all these wonderful things the Indians had given us. Whereas we Europeans had been over here for 500 years and had yet to domesticate a single food plant from wild stock.

The two females left in camp were Gail and Denise, both a little plump, with their brown hair cut short, so that you could see the backs of their necks, all the way up to where the mowed stubble began. Gail was the quiet one. I took her for a mouse and I was wrong about that. She prepared a tray of food to take to Dr. Ritchie.

"No, no," said Skinner. "He's coming. He's up on his feet now. I just went over the work log with him. He'll be along."

Rudy asked if they used a caesium magnetometer in their work. I was uneasy. This had an extraterrestrial ring to me. But no, there was such a device, something like a mine detector, I gathered, for sensing underground anomalies, buried stelae and the like, and they did have one here, though it was down. High tech or low, almost everything here was down. I was proud of Rudy for knowing about the thing.

Dr. Ritchie came stumbling in, and Gail got up to help him along.

Skinner said, "Here's our warlike Harry now. Look, there's a leaf on his shoe."

"Greetings, greetings. Anything left?"

Gail seated him across from me and took off his hat and served him. He was trying hard to be chipper. "Sure smells good. We're in your debt, Jimmy, for this fresh seafood."

"We can pull out tonight if you want to, sir. I can have you in the hospital by midnight. No use putting it off."

"Well, maybe tomorrow. I'm certainly no good to anybody like this. What do you think, Gene?"

Skinner shrugged. "Whatever you say. What's your fee on a deal like that, Burns? Double rate on a hospital run?"

"For you it would be double."

Dr. Ritchie jiggled his soup spoon. "Boys, boys."

Lund picked up on the theme of Indian superiority. He talked about their natural ways, how they were attuned to the natural rhythms of life, their natural acceptance of things, natural religion, natural food, natural childbirth, natural sense of place in the world, natural this, and natural that. All true enough, perhaps, but there was something a little bogus and second-hand about his enthusiasm. It was like some poet or intellectual going on and on about the beauties of baseball.

I lit a cigar and tuned out. We had the Indians to thank for tobacco too. They had given us these long green *puros* for solace. I watched the flashes of bugs being electrocuted. You couldn't hear the crackling sounds, or even the chugging of the generator, for the rushing noise of the river.

Skinner was soon at it again. ". . . an old and honored tradition, I know, this robbing of travelers in out of the way places of the world, but I broke your pal Bautista from sucking eggs and I'm going to break you too."

"You've already broken me, Skinner. I'm cured. I won't be back."

"No, you don't get off that easy. You can't just turn this away. You'll be back. Guys like you are always hanging around where there's a quick buck to be made. You'll be back, but on my terms. No more grand larceny. Next time there'll be a clear understanding."

"We'll see."

I noticed that Dr. Ritchie's jaw had dropped. Flies were walking around on his lips and teeth. The flies know right away. The man was dead. He had just quietly stopped living. As a child I thought you had to go through something called a death agony, certain pangs and throes. They were not incidental but a positive visitation. Death came as a force in itself. We laid him on the ground, and Gail gave him mouth to mouth resuscitation. Burt pounded on his chest. I turned him over and pitched in with my method, long out of date, of pumping up and down on his back. Lund said, "All right. That's enough."

We carried the body to his tent and zipped it up in his sleeping bag. Skinner was shaken. "I thought he just had the flu." He said we would sit up with the body through the night, turn and turn about. He took the first watch. I slept in my truck, after moving it beyond the glow of the electric bug killer. My suspicion was that those things attracted more bugs than they killed. The trick was to lie low. Later it rained a little and that shut up the monkeys. No one called me for my watch. Skinner sat up alone with the body all night.

At breakfast he announced that he and Lund—the Mexicans might want a second witness—would take it out in the Toyota. I was to follow behind in my big truck to see that they made it across the ford. The river was up a bit. They would take the body to Villahermosa, the nearest town of any size, there to make the necessary calls home and to see to the legal formalities and the shipping arrangements. They would return in a day or two. The rest of the crew would carry on here under Burt's direction. He had his trail bike, if any emergency came up. Dr. Ritchie's achievements were well known, his brilliant work on the Tajín horizon, his reconstruction of the Olmec merchant routes. The Bonar expedition could best serve his memory by finishing the job here.

Gail said, "Denise and I are going out, too."

"No need for that."

"I mean we're leaving the dig. We're going home."

"Why?"

"We have our reasons. One reason is that we agreed to work for Dr. Ritchie and no one else."

Skinner looked at them and brushed crumbs around on the tin table. It was a bad moment for Denise. She was almost in tears. Gail turned to me. "Can we ride back to Mérida with you?"

"Sure."

"Can you fly out of there to the States?"

"Yes, of course. Daily flights to New Orleans and Houston."

Skinner said, "Well, I see it was a mistake to bring you along. You've wasted a lot of my time. I thought you were serious students. You realize how this is going to look in my report?"

Gail was calm. "We may have some things to report ourselves."

He thought that over and then came quickly to his feet. "All right, suit yourself. Anyone else. No? Then let's get on about our business."

At this rate Rudy would soon be in charge. The girls went to pack their things. We lashed the body down in the bed of the Toyota so it wouldn't roll about. Skinner said, "I really thought he just had the flu." I drained my two tanks and left the gasoline for Burt, or almost drained them. I kept just enough to make the run back to Palenque.

Rudy gave me a manila envelope to take back to Louise. It was all sealed up with tape. Today he was dressed in camouflage fatigues and black beret with a brass badge on it. I couldn't believe the National Guard had ever issued that cap. From his web belt there hung canteens and other objects in canvas pouches.

"Rudy, I wouldn't wear that military stuff around here. Just down the way there, through all that greenery, is the Usumacinta River, and on the other side of the river is Guatemala."

"So?"

"You might get shot. They're shooting at each other over there, guerillas and government troops. Sometimes there are skirmishes on this side of the river. A lone strag- gler in that outfit—you're just asking for it."

"With my blond hair they can see I'm a gringo."

"And maybe shoot you all the quicker for that."

"I can take care of myself. I've been out in the field before. You never give me credit for knowing how to do anything."

He was right. I liked Rudy but something about him aroused the bully and the scold in me.

"Look, Burns, don't worry, okay? I always have this stuff right here in my shirt pocket where I can get at it. I have my tourist visa and my car papers and my letter of introduction from Professor Camacho Puut. I know how to get along with people. Nobody's going to bother me when they find out who I am. I have my press card taped to my chest."

"Who you are?"

"That I'm a writer. Down here they respect artists."

"Well, I wouldn't go wandering far in that rig. The Mexicans don't like it either."

"There's a ninety-minute cassette in that envelope. Keep it out of the heat. I've sealed it up in such a way that Louise will know if it's been tampered with."

"Okay."

"And don't tell anybody where I am. Just say I'm at—Chichén Itzá."

"Right. The sacred well."

We stopped at the fording place on the Tabí and loosened the fan belt on the little truck, to keep the fan from turning and throwing water back on the distributor. A family of rusty brown iguanas watched us from an overhanging limb, then plopped into the water on their lizard bellies, a family dive. Skinner dithered and stalled around. Finally he took the plunge in his truck and made it across without mishap.

I was busy dodging roots and hanging onto the gearstick. The girls talked between themselves, about some certificate they probably wouldn't get now. Denise asked me if there were any drugstores in Mérida.

"There's one on every street corner."

Once out on the wider road I dropped back and let Skinner and Lund pull ahead, out of sight. There was no dust, but I disliked being part of a convoy. Denise said she and Gail had not been sick a single day and had washed more potsherds than any four of the others. She wanted me to know that their departure had nothing to do with female hysteria but was rather a carefully considered and justifiable move.

I agreed. "You stayed longer than I would have."

We picked up a hitchhiker, an old man, who piled into the cab with us and sat by the door, silent, with his stick between his knees. He rolled up the window, as I knew he would, to keep the *aires*—evil winds—from swirling about his head, seeking entry. These dark spirits penetrate the body by way of the ears and nose and mouth, and cause internal mischief. He would suffocate on a bus before he would crack a window.

At Refugio's place we had some coffee with hot milk. He was sitting under a shade tree, bolt upright on a wooden chair, with his hands placed stiffly on his knees. He was a pharaoh. Sula was trimming his hair. Manolo was polishing the new red truck.

"No!" said Refugio. "But this is terrible news! Dr. Ritchie! Such an amiable man! There was a light in his eyes! So quiet! Always dedicated to bennee! He leaves small children?"

"I don't know. I wouldn't think so."

He said he had seen the *pagano* Skinner go by in his truck and had wondered. Now Skinner was a pagan monkey. Was his stupid *cloche* then fixed? Yes, I said, but they were going to the wrong town, to Villahermosa. The death had occurred in Chiapas, and the proper place to deliver the body and make the report was Tuxtla Gutiérrez, the state capital. They didn't know that Villahermosa was across the state line in Tabasco, or didn't think it important. There would be bureaucratic delays, various Mexican hitches. Skinner's temper would flare. He would insult the officials and his problems would be compounded tenfold. He and Lund would be gone for days. The fellow with the motorcycle, Burt, was now the boss at Ektún. He was an agreeable young man. Refugio could now resume his deliveries to the site and perhaps even sell the boy some odd lengths of plastic pipe.

"Yes, this is good thinking, Jaime. But my little green man? You won't forget him?"

It took me a moment to make the connection. His Olmec jade piece, my photograph of same. "No, I won't forget."

The fuel gauge needle had long been resting on E when we reached Palenque. The old man got out at the

CHARLES PORTIS

town plaza. He took off his straw hat and said, "You have my thanks, sir, until you are better paid."

If the girls offered to help pay for the gasoline I would accept. We would split the cost three ways. But I would let it be their own idea to give me money. As they say in New York, I should live so long. They drank Cokes and ate potato chips at the Pemex station while the boy pumped 160-odd liters of leaded Nova into my two tanks. They watched with mild interest and said not a word as I stood there for some little time peeling off fifty-peso notes. Gasoline was fairly cheap then, but they didn't give it away.

On the drive to Mérida the girls played around with the CB radio and scratched at tick bites on their ankles. Denise was a laugher. Her Spanish was excellent and she made jokes with the Mexican truck drivers. She kept asking me what people were doing along the way. "Now what is he doing?" A man lashing milk cans to a motorbike. A man selling bags of soft cheese. A woman bathing a child. If it was some activity I didn't understand, I said it was a local custom, a ritual, just a little thing they did around here to insure a good crop. This was a line I had picked up from the anthropologists.

North of Champotón where the road runs along the Gulf there is a rocky promontory and a small sandy crescent of beach. I stopped to see if anything of value had washed up. Sure enough, there were two mahogany planks bobbing about in the eddy. They were fine wide planks, newly cut, unplaned, about twelve feet long, soaked and heavy. Gail and Denise helped me drag them up the bank and manhandle them into the truck. When I was going with Beth, she said it was awkward introducing me to her friends as a scavenger. I called this foraging. We had other differences.

How were they fixed, these two girls? Poor graduate students? Was there family money? Neither of them had ever seen a CB radio before. Did that place them socially? Or just regionally? Assuming them to be at least temporarily short, I recommended the Posada Fausto. It was cheap but clean, I told them, certainly no flophouse, and handy to everything. Calle 55 was dark when we arrived. There was a feeble yellow light in the hotel doorway. Fausto's twenty-watt bulb put them off a little. They were expecting a place that offered two complimentary margaritas on check-in.

Denise said, "This is where you live?"

"I keep a room here for when I'm in town, yes. It's all right after you get inside. The rooms are okay. They have high ceilings and ten-speed ceiling fans. You don't need air-conditioning. The doorknobs are porcelain with many hairline cracks. The towels are rough-dried in the sun. Very stiff and invigorating after a bath." I caught myself overselling the place, making it out to be a charming little hotel. It wasn't that but it was all right.

Gail said, "Is that it, next to the shoe place? It doesn't even look like it's open." That was the first peep I had heard out of her for many miles.

What they wanted to do was ride around town some more, make a hotel inspection tour, find a properly lighted one that accepted credit cards but was at the same time reasonably priced, with maybe a swimming pool and a newsstand. This was why I no longer worked with other people—Refugio, Eli, Doc, whoever. The great nuisance of having a debate every hour or so and taking a vote on the next move.

I took them out to the Holiday Inn and dropped them. Then I made a jog over the Calle 61 to deliver Rudy's package. He and Louise had rooms at a place called Casitas Lola. I found her working away, typing up taped dictation from Rudy. What a job. The machine ran a little fast, and he sounded like a castrato. "Just five more to do and I'm caught up," she said. My gift of cacao beans delighted her. It was Christmas again.

"Did you see Rudy at Tumbalá?"

"I'm not supposed to say. You'll have to read his letter. It's written in lemon juice."

"You think you're oh so funny. Well, there's nothing funny about our security methods. There are people who would pay thousands of dollars just to get a peek at this material. You never have grasped the importance of our work and you never will. Did you know I was a late child?"

"No, I didn't."

"My mother was forty-three years old when I was born. There are so many interesting things you don't know about me. I may tell you some of those things later. I may not. It all depends. I haven't decided yet. Whether to confide in a vandal."

It was a shadowy room with a raftered ceiling, very low, and a single old-fashioned floor lamp with a parchment shade, a good room in which to carry on some quiet mad enterprise. Louise worked at a long table in the pool

of light. She sat erect before her typewriter, the perfect
secretary, in fashion eyewear, white blouse and floppy red
bow tie. She had blue eyes set far back in her head, so that
they appeared to be dark eyes. Her blond ringlets were
trimmed short and sort of tossed about. Next door I could
hear a child singing, in English. The new people in the next
casita, a family from New Jersey. They had moved down
here to escape the blast from the coining nuclear war.

"Do you mind very much being called a vandal?"

"No, go ahead."

"I mean after all that's what you are. I've never
known one before. I mean who worked at it full time.
You'll never guess what I dreamed last night. I dreamed
I had a baby and gave it away to Beth. Can you imagine
that? Just gave it away. The same day. I said, 'Here's a little
baby for you, Beth.'"

"Maybe it was a mutation. A rejected sport."

"I hadn't thought of that. A space baby. Genetically
altered. You're joking, but it happens, you know, all the
time. The hospitals aren't permitted to report it. But even
so, why would I give it away? I would never give my baby
away, even if it was a mutant. With his tiny knowing eyes
following me around the room."

"I've got to go, Short Stuff. It's late. I've been on the
road all day."

"Don't call me that. Wait. I was just going to make
some hot chocolate."

"Thanks anyway, no, I'm beat."

"Is it very far away? Where Rudy is? I worry about
him traveling all alone in that old car."

"Rudy's okay. He's down in Chiapas with some college people. He'll be back in a few days. The mosquitoes will soon run him off."

"Thanks for bringing the tape. Watch your step. There was a lot of slick stuff out there today."

She meant outside Dr. Estevez's House of Complete Modern Dentistry, where the sidewalk was spattered daily with gobbets of bloody spit.

THE MAYAS had a ceremonial year of 260 days called a *tzolkin*, and then they had one of 360 days called a *tun*, and finally there was the *haab* of 365 days, the least important one, not used in their long calculation. This was simply a *tun*, plus five nameless days of dread and suspended activity, the *uayeb*, corresponding somewhat to our dead week between Christmas and New Year's Day.

Here in Mérida the sky was blue and the air soft, no driving sleet, no dense waves of northern guilt, but there was a seasonal lethargy all the same. The year had run down and nobody was quite ready to start the grind again. These were our nameless days.

Beatriz was moping at the desk the next morning. She said Doc Flandin had called three times asking for me. There was no letter from Ah Kin, only a sharp note from Frau Kobold. Her cakes again! I picked them up for her weekly when I was in town, a big plastic sack of stale muffins and *pastelitos* and broken cookies, which she got from the Hoolywood Panaderia for next to nothing.

It was a long-standing arrangement, and this was all she ate, as far as anyone knew. It seems you can live for years on *pan dulce* and Nescafé and cigarettes, and even thrive. She appeared to be none the worse for having smoked 900,000 Faros cigarettes.

I walked over to the Hoolywood and waited for the rejects to be bagged. Someone clapped a hand on my shoulder from behind. It was a man named Beavers and he wanted to borrow ten dollars. I barely knew him but he was on me so fast I couldn't think of a way to say no. He said Flandin was looking for me.

On the way back I paused at the *zócalo* to watch the Mexican flag being raised. There was a color guard and a drum and bugle platoon from the army barracks. I had seen it all many times but I could no more pass up a display like that than I could a car wreck with personal injuries. They were smart looking troops, with one or two corny touches—chromed bayonets and white laces in their black boots, all back-laced and looped about. The rifles were real, though the M-16 makes a poor ceremonial piece—ugly, too short, too black, too much plastic. More a weapon to be brandished defiantly above the head by irregular forces. There it went, the big tricolor, as big and soft as a bedsheet, creeping up inch by deliberate inch. I was trained to run the colors up briskly and bring them down gravely, but this way was all right, too, I suppose.

I saw Beth across the plaza. She was smiling and must have been watching me. Had she caught me muttering to myself? With that bag of crumbs slung across my back I was a cartoon burglar making off with his swag in a pillowcase. She looked good, in her washed-out, pioneer woman way, with little or no makeup, with her hair parted in the middle and pulled back into a knob. She wore a peach-colored dress with shoulder straps. Bollard was with her, sitting lumpily on a bench with a newspaper. What did she see in that cinnamon bear? There's always some jerk who won't rise for the national anthem, his own or anyone else's. No wait, now he was getting up, but grudgingly, humoring Beth, and the natives, in their absurd ritual.

Bollard lived on the top floor of the Napoles Apartments and wrote novels. Of the grim modern kind, if I can read faces. I hadn't read his books. My fear was that they might not be quite as bad as I wanted them to be. Art and Mike said they were no worse than other books. He had a certain following. He called me The Great Excavator, and also, Our Mathematical Friend, after I had once corrected him on a compound interest calculation. He thought he was going to make a fortune off his Mexican telephone bonds. Bollard wasn't always lost in his art, up there in the penthouse. It was a nice place. I had once lived in the Napoles myself, when I was selling those long leather coats.

Beth gave me a mock curtsy. I nodded. Our flickering little romance had just about flickered out. She had taken me at first for a colorful Cajun, sucker of crawdad heads, wild dancer to swamp tunes, then lost interest when she found I was from the Anglo, Arkansas-Texas part of Louisiana. Of our Arklatex folkways she knew nothing. She suspected them to be dark ways, a good deal of sweaty cruel laughter, but of a darkness that wasn't particularly interesting.

Then she began to cultivate me again when someone told her I was a pretty fair hand at sorting out genuine Mayan pieces from the modern forgeries. Then someone else told her how I came by my knowledge and she got frosty again.

Frau Kobold was waiting for me in her wicker wheelchair. She wasn't exactly lame, just old. Her bones were dry sticks. I went carefully over the explanation again, how other cake arrangements were going to have to be made when I was gone.

"I don't like people knowing my business," she said.

Her pride, yes, I understood that, but Fausto and Beatriz and Agustín already knew her business, her situation. Louise was right, there was too much stuff in this room. There were bulging pasteboard boxes, packed with clothing and dishes, as for an immediate move. They had been sitting here for years. Mayan relics were jumbled about on tables and chairs. On the walls there were framed photographs of temples and carved stelae taken by her husband, Oskar Kobold, long dead. Some of these prints were fifty years old but they were still the best I had ever seen of low-relief carvings. With all their fierce lighting and fine lenses and fast film, the modern photographers still couldn't capture those shadowy lines the way Oskar Kobold did, which is why the inscription scholars have to rely on drawings.

He died a poor and bitter man, having been cheated of both recognition and money by museums, universities, governments, publishers, all manner of high-minded institutions. They had used his work freely, were still using it and had paid him trifling fees when they paid at all.

Mostly they sent him remaindered books. But then he had a reputation for being prickly and hard to deal with, too, something of a nut. Frau Kobold, the former Miss Alma Dunbar of Memphis, had traipsed about in the bush with him in jodhpurs and pith helmet. She carried his tripod and mixed his chemicals and prepared his wet plates and kept his notes. None of it seemed to mean much to her now. She seldom talked about the old days, except for the time she and Oskar had appeared in a Fox Movietone Newsreel—*Bringing an Ancient Civilization to Light!* Doc said it was a segment lasting two or three minutes. Nothing much pleased her anymore or engaged her interest. She said her sleep was dreamless.

I sat on the bed and had coffee with her. Stale cake is not bad. The shaggy balls of the chenille bedspread were worn down to nubs from countless washings. The mystery novels were within easy reach of the insomniac, all lined up on improvised shelving of pine boards and bricks. She had some new reading material, too, a newsletter called *Gamma Bulletin*, which came once a month from the States, and which I took to be some archaeological journal. She boiled the water with an electric immersion coil in plastic cups.

I said, "Alma, you were rude to a friend of mine the other night."

"Oh? Who?"

"A girl named Louise Kurle. She took the trouble to come by here and wish you a merry Christmas."

"Oh yes. She had been here before. I didn't want to encourage her. I thought she might become a pest. I don't care to make new friends at my time of life."

"You might make an exception. Stretch a point."

"No, I don't think so. I didn't like her manner. She doesn't appreciate who I am."

"She'd be glad to do things for you."

"No, she doesn't fit in around here. Do you think because I'm poor I should have to tolerate fools?"

She showed me her coins, knotted up in a hand-kerchief, schoolgirl style, and said I had also forgotten about her appointment at the beauty shop. Once a month I rolled her down to the *sala de belleza* to get her hair done, and air her out a bit. She still paid the girls at the *sala* five pesos, having no idea of what the peso was worth these days. Fausto and Doc and I made up the difference behind her back, as we did with her other creditors. Coffee was cheap enough, and postage stamps. She ran through a lot of stamps. But the expenses didn't amount to much, except for the medicine. Terry Teremoto, the crank sculptor, had helped too, with a regular check, until his recent death in Veracruz.

"Well, make another appointment and let me know. I should be in town for awhile. Here, let me see your glasses." They were smeared. I breathed on them and wiped them on the bedspread.

Now it was time for a real breakfast, and I went along to the Express, a sidewalk café where the gringos gathered. Here I was greeted by Vick, Crouch, Cribbs, Bolus and Nelms, who feigned surprise.

"I wish you would look."

"Not him again."

"You still hanging around?"

I had announced recently, as I did once or twice a year, that I was leaving Mexico for good, going back to Shreveport to join my brother in the construction business. "Yes, but not for long," I said. "You better make the best of me while you can." I chose to sit at another table, one offering a better view of street events, with Simcoe, Pleat, McNeese, Coney, Minim and Mott. Already there was something to see, a car fire in the cab rank across the street. The cabbies were throwing clods of dirt at it and slapping at it with rags.

Pleat, great favorite with the ladies, said he had owned thirty-odd cars in his lifetime and never once had an engine fire. Coney, the English painter, whose tuneless humming drove people away, said he once had a car fire so hot that the aluminum carburetor melted and ran down over the block. Minim was in the Bowling Hall of Fame. He was a retired bowler and sports poet, and he maintained that bowling was held in even lower esteem than poetry, though it was a close call. He had made more money with his short sports poems, he said, than he had ever made on the bowling circuit, though not much more. Mott always looked sprightly and pleased with himself, like Harry Truman at the piano, with his rimless glasses and neatly combed hair. He had gone crazy in the army and now received a check each month, having been declared fifty percent psychologically disabled. Had they determined him to be half crazy all the time or full crazy half the time? Mott said the VA doctors never would spell it out for him. He had whatever the opposite of paranoia is called. He thought everybody liked him and took a deep personal interest in his welfare. But then everybody did like him.

"Don Ricardo is looking for you," he said.

"So I heard."

Let him look. He knew where to find me. "Don Ricardo" was another of Flandin's self-bestowed titles. This one had never caught on outside his own household. His wife, Nan, had pushed it, and of course the servants had to call him that. The rest of us refused to do so, out of pettiness no doubt. All except for the guileless Mott.

Simcoe said he had seen an interesting thing in the *zócalo* that morning. He had spied a rat high up in the topmost branches of a laurel tree. Minim said rats didn't climb trees and that it must have been a squirrel or a gray bird. Simcoe didn't like having his eyesight or his honesty questioned. He said, "A gray bird eating a Baby Ruth from the wrapper? What speeshees of gray bird might that be?" In the end we agreed that city rats could climb trees but did not often choose to climb trees and that Simcoe was right to report his sighting.

A portly hippie with a two-stranded beard went ambling past our table. McNeese said, "Look at that morphadite creep. On his way to shoot some dope into his old flabby white ass, I'll bet."

Mott said, "Is that the way they do it? Wouldn't he need an assistant? An accomplice?"

Coney said, "I wouldn't touch him with a barge pole."

"What are they up to? Is there some hippie convention?"

"I don't understand how they get across the border."

I had a boy polish my shoes. Coney sketched and hummed. Simcoe read a book. It was all right to do that here. In the States it was acceptable to read newspapers and magazines in public, but not books, unless you wanted to be taken for a student or a bum or a lunatic or all three. Here you could read books in cafés without giving much offense, and even write them. I had seen Bollard doing it, scratching many life-destroying things on a legal pad. McNeese said, "Speaking of hippies, I heard they picked up your man in the station wagon."

"What, here?" I said.

"I don't know."

"Did they get the little girl back?"

"I don't know the details. I just heard something at Shep's about it."

Just then Doc Flandin came up in his slippers. When I first met him he wore a seersucker suit and a spotless Panama, day in and day out. Now he looked like a wino. He was unshaven, and his shirttail was out, and he had an odd little brimless cap pushed down on his ears, of the kind James Cagney used to wear in prison. He beamed down on us with one fist on his hip. We amused him.

"Well, boys, what is it this morning? Pork Chop Hill? Leyte Gulf? Chesty Puller? Service-connected disabilities? Fort Benning?"

Supposedly we sat here all day drinking coffee and telling grotesque military anecdotes, impatiently waiting our turn in a round-robin. Bollard called us the Private Slovik Post of the American Legion.

Minim said, "No sir, our topic today is the sinking peso. We were hoping you might come along and shed some light on the matter."

"What? Economics? Good God. No, not my line, gentlemen."

Coney said, "Do join us, sir, in our banter. Your presence alone would raise the tone of things."

"Oh, I'm not so sure of that. Jimmy, I'd like a word with you."

I followed him across the street to the little park. The old man was in bad shape. His plum face had gone off to the color of lead.

"Where in the world have you been?" he said. "I need to talk to you. Big news. You never come by to see me anymore."

"I've been to your house three times since Nan died."

"What, I was out?"

"Mrs. Blaney said you couldn't be interrupted. I finally got the message."

"Lucille told you that? Well, things have been all balled up lately. Look here, I want you to come by Izamál for lunch at two. Can you do that? It's important."

"Have you cleared this with Mrs. Blaney?"

"I believe you're sulking. A fancied slight? Let me tell you frankly, it's not very becoming. The poor woman made a mistake, that's all."

"Did you hear about Dr. Ritchie?"

"Yes, I did. Too bad."

"It was his heart, I think. I was there. A bad business. He was quite a man in his field, wasn't he?"

"Ritchie was adequate. Undistinguished."

He left me abruptly, and I went back to the Express to use the telephone. I called a man named Lozano, with the Judicial Police, to whom I had made my report about Dan and the runaway girl, LaJoye Mishell Teeter. But no, McNeese had gotten it wrong, Big Dan had not been arrested. Or rather the Municipal Police in Valladolid had picked him up, then let him go. Lozano said the patrol-men had not seen the bulletin on him. Three of them had gone to answer a call about a big gringo who was trying to entice a small boy into his spotted car. They came and handcuffed him, but it was at the end of a shift and they didn't want to bother taking him back to the station, going through all the paperwork, with a foreigner. So they ham-mered him to his knees with their sticks, gave him a good bloody beating, and turned him loose with a warning.

Lozano said, "We'll have him in a day or two. A car like that."

Hard to say. I wasn't so sure. The Jumping Jacks might well have another car by now. They might be in Belize or Guatemala. Off to their City of Dawn, beyond the range of my understanding.

As for Doc's big news, I could make a pretty good guess at that. His book was finished at long last. Well, it *was* big news. He had been working on the thing for almost forty years, his masterful survey of Meso-American civilization, from Olmec dawn through the fall of the Aztecs. It was a grand synthesis, he said, proving that the several cultures were essentially all the same, or closely related. Along the way he would clear up all the old mysteries. He would show that Quetzalcoatl or Kukulcán was a historical figure and not just some mythical "culture hero," and he would explain the basis for the 260-day year (the human gestation period, with the odd days lopped off) and the twenty-day "month," which seemed to have no astronomical significance. He would set forth in detail the real reasons for the collapse of the Mayan high culture in the ninth century. He would tell us who the Olmecs really were, appearing suddenly out of darkness, and why they carved those colossal heads that look like Fernando Valenzuela of the Los Angeles Dodgers. He would give the location of Aztlán, the original home of the Aztecs, and he would end speculation once and for all on transoceanic contacts, by revealing the simple truth of the matter. He would identify "the dancing men" at Monte Alban, and he would settle the question of the "elephant" carving at Copán. For good measure he would decipher the Mayan hieroglyphics.

Some of it would be nonsense and perhaps a lot of it but not all of it. Flandin was formidable in his way. I was eager to read the part about the glyph translation, hoping it wouldn't be silly. For some time now he had told me he could read the inscriptions. When I pressed him he was evasive. "I can tell you this much and no more, for the present. These writings are not just calendric piffle." Some other kind of piffle then. Thousand-year-old weather reports. *Champion Spark Plugs*. I knew he hadn't actually broken the code, but it was possible that he had hit on some useful new approach to the problem.

Beth was waiting for me in front of the Posada Fausto. She wanted me to haul some chairs for her. They wouldn't fit in Bollard's Peugeot. If you have a truck your friends will drive you crazy. We drove out to a carpentry shop on Colón, where a man named Chelo made tables and things out of withes and sticks and swatches of rawhide leather. He made baby furniture, too, strange rough cradles with a lot of bark showing and little Goldilocks chairs. I tried to sell him my big planks. Chelo said he never worked in mahogany, seeming to suggest there was something vulgar about it. Another artist.

Beth had bought a round table and four chairs, bulky pieces but not heavy, and I transported them and set them up in her courtyard. She had a nice roomy place all to herself behind the museum. There was a flowery patio with bees and paper lanterns and wind chimes and two prowling cats. These people on grants did all right for themselves. She had a grant from some foundation to manage this children's museum, which was a very good one, no expense spared, the idea being to march the local *niños* through in troops and give them some appreciation of their Mayan heritage.

Beth wiped her hands on a fresh towel and tossed it into the hamper. It was one use and out for her. She didn't have to wash them. She made a pitcher of limeade, and we sat in the new chairs. The rawhide was smelly. Bits of flesh still adhered to the skin. I knew a little about the leather business and even I knew that rawhide must be scraped and dried and stretched properly. Beth denied that there was any smell and then denied that the smell was unpleasant. To her it was agreeable and even bracing. She defended all things Mexican.

"I haven't seen you around. What have you been doing with yourself?"

"Nothing much," I said. "Trying to save some money."

"Out at night drinking with your buddies, I suppose. Ike and Mutt, are they? Those two you're always quoting?"

She meant Art and Mike, the inseparable Munn brothers.

"No, I haven't been drinking at all."

"Will you read something if I give it to you?"

"Sure. What is it?"

"I don't mean now. I'm still working on it. Just some observations. A kind of list. It's about the kind of person you've become."

"A list of my shortcomings then."

"Not exactly that. More about personal growth. Our repetitive acts. How our growth can be arrested and we may not even be aware of it."

"Growth? That sounds like one of Bollard's words."

"Do you think I can't have my own ideas?"

"I think you'd do better to stay away from people like that."

"Like what? Look who's talking. Carleton had nothing whatever to do with this and you know it."

"Well, no, I don't know it. I see you all over town with him."

"Will you read it?"

"I'll read it if you can put it on one sheet of paper."

"Now what is that, some military thing?"

"No, I read about it in a business book. The need for keeping memos and reports short. How it concentrates your thinking and saves time for everybody along the line."

"You're afraid of smart women, aren't you?"

She had used this ploy before, having heard via the female bush telegraph that it was unanswerable. She was right though. I was leery of them. Art and Mike said taking an intellectual woman into your home was like taking in a baby raccoon. They were both amusing for awhile but soon became randomly vicious and learned how to open the refrigerator. Beth asked if I remembered her green sofa that the cats had scratched up. I said I did but I had no memory for particular pieces of furniture, having hauled so much of it. She told a long story about how she had given the sofa to an ungrateful person who had in turn given it away to someone else.

"You're not even listening to me."

"Yes, I am. The green sofa. I tell you what. I've got some things to do. Let me know when you've finished the paper and I'll read it and think it over."

"You're too kind. How much do I owe you for the delivery job?"

"No charge."

"I saw that mud on your truck and all those branches caught up underneath. You've been out ransacking temples again, haven't you? You never did really stop. On top of everything else you're a liar."

On top of all my other defects, too many to be recorded on a single page. I had meant to ask her if Bollard brought cat treats when he came calling, as I had done, but I let it go.

MEXICAN HOMES as a rule are closed off to the world by high blank walls of yellowish masonry, topped with broken glass to discourage *escaladores*, or climbing burglars. The gardens and fountains and other delights are hidden, as in an Arab city. Each city block is a fortress. But on the Paseo Montejo in Mérida there are two-story houses standing detached with their own lawns and tropical shrubbery. The Paseo is a shady boulevard where the sisal millionaires once lived, a short version of St. Charles Avenue in New Orleans, and a very un-Mexican street.

Doc Flandin lived on the near end of it in a fine white house with a wraparound porch and a little round tower on top, a cupola. Izamál, it was called, or place of the lizard. Doc had come late in life to this luxury, when he married Nan. She had the money.

Mrs. Blaney admitted me this time, making a show of checking her watch. This was to let me know that formal luncheon appointments are one thing and drop-in calls quite another.

"Don Ricardo will see you in his bedroom. Can you find your way? Just follow the music."

"I think I can find it."

I was wandering around in this house before Lucille Blaney had ever set foot in Mexico. I had met Eric Thompson, the great Mayanist, in this very room, with its cold tile floor and grand piano. No one played the piano, but the lid was always propped up on its slender stick. Sir Eric, I should say. He called Flandin Dicky. It was Eric this and Dicky that. I still cringe when I remember how I talked so much that day, trying to show off my piddling scraps of knowledge.

The music came from an old wind-up phonograph. Doc was listening once again to Al Jolson singing "April Showers." I found the old lizard upstairs in his bed, a big canopied affair made of dark oak. The posts and beams were carved with a running fretwork design in the Uxmal style. The room was long and sunny. There were casement windows and a fireplace and a balcony. He allowed Al to finish, then lifted the arm from the thick black record.

"Do you mind if we eat here?"

"No, of course not."

"It would be nicer by the pool, but this way we can have some privacy. Lucille has the ears of a jackrabbit."

"You're no match for that woman, Doc. Nan could handle her, but you can't. She's got your number."

"Well, I can't kick her out now."

"No, it's too late in the day for that."

The maid, Lorena, served crabmeat salad in avocado halves. I told Doc about my run to Ektún, the death of

Dr. Ritchie and how that Refugio had asked about his book and his tobacco pipe. He found that funny. He and Refugio had some running joke about the pipe that I wasn't privy to. A little reminder that they had worked together before I came along.

"Was Ritchie one of these trotters or joggers?" he asked me. "Some exercise nut?"

"I don't know. You couldn't do much jogging at Ektún."

"He was not really a good field man, you know."

"No? He had a good reputation."

"Look at all the staff support he had. If I had been set up like that in my sixties, I would have accomplished great things. I would have shown them a thing or two."

"You've done all right. You found the Seibal scepter. That should be enough for one man. Nobody can do very much. Then there's your book."

"They won't acknowledge that I've done anything."

"I saw you in church on Christmas day."

"Well, why not? I'm an old sinner."

"No, I approve. It's just that I hadn't seen you in church before."

"But I was never a public and obstinate sinner. No one can say that."

"No."

"A love for truth too. I've always had a love for truth and that in itself is a sign of grace. Did you never hear that?"

"I don't think so."

"I'm dying, Jimmy. You're talking to a corpse."

"What?"

"It's prostate cancer. I'm waiting for the biopsy report from Dr. Solís, but that's only a formality. I wanted you to know. We won't talk about it. I've arranged for Father Mateo to say some masses for me."

"Have you seen Soledad Bravo about this?"

"No, I haven't consulted any witch doctors, thank you."

"When do you get the report?"

"I don't want to talk about it."

"We don't have to talk about it for three hours, but you can't say something like that and then just drop it."

"There's nothing to be said or done. You can't beat the slowworm. Sometimes he's not so slow."

"L. C. Bowers beat it. He went up to the Ochsner Clinic in New Orleans, and they cut it out. That was what, three years ago, and he's still walking around."

"Bowers had some lesser form of the thing."

Doc's diseases had to be grand, too. He had never shown much sympathy for the sick, not even for Nan when she was dying, believing as he did that illness was largely voluntary. Giving way. Then whining. He took no medicine himself and he seemed to think that Nan had killed herself through a foolish addiction to laxatives and nasal sprays.

And Soledad Bravo was no witch doctor. She was a modest lady who practiced folk medicine in her home on Calle 55, just down the street from me. She was a *curandera*, who could deliver babies, remove warts and pull single-rooted teeth, no molars, and she could put her ear to your chest and look at your tongue and your eyes and feel around under your jaw, then tell you what was wrong and give you a remedy. It might be something old-fashioned like arnica or camphorated oil, or it might be some very modern drug, or some simple dietary tip. She kept up with things. Soledad had a gift. She got results. What more can you ask than to be healed? I wouldn't go to anyone else.

"That little round cap you're wearing," I said. "Does that have something to do with your condition?"

"No, but it keeps the vapors in. Vapors were escaping from my head."

"Why not let them escape?"

"I don't care to discuss the cap. My death is imminent and I have some important instructions for you."

"This is not the razor blade deal again, is it?"

"The what?"

I had to remind him. Some years back, fearing a stroke, he had given me a package of single-edge razor blades. Should he be struck down and incapacitated, unable to move, I was to sneak into his room at night and slit his wrists with one of those blades. Others would string him along, he said, but he knew I would do it. This, I think, was intended as flattery. I still carried those Gem blades around in my shaving kit.

"Oh no, there's no question of paralysis with this thing," he said. "I have some morphine tablets that will do the job when the time comes."

"I came over here thinking I would hear that your book was finished. Now you tell me this."

"The book is coming along, don't worry. I'm still at it. Answering a lot of questions that nobody has asked. If I had had any decent staff support, the thing would have been finished long ago. But you know, I made a late discovery. Working fast suits me. It reads better. I learn to write on my deathbed, you see. The schoolboys won't like it but by God they'll have to take notice this time. Oh yes, I know what they say. 'What can you expect? He's French! Brilliant but unsound! I can't keep up with him! This old flaneur has too many ideas! Too many theories!' It's my brio, Jimmy, that they can't stomach. My verve. It sets their teeth on edge. I know how these drab people think and I know exactly what they say about me."

It was worse than that. They didn't say anything. The academics, or schoolboys, as he called them, didn't even take the trouble to dispute his theories. The papers he submitted to scholarly journals were returned without comment. He was never invited to the professional conclaves, other than local ones that the Mexicans sponsored. Mexicans weren't quite as rigid as the Americans and the English and the Germans in these matters of caste.

It seemed to me that he deserved better treatment. Perhaps not complete acceptance, or the centerfold spread in *National Geographic* that he so longed for, but something, a nod in the footnotes even. His great find, the manikin scepter at Seibal, was widely published but never attributed to him. And it was Flandin, with two or three Mexicans, who had argued years ago that it was the Olmecs and not the Mayas who had invented glyph writing and the bar-and-dot numeral system and the Long

Count calendar, when American and English scholars—Thompson himself—refused to hear of such a thing. Being prematurely right, and worse, intuitively right, he got no credit for it. Rather, it was held against him. His field work was good and his site reports were, in my lay opinion, well up to professional standards. No brio here; they were just as tiresome to read as the approved ones. His crank claims and speculations made up only about twenty percent of his work but it was a fatal sufficiency. Or say thirty percent to be absolutely fair.

"When do I get to see the glyph chapter?"

"In good time. Camacho Puut is looking it over now. But we're not going to talk about the book."

I wondered what we were going to talk about. Lorena brought us a pot of coffee and some strawberries in heavy yellow cream. Doc asked her if she would go to his office and bring back his—*pistola*—I thought he said. Lorena was puzzled, too, and then seemed to work it out. Doc spoke fluent Spanish, but it was incorrect and badly pronounced.

"I'm worried about Camacho Puut," he said. "I do believe the old fellow is taking some dangerous narcotic drug."

"Oh come on. The Professor?"

"You weren't here. He was sitting right there. I was reading my revised prologue to him and his head was lolling and he could hardly keep his eyes open. It's none of my business if he wants to kill himself with dope but I do think he might consider his family and his own dignity. What about Alma? Have you seen her?"

"I saw her this morning."

"Is she doing any better?"

"About the same."

"Don't say anything but I'm leaving her a small annuity. A little something to help with the rent."

"She won't accept it."

"I'm rigging it up so she'll think it came from Oskar's work. But keep it under your hat."

"Did you ever work with Oskar Kobold?"

"No, never. We hardly spoke. He was an artist of the first rank, I grant him that, but he couldn't get along with anybody. An awful man. He treated Alma like a mule."

"I can't imagine her putting up with that."

"Well, she did. She wasn't hard then. Just a little pale Southern lily with a love for those travel books of John Stephens."

Lorena came back and yes, it was the *pistola* he had asked for. Gun, holster, belt, the whole business coiled up on a wooden tray. She held it forward, not wanting to touch it. Doc said, *"Por mi amigo Jaime,"* and so she served it up to me, a .45 automatic on a platter.

Until very recently he had worn this big-bore pistol openly around town, and he always carried it in the bush. At our campsite, just before turning in at night, he would fire it twice into the air. This was an announcement to anyone who might be in the woods nearby. *Here we are. We're armed and we're not taking any crap.* Or sometimes I fired my shotgun, or Refugio his army rifle, an old Argentine Mauser with a bolt handle that stuck straight out.

I slipped the pistol out of the holster. Most of the blueing was gone, and there was a lot of play in the slide. It still looked good. The 1911 aeroplanes and the 1911 typewriters were now comic exhibits in museums, but this 1911 Colt still looked just right. It hadn't aged a day. The clip was crammed from top to bottom with short fat cartridges. I shucked a couple of them out.

"You'll weaken the spring," I said. "Leaving it fully loaded like that."

"Damn the spring. Put them back. I like it full."

So, he was disposing of his things.

"This is for me?"

"No, no, not the gun. That's for Refugio. I want you to see that he gets it. My binoculars too, if I can ever find them, and all my field gear. I'm putting some stuff together in boxes for him, but the pistol is the main thing. You know how he admires it."

Not the gun. So. I was to get something else. He was clearing the small bequests out of the way first. I saw where this was leading, I was staggered. Flandin is going to leave me this big white house. There was no one else. Nan was gone, as was his first wife, and the blind sister in Los Angeles. Mrs. Blaney, an old friend of Nan's, was here on sufferance. I didn't see Doc as much of a public benefactor. It was unlikely that he would endow an orphanage or set up a trust to provide free band concerts for the people of Mérida. All his old cronies were gone except for Professor Camacho Puut, who, properly, would get the library and the relic collection. That left me. I had served him well. My reward was to be Izamál.

Mrs. Blaney poked her head into the room. Always looming and hovering, this woman. "Oh. I thought you had gone, Mr. Burns. Don Ricardo usually has his nap at this time."

"No, I'm still here."

Doc said, "It's all right, Lucille. We're talking business."

"Oh. Well, then. I'll just—leave you two."

She left and I asked him if she knew about the cancer.

"Not yet but she suspects something."

That meant she probably did know. Nothing was said about the house. We got down to my instructions. Dr. Solís was to send for me the moment that he, Flandin, died. There would be no lingering decline in a hospital. He would die in this room. I would come at once and stand guard by his bed, allowing no one to move his body for thirty-six hours.

"Are you willing to do that? Without asking a lot of questions? Don't humor me along now. I want an honest answer."

"Yes, I can do that. Do you mean exactly thirty-six hours?"

"No less than that. I want your solemn word."

"You have it. What else? What about the funeral?"

"I've already gone over that with Huerta. You just do your job. You just make sure I'm dead."

He was afraid of being buried alive. A childhood nightmare of screaming and clawing and tossing about in a dark box. It wasn't an unreasonable fear. Any doctor can make a mistake. Funerals were carried out promptly here, and usually there was no embalming. Some morticians offered same-day service. Harlan Shrader died one morning in his hotel room, and we buried him before the sun went down, in a coffin too narrow for his shoulders, and they weren't broad. The box was made of thin pine boards and six-penny nails. Huerta charged us $40 for everything, including the grave plot, and he even put some cowboy boots on Harlan's limp feet. I don't know how he did it, slit them perhaps. We found them in Harlan's closet, but I think they must have belonged to some former occupant. In life Harlan tramped around town in threadbare canvas shoes with his toes poking out, and in death he became a member of the equestrian class. Mott and I paid Huerta. Shep applied to the Veterans Administration for the $250 burial allowance but said he never got it.

"Not a word about this to anyone," said Doc. "I know I can count on you, Jimmy. Now I want you to go up to the attic. The black steamer trunk. It's not locked. Open it up and you'll see a pasteboard box tied up with rope. It's marked notes. I want you to bring it down here."

I went up to the attic, an oven, just below the round cupola, and made haste to find the thing. It must have been 150 degrees Fahrenheit in that room. While poking around in the trunk, I came across a blue case with gold lettering. It held a Carnegie Medal for heroism and a citation on thick paper telling how young Richard Flandin, a grocer's delivery boy, had rescued an old lady and her dog, both unconscious, from a burning house in Los Angeles. Quite a little man. Doc in knickers. Sweat dripped from my nose and made splotches on the soft paper. Great boaster that he was, he had never told me about this. Had he forgotten? It served to remind me, too, that he was an old Angeleno, American to the bone, for all his French posturing. In a rare moment of weakness, he confessed to me one night that he was only five years old when his widowed mother made the move from Paris to California with him and his sister. He saved coins. I found a cigar box filled with silver pesos, and I bounced one, nice and heavy, on my hand. It was once one of the world's standard currencies, like the Spanish dollar, or piece of eight, and now a single peso was all but worthless. It was worth less than a single cacao bean, which the Mayans had used for money.

My first improvement to this house would be some roof turbines. Clear out all of this hot air. Would I allow Mrs. Blaney to stay on? Perhaps, but with much reduced authority and visibility.

The pasteboard box was packed with Doc's old notebooks. They were engineers' field notebooks, with yellow waterproof covers and water-resistant pages, each sheet scored off with a grid pattern. On the inner sides of the covers there were printed formulas for solving curves and triangles. I lugged it down to the bedroom and began untying the ropes. I thought he wanted the notes for reference. I thought this had something to do with his book.

"No, bind it back up," he said. "They're yours, Jimmy, to do with as you please. All my early field notes. I want you to have them."

His notes? Not the house then. I was to receive instead this dusty parcel of data. Unreadable scribbling and baffling diagrams with numbers, and here and there the multi-legged silhouette of a bug smashed between the pages. Did the stuff have any value at all? It was like being told that you had just inherited a zircon mine, unless zircons are quarried, I don't know. I was caught up short. I was at a loss.

"This is very good of you, Doc. I wonder though. Shouldn't valuable material like this go to some library or museum?"

"They had their chances. You're not pleased?"

"Yes, of course I am, a great honor, but you know how I live. Right now I'm camping out in a room at Fausto's place. You know how I move around. These notebooks should be catalogued and stored somewhere. I'm no scholar."

"It doesn't matter. You're my good friend. You've been a loyal friend. They're yours. Enough said."

Lorena came back to collect the dishes. Doc told her to go to the bureau and bring out all his—handkerchiefs— I thought he said. *Pañuelos?* She got one, and he said no, all of them, *todos*. They were plain white handkerchiefs, and she made stacks of them on a tray. He indicated that they were for me.

"I want you to have my handkerchiefs, too, Jimmy. All my old friends are dead now, and most of my new acquaintances are ill-bred people of below-average intelligence. Mental defectives for the most part. They don't use handkerchiefs."

Lorena served them to me. Doc waved off my thanks. "You do carry one, don't you?"

"Sometimes."

"I want you to feel free to use them. They're not to be put away now. They're for everyday use. There's plenty of service left in them."

"Well. They're nice handkerchiefs."

"Nothing fancy, but you can't beat long-staple cotton for absorbency and a smooth finish. How many are there?"

Now I had to count them. He wanted to draw this out.

"Twenty-two."

"So many? Well, there you are. Twenty-two flags of truce. You never know when you might need one. Take them, enjoy them. Properly cared for, they will give you years of good service."

"You mean I'm to take them now?"

"Absolutely. They're yours, enjoy them. The notebooks, the handkerchiefs. A lot of good reading in that box. I never could understand these selfish old people who hang onto everything till their very last gasp."

A little later he dozed off. I left through the back door, through the kitchen, by way of all the copper pots, thinking to avoid another encounter with Mrs. Blaney. But there she was, poolside, with her English class. She taught English conversation and ballroom dancing to young Mexican matrons. They were sitting in a half-circle, six or seven of them, holding cups and saucers. Mrs. Blaney was drilling them in garden party remarks.

I made a detour around the swimming pool. Purple blossoms were floating in the water, and a blue air mattress, deflated, swamped and becalmed. Mrs. Blaney called out to me. "Mr. Burns? One moment please. What is that you are carrying away?" The young matrons looked at each other. This must be what you said in English to a person who was leaving your grounds at a smart clip with a box on his shoulder and a gun belt draped around his neck. I kept moving. I was thinking about the cancer demon and other things and I had no time for Lucille Blaney's nonsense. Sometimes I thought she was the one who was sending me the Mr. Rose letters.

HUERTA'S FUNERAL parlor was out by the old city wall, with a white glass sign in front, lighted from within. *Inhumaciones Huerta*. I drove around to the workshop and got Huerta out to look at the mahogany planks. Was that enough wood to make a coffin for Dr. Flandin? Or perhaps other plans had been made. I didn't want to interfere. Huerta ran his fingers along the grain. Oh no, this was a wonderful idea. This was more than enough. The mahogany would take a nice finish and would make a much more suitable *ataud* for the Doctor than the ugly metal casket he had chosen. He would dry the wood and stain it and buff it with wax and fashion a fine work of mortuary art. He would use bright copper hinges and fittings. Ulises could do some carving on the lid.

"Not too narrow now," I said.

"Oh no. *Amplio*." He spread his hands to show just how wide. "*Asi de amplio*." But how much time did he have? The Doctor had not been clear about when death would come. I said he had been vague with me, too, but I thought there would be time enough.

On a wooden table nearby a boy was washing down a corpse with a water hose. I stopped to look at the face. Huerta said, "Did you know Enrique? He had a short fit and then dropped dead in his box. Just the way he would have wanted it." The name meant nothing to me, but I recognized him as a man who had kept a newsstand downtown. He had sat half-hidden in a wooden box behind drooping curtains of newspapers and comic books, deaf, addled, smothered in news. It was a shock to see him outside his nest and laid out dead and cold on a wet table into the bargain.

That night I went to Shep's bar for the first time in weeks. There was a going-away party for Crouch and his wife. Shep's In-Between Club was the proper name, and from the outside it looked like a *pulque* joint in central Mexico, a hole in the wall with slatted, swinging saloon doors. No *pulque* was served here, however, and women were allowed to enter. It was bigger inside than you expected it to be and not as dark as you expected. Shep had a Mexican wife, and the place was registered in her name.

Nelms was intercepting people at the swinging doors. He was eating a curled hunk of fried pork skin that had been dipped in red sauce. He started eating street food at mid-afternoon and ate steadily along until about 11 at night. There was a whine in his voice.

"How long have I been coming in here, Burns?"

"I don't know. A long time."

"Shep won't cash my check."

"Why not?"

"I've bought 50,000 drinks in this place and he won't take my check. Can you believe that guy?"

It was hard to get a straight answer out of Nelms. The drinkers were standing two deep at the bar. A good turnout. Crouch and his jolly wife were popular and would be missed. She said, "I like Mérida all right but there's nothing to do here." They were seated at a table amid well-wishers. There was a pink cake. I hoped she would find some interesting activities in Cuernavaca. It would be cooler there anyway, and the gringo drunks would be richer and drunker.

I stopped to wish them luck and then went to the bar, which was a long flat slab of cypress. A man in a base-ball cap made room for me. I knew his name, Nordstrom, and he knew mine, and that was about it. He was looking at the ice-skating scene behind the bar, perhaps longing for Milwaukee. The two skaters were dolls on a round mirror. There was some fluffed-up cotton to represent snow. This was Shep's annual Christmas display.

Shep hopped about on a twisted foot. The crowd was such that he himself was serving drinks and washing glasses tonight, along with the regular bartenders, Cosme and Luisito. Cosme gave me a look as he made change. He had an unspoken agreement with a few old customers. We paid only for every other drink and then tipped him the difference, or a little less. Everybody won but Shep, and with his prices he didn't really lose. But tonight, with the boss hovering, the deal was off. I gave Cosme a tiny nod of perfect understanding.

Mr. Nordstrom showed me a piece of engraved amber in the shape of a crescent. He wanted to know how much it was worth and where he could sell it. He said he had paid $50 for it.

It was an ornamental nose clip of a reddish cast, finely worked, probably from Monte Albán or thereabouts, certainly not Mayan, but rare in any case. I had never seen a piece quite like it and I wouldn't have hesitated to ask $750 for it, though there really wasn't enough amber on the market to establish a price range.

He had made a great buy, beginners luck, but I didn't want to encourage him. Still, it was a bit early in my conversion for me to be lecturing others on the evils of the trade. A decent silence was indicated, and I was no good at that either.

"You don't want to get mixed up in this business, Mr. Nordstrom. When you buy this stuff you'll be cheated, and when you go to sell it you may end up in big trouble. It's not worth it. Leave it at the museum. Drop it in the church box."

"I got stung?"

"It's not a bad piece but I really can't advise you."

"Shep said you would know."

"That tall fellow back there in the T-shirt and cowboy hat. He might be able to help you. His name is Eli. But don't go showing it around to just anyone."

Along the bar various claims to personal distinction were being made.

"I have a stainless-steel plate in my head."

"I am one-sixteenth Cherokee."

"I have never voted in my life."

"My mother ate speckled butterbeans every day of her life."

"I don't even take aspirins."

Suarez, the Spaniard, the old *gachupín,* was standing at my right with his newspaper and his glass of Ron Castillo. The chest-high bar was a bit high for his chest. He was a little man who drank alone in public places. He lived and drank alone and unapproached. Once in a while you would catch him shaking with private laughter. He hissed at me and nudged me and pointed to an item in the paper. "*Señor Mostaza.* Read that if you please." He called me that, Mr. Mustard, having once observed me spreading what he thought was far too much mustard on a ham sandwich. I read it, a single paragraph in *Diario Del Sureste,* about an exchange of gunfire between some squatters and a landowner near Mazatlán.

He said, "The straw is beginning to burn, no?"

"No, I don't think so. Too early. This means nothing."

Suarez was always looking for signs of revolution and finding them. It couldn't come soon enough to suit him, this great wind that would blow all the monkeys out of the trees. He was an old communist who had fled Spain in 1939, only to become a fascist here in Mexico, a Gold Shirt. But then he left that banner too and now he had some sort of *pan-hispano-anarcho-rojo-swino-nihilo* program of his own devising. There would be a good many summary executions, with Jews, Masons, Chinamen, Jesuits and Moros heading the list, and with no parliamentary nonsense—no republican *tontería.* He would close the borders for a period of national cleansing. He would change the marriage laws for some eugenic purpose. It nettled him a little when I called him a *comunista*. He said it made him sound like a pansy (*hermanita*). Back in the days when he was eviscerating priests and burning down churches in Barcelona (Barthalona), he told me, the communists were the squeamish moderates. He had contempt for Mexicans, even though they had given him refuge, or perhaps because of it. It showed their weakness. The French and the Italians were soft too. Spaniards were the only hard Latinos. Julius Caesar would have none but Spaniards as bodyguards—for all the good it did him. Nor did he think much of Americans. We were not a tribe he admired. We were the *Alemanni,* the hairy and dull-witted barbarians from across the Rhine, or in this case the Rio Grande, jabbering away in a Low German dialect called English.

He placed his finger on the Mazatlán dateline. "There. This time the rising will come from the Pacific. The *Alzamiento*."

"You once told me Veracruz."

"*Habladores,*" he said, showing me with thumb and fingers how the *Cruzanos* chattered away to no purpose. "No, I am looking to Sinaloa now. I am watching the west."

A hippie with his hair pulled back in a ponytail came traipsing along behind us. Shep reached across the bar and gave him a flick with his fly swatter.

"Just where do you think you're going, pal?"

"To the head."

"No, you're not. You people come in here and never buy anything and what, I'm supposed to provide facilities for you?"

"Hey, what is this? I just walked in. I may get a beer or a Coke or something. I don't know yet. First I got to go to the head."

"Okay, but in and out. Number one and that's all. I don't want you taking a bath back there."

It was too crowded at the bar. I went to the Crouch table and had a piece of cake. Minim recited some verses he had composed for the occasion, a long poem for him, which ended with these words: "And so we say goodbye for now to Peg and Vernon Crouch." Beth was sitting there with Bollard. He wore a white turtleneck sweater. She couldn't stay away from these literary fellows, poets for preference, and they invariably let her down. Last spring there had been Frank, the uninspired poet. She listened to his complaints. She lent him money. It was Minim who told me he was uninspired, though I don't see how he could know. Frank didn't write anything, or at least he didn't publish anything. Beth claimed he burned with a nonluminous flame, and all the hotter for that. Perhaps. A nonflowering plant. He soon drifted away. The Olmecs didn't like to show their art around either. They buried it twenty-five feet deep in the earth and came back with spades to check up on it every ten years or so, to make sure it was still there, unviolated. Then they covered it up again.

Bollard talked about his investments. I had to get away from these poems and telephone bonds, and I moved on to another table, with Art and Mike and a young man named Jerry, who called himself an "ethnomusicologist." He was supposed to be out in the villages spying on people and recording Mayan songs, but he preferred to spend his time and his grant money here at Shep's. We sat there drinking and talking foolishly under the huge fresco map of the Yucatán peninsula. There are many fine wall paintings in Mexico but this wasn't one of them. As a map it was so distorted as to be useless, and it didn't please as art either, or it didn't please me. I know nothing about art, but in my business we gave ourselves these airs. Even Eli had opinions.

The hippie came out of the toilet, having bathed and washed his hair and generally freshened up. He stopped at the bar to bum a cigarette. Vick gave him one and he also gave him some Scripture to think over. " 'If a man have long hair, it is a shame unto him,'" he said. "First Corinthians, eleven, fourteen."

Shep swatted the hippie again. "You. Stop hustling the customers. Out."

"Hey, man, you never been down and needed a smoke?"

"Yeah, I have, and you know what I did? The first thing I did was quit smoking and the next thing I did was get a job."

"You can't get a job in Mexico. A gringo can't."

"The hell you can't. You want a job? I'm calling your bluff, pal. I got a job right here for you."

It was a dilemma for the hippie. He knew the job would be something like cleaning out a grease trap and that he would probably be paid not in cash but with some old clothes and broken-down shoes. But then he was shown up if he didn't accept.

"All right, but first I need to see this guy. I'll be back."

"No, don't bother."

Art and Mike didn't believe the story of how Shep, finding himself up against it, had given up his Chesterfields and knuckled down in earnest to a life of hard work. I was inclined to believe it. Jerry sat on the fence. Judgments came hard to him. It was true that Shep didn't exert himself much these days, but I was thinking of a younger Shep, hopping from door to door selling term life insurance, and later, peddling badly worn furniture and carpeting from bankrupt motels. I wondered who bought those rugs. People make fun of salesmen, people with salaries or remittances, who don't have to produce. They have no idea of what a tough game it is. Art and Mike said Shep had a dog's name. Jerry said he had no manners. Art and Mike went further and said he had no soul, or at most the soul of a bug, an ant-size portion of the divine element. I thought they went too far.

Nelms was going from table to table seeking sympathy. "How long have I been coming here? . . . This is how he repays me . . ." He had a drink in one hand and a boiled pig's foot in the other. His lips were frosted with coarse grains of margarita salt. Nardo Cepeda had announced his presence at the bar, crying out every few minutes, "*Beebah Mehico!*" and "We want Nardo!"

Louise and Emmett and a young man in a blue suit joined us. They had been to a movie. The young fellow was introduced to us as Wade Watson, a government clerk from Jefferson City, Missouri, who wrote science-fiction tales in his spare time. "I just flew in this afternoon," he said. "I had seat 28F at the back behind the emergency door. You get more leg room that way. I still can't believe I'm actually in Mérida. The ancient name, you know, was Tiho, or more correctly, T'ho. I won't have time to inspect all the great pyramids and monuments because I have an appointment at the City of Dawn. After I see *El Mago*. First I have to meet with him in the town of Progreso."

Wade's fingernails were bitten down to the quick. Louise had found him wandering the streets and she took him in tow. Art and Mike cautioned him that the Maya-land picture books made things appear bigger than they were, and that the colors were touched up, as with picture postcards. Even so, the ruins were magnificent, and he wouldn't be disappointed. Wade asked where he could catch a bus to Progreso.

Louise had little to say about the movie, something called *Amor sin Palabras*, only that it was "thought-provoking." That was her lowest rating.

Jerry said, "But 'Love without Words'? How did they manage that?"

"Well, of course they didn't," said Emmett. "You never heard so much gabble and twittering in your life."

He bought a round of drinks and said that Louise had been right, this night on the town was just what he needed. He had been cooped up in the trailer too long. He was feeling much better. The new medicine worked better than the old medicine, and the only side effects so far were blurred vision, hair loss, vertigo, burning feet, nightmares, thickened tongue, nosebleed, feelings of dread, skin eruptions and cloudy urine. Art and Mike said it was a scandal the way she went gadding about town with this old man. She said she was only trying to protect him from fortune-hunting women. Emmett said she was much too late for that. Nelms came by and appealed to her, and she went off with him to see why Shep wouldn't accept his check.

The City of Dawn. That was where Dan and his people were going. I asked Wade about it. "Is it a place or what?"

"Yes, a place, of course, but much more than that. Much more!"

"Where is it?"

"Where indeed."

"You don't know?"

"I see what you're trying to do. You're trying to trap me into an indiscretion."

"Hardly a trap. I simply asked you where it was."

"Aren't we curious!"

No use to press him. Smirking and coy, he was like all the others of his breed. I would have to grab him by the throat to get any sense out of him and I couldn't do that here.

A strolling mariachi band came in and added to the din. We had to raise our voices. Over at the Crouch table they were laughing and shouting in each other's faces, taking feverish delight in their powers of speech. They appeared to be practicing words and phrases on one another, drunken delegates at an Esperanto congress.

Mott led the applause for the band and gave the cornet player a handful of money. Louise was at the bar demanding answers from Shep. I caught sight of Eli up there, waving me over. Mr. Nordstrom had gone, and Eli was drinking with Nardo, the lawyer.

They were both drunk or close to it. Nardo clapped me on the back. "What is this, Boornez, you're not in jail?" *Boornez* was his rendering of Burns.

"I'm out on work release."

"No, you're a shadow and they can't see you. They can't see a ghost. You have Don Ricardo looking after you too."

"Speaking of that, why aren't you locked up?"

"Me! Nardo in prison! What an idea! But look. Eli here is a real criminal. The question is, how does he stay out?"

"I mind my own business," said Eli.

"And what business is that? Let me tell you something, my *zopilote* friend. The days are over when you gringos can come down here and use my country for a playground."

"I don't think them days are quite over yet, Nardo."

"We'll see! Luisito! Give these two *coyotes* whatever they're drinking and bring me the telephone!"

There was no telephone at the bar and never had been. He and Luisito argued the point once again.

Eli was a solemn drunk with a slightly curved spine and a drooping head. The Mexicans called him The Vulture, *El Zopilote*. He had a pointed beard and long ropy arms with Disney bluebirds tattooed on them. There was a black leather strap on his left wrist, which had no function that I could see, other than to be vaguely menacing.

"What was wrong with that amber piece?" he said.

"Nothing. You didn't buy it?"

He stared at me and went back to his drink. I could see his difficulty. Why would I be sending him such a sweet deal? He couldn't believe that I was really out of the business. Tiny blood vessels were breaking inside his head as he tried to think it out.

"Where was it from, Tepíc?"

"I thought Oaxaca. Zápotec."

"How did he come by it? I mean a guy like that."

"I didn't ask him."

"There's nothing funny about it?"

"Not that I know of."

"Damn. Now he's gone. He only wanted a hundred for it. The amber itself is worth more than that. Where does the old man live?"

"I don't know. You mean where he stay?"

"I mean where he be staying."

"You must mean where he be staying when he at home."

Eli was from Mississippi, and we sometimes fell into this black man patter. "What time it is?" and such stuff as that. We had a lot in common. One difference between us was this: He said shevel and I said shovel. Trust me to go with the crowd. Luisito pushed more glasses at us. "Señor Mott," he said. Mott was treating and circulating about like a host, with a word of welcome for everyone.

"Come on, come on," he said, urging us to clap for the band. "Let's show some appreciation. Isn't that trumpet player great?"

Nardo said Mexicans were the only people in the world who could play the trumpet. Nobody else had the heart for it. Mott said all his life he had envied Harry James, who would go out at night to some ballroom and knock everybody dead playing "Ciribiribin," and then when he got home Betty Grable was there. Nardo said Harry James was a Mexican and that Mexican trumpet players and athletes were the envy of the world.

Mott moved on to greet the others. Eli said that he, too, would go around grinning at the world and buying drinks for everybody if the government sent him a disability check every month. I told him I didn't think he would. He went off to search for Mr. Nordstrom.

Shep was trying to explain things to Louise. "But I'm not running a bank, little lady." She hated those diminutives. "I'll take his check for the amount of his drinks but I'm through handing out cash. With the peso changing from day to day, I can't sit on the paper. I can't afford it no more and I can't make no exceptions."

Nardo had gone into his football chant. He was slapping the bar with his hands. "Nar-do! Nar-do! We want Nar-do!" That was from the stadium fans at Bonar College. They wanted to see Nardo on the field, running back a punt or a kickoff, or knocking some pass receiver cold. He had played both ways, and he was a real player, too, no mere place kicker, as the rumor went. I had seen the newspaper clippings.

He held up a fist to his mouth, a microphone. "Oh yes, that's Nardo Cepeda, and let me tell you something, this little guy never calls for a fair catch! Oh brother, can he scoot! He's a little man, only five-six and a hundred and forty pounds soaking wet, but can he fly! Will you look at that! The little guy can turn on a dime! You can't coach those moves! He's gone! Cepeda is gone! See you later! No way that kicker will catch him now . . ."

It was one of his weaker performances, and suddenly he just stopped. "They think I'm a clown. These people don't know anything. We went twenty-eight and two in three years. I was pretty good for my size, Boornez."

"I know that."

"No, you don't. You think I was just a Division II player. Let me tell you something. If I weighed another ten kilograms I could play for anybody."

"Fausto says you're a good lawyer."

"Not only Fausto. I could get you out of jail in five minutes. Like that." He tried to snap his fingers but they were wet and wouldn't snap. "I know the law, Boornez. Would you like to know how many laws we have in Mexico? We have more than 72,000 laws and regulations. What do you say to that, gringo?"

"I say that's pathetic. That's pitiful for a progressive nation. In my country we have 459,000 laws and regulations. You'll never catch us."

"I know the law. I know how things are done. I could get you out of jail in five minutes. Your friend Eli? No. I wouldn't bother with him. He's looking at Article 33 right now. Did you know that?"

"Well, it's better than jail."

"He may get both. Why don't they let you use the phone up here anymore?"

"I don't know."

"Luisito!"

Article 33 hung over all our heads. This was a catch-all provision in the Mexican constitution whereby any foreigner could be kicked out of the country at any time for any reason at all, or for no stated reason. That was my understanding of it. Not that reasons would be lacking in Eli's case, or in mine. But I had worked with a certain amount of protection, being associated with Doc Flandin, who had friends in Mexico City. He knew all the old-timers at the Instituto Nacional de Antropología, and they allowed him a good many liberties. Nardo, as an active party man, had political influence. He had arranged the dig at Ektún for his small and obscure college in Illinois, which was quite a feat, seeing how few permits were given to foreigners these days. Most of them had to settle for secondary sites in Belize or Guatemala. Just how great a feat it was, I don't think Nardo ever appreciated, or he would have made more of it.

I told him about the Bonar College troubles at Ektún. It came as news to him and not very interesting news. He thought too much fuss was made over all this ancient masonry. What was the appeal of these old *Indios* (the *naturales*, he called them) and their ruined *templos?* It was all a great bore to him, the Maya business, except for the tourist aspect. It gave people the wrong idea about Mexico. Departed glory. Blinking lizards on broken walls. He wanted his country to be thought of as Euro-America or Ibero-America and not Indo-America.

The hippie came back, to my surprise, and with a friend, an older and thinner hippie, who had long brown hair breaking over both sides of his shoulders. They went directly to Vick at the bar. The new hippie said, "You never heard of Samson in the Bible? Samson's strength was in his long hair."

Vick said, "I've heard of Absalom. He was in rebellion against his father. His pride and vanity were in his long hair and it got him hanged from the thick bough of a great oak."

"What about Samuel? Samuel found favor with both God and man and a razor never touched his head. You never heard of Samuel?"

"Nebuchadnezzar had long filthy hair and long green nasty fingernails. He ate grass with the beasts of the field. That was where his pride and vanity got him. He was swollen with pride just like a dog tick all bloated up with blood."

"You're way behind the times, old man. You've got a lot of unresolved anger there too. You belong in an old man's home."

The other hippie corrected him. "Old folks home. Nursing home."

Vick said, "You two belong in the hall of shame."

They laughed at him and went away, the two hippie pals, off to wherever they were bedding down for the night. They had their campgrounds, and their fleeting friendships, too, I suppose.

Nardo challenged me to a 100-meter footrace out in the street. The time had come for barroom displays of strength. I told him I was gone in the knee but would be glad to arm-wrestle him for a drink. He didn't want to do that. I had the reach on him and the leverage. He went off into a dream, brooding and muttering.

One of my quirks too. I didn't do it in the street like *El Obispo,* not yet, but in my room, in the woods, on long drives, I spoke softly but audibly to myself, in the second person, as was only proper. I spoke to a child or a half-wit. *Why can't you put that bottle-opener back in the same place each time and then you'll know where it is.* Doc had called my attention to it. I was trying to get a job with a crew of Mormon *arqueos* in Belize and I gave him as a reference. At the bottom of their letter of inquiry he scribbled, "Jimmy Burns is a pretty good sort of fellow with a mean streak. Hard worker. Solitary as a snake. Punctual. Mutters and mumbles. Trustworthy. Facetious." Doc gave with one hand and took away with the other. The Mormons must have scratched their heads over those last two things. How could he be both trustworthy and facetious? They hired me anyway, and soon I was doing all their hauling. The trick is to make yourself first useful and then necessary. Punctual! Yes, the puniest of virtues, nothing to brag about, but Doc was right, I was always on time. Unheard of here in Mexico.

Now here came Harold Bolus on his two canes, taking his stiff and well-planned steps. "Great news, Jimmy. The Crouches have decided to stay on after all. It was this wonderful party that did it. This is a Who's Who of Mérida and they were touched. They're not leaving." Bolus had lost his legs, the lower parts below the knees, in the Chosin retreat. "My heart's in Oklahoma," he would sing, "but my feet are in Korea." That was his song. He sat on park benches and showed his willow-wood shins to children. This was what came of too much dancing, he told them. As a foolish boy he had danced his feet off. Let this be a warning to them. Go easy on the dancing and particularly the spinning about, or when the music was over they would end up like him with nothing left to stand on but two bloody stumps.

I was exhausted. All this talking and listening, a six-month quota for me in one night. My neighbors, Chuck and Diane, stopped to speak. That wasn't quite their names but some names you can't take in. They could have spelled out their names for me every day for six days running and on Sunday morning I would have drawn a blank again. It was embarrassing. They were a nice young couple with a room down the hall from me at the Posada. They were my neighbors and it would be my duty to denounce them after the Suarez revolution, but first I would have to get their names straight. Something like Chick and Diane but not quite that. I wouldn't be permitted to sit it out. Suarez had warned me that anyone who sat back and tried to mind his own business would be arrested and charged with "vexatious passivity."

Back at my room I found a note under my door from Beatriz. Refugio had called from the bus station in Palenque. "He says he is bringing the car back to Mérida tomorrow." What car? I didn't understand the message. Then Nardo and Sloat, drunk, came by my room and woke me up. Shep had closed his place, and the gang was moving on to the Tiburón Club. I told them I was too tired.

Besides, I didn't go to disco joints, with all that noise, and I didn't like bars that were upstairs. I ran them off.

A few minutes later there was more rapping at the door. It was Nardo again. He had to brace himself with both hands against the door jambs. "I forgot to tell you something," he said. "Did you notice I was feeling low tonight?"

"No, I thought you were in good form."

"It was off just a little, my natural charm, you know, that everybody talks about. You must have noticed. A touch of *opresión*. I wanted to explain."

"I didn't notice anything."

"But you already know, don't you?"

"Know what?"

"Is there any need to explain? I think you can guess why I'm feeling low."

"No, I can't."

"The *yanquis* took half my country in 1848."

"They took all of mine in 1865. We can't keep moping over it."

"Why not?"

"I don't know. That's what they tell us. We just have to make the best of it. They say we should just go on about our business and leave all that to them."

"Is that all you have to say?"

"That's all I have to say tonight."

"The *coche* is waiting. Come on. Everybody's going to the Tiburón."

"Another time maybe."

"Sloat wants to talk to you downstairs."

"No, you go on. I'll be over later to help mop up the cripples."

"Half my country."

"A few border corrections, that's all."

I had to take him down and put him in the taxicab with the others and give it two hard slaps on the fender, which meant, *go!* Maybe he would manage to forget the old grievance out there on the dance floor. If I knew Nardo he would still be leading the conga line when the sun came up. He spoke good English but his *"yanquis"* came out something like "junkies."

AT MID-MORNING Refugio came rolling in with Rudy's bulbous yellow car. The first thing he wanted was a red snapper, broiled with tomatoes and onions, and a stuffed pepper on the side. We ate at the Express, where you could get anything you liked. There were forty-odd entrees on the menu, and if you wanted something else, an artichoke or a piece of baby shark liver, they would send out to the *mercado* for it and cook it to your taste. Refugio said he had also brought the camping trailer out of the jungle, but then a hub bearing had burned out on the highway and he had left the rig with a friend. He had the bearing with him, and he had the little Olmec jade man, too, in a jar of water. It looked like an evil fetus. He thought jade would crack, as opals sometimes do, unless you kept it soaked. He planned to sell it while he was in town.

Yes, yes, yes, but what was he doing with the car? What was all this? Where was Rudy? The young man who owned the car?

As to that he couldn't say. He and Manolo had gone to Ektún with some gasoline and odds and ends to sell.

All was confusion there. Skinner was still tangled up in Villahermosa, but Lund had come back to find that this Rudy had disappeared. He had strolled off into the woods and vanished. They had searched for him all around the site and as far downstream as the Usumacinta River. Lund, the bearded *ingeniero,* was unnerved, and furious too, calling me terrible names. He had directed Refugio to deliver the car and trailer to me, along with this note.

> Mr. Burns
>
> Your friend Kurle has disappeared. I am in no way liable. He was on his own here as you well know. He walked off down the river alone. He was not invited here and he was not authorized to be here and neither I nor Bonar College can be held responsible. You brought him here uninvited. There are witnesses to that fact. Therefore I am sending his car and his things to you by way of Señor Bautista. I have notified the police in Palenque and I disclaim any further responsibility.
>
> Sincerely yours,
>
> C.A. Lund
> Chief Surveyor

I could see that Lund, having come so recently from the States, was living in terror of lawyers and courts and insurance companies. He feared legal reprisals but he need not have worried. It wasn't so bad down here yet, where extortion was still largely a private matter, arranged quietly and informally between the parties, and cheaper all around for everyone. But he was right, I was in some sense responsible. I had, in a manner of speaking, taken Rudy in to Ektún.

Refugio wanted money. He wrote "$100" in the hollow of his hand and showed it to me. Lund had told him I would pay him a lot of money for delivering the car.

"And look," he said. "I make that long drive with no company."

Solitude was agony to him. A few hours alone with your thoughts could drive you crazy.

"We'll see. The car is just part of it. You'll have to help me find him too. These people don't have much money."

"They have a nice car. They have a nice sleeping trailer and a nice CB radio."

"We'll talk about that after we find him."

He showed me the wheel bearing and told me how it had screeched and smoked. It looked okay to me. The rollers were unscored and they still turned freely in the race. There was too much talk about this bearing. Then it came to me. There had been no breakdown. He was holding the trailer as security against his fee. He was hiding it somewhere. A bird in Refugio's hand was worth thirty or forty in the bush.

He thought the boy would turn up in a day or so, if he was merely lost, and if he was prudent enough to keep going downstream. Once on the big river he was bound to encounter a boat or someone along the banks. And even if he was wandering around in the *selva* he would soon run across a trail and, eventually, a Lacondón village. The Lacondones would bring him out. It was all a big fuss over nothing, a gringo *bulla*, a *bagatela*.

Possibly, but he went too far in assuming that Rudy would do the sensible thing. I suspected that Rudy had gone down the Usumacinta, walking the banks, in search of Tumbalá, the place of the little temples. He was there or he was lost or he was drowned or he was dead of snakebite or he was shot or captured in the guerilla war across the river.

We lingered over coffee. The ragged old man called *El Obispo* passed by on the sidewalk, and we all turned our heads away so as not to meet his evil eye. The danger was small, he never looked up from the ground, but one day he might raise those red eyes. Pedestrians gave way. They peeled off left and right about six paces ahead of him. The effective range of his gaze was not thought to be great. He jabbered away as he walked, saying the same thing over and over again, and today he was moving right along. Some days he took it slow, placing one foot directly in front of the other with the care of a tightrope walker. He was called The Bishop because he slept in a shed behind the cathedral.

Refugio spit between his legs to neutralize the evil. What he hawked up, this heavy smoker, was a viscous ball of speckled matter resembling frog spawn. I had put off telling him about Doc. Now I told him. His hands flew up in alarm. Cancer is cancer in Spanish, too, and the word is avoided in polite company.

"No! Not the Doctor! This is too cruel! I must go to him!"

"Yes, but let me call first. They have a new set-up at that house."

I called Mrs. Blaney and simply told her that we were coming by, and then I dropped Refugio off at Izamál, he carrying his gift .45 in a paper sack. Doc was waiting for him outside. They embraced on the lawn, with Doc calling him by an old nickname, Cuco.

There was another unpleasant duty to perform. I tracked Louise down to the museum, where she was helping Beth take some school children through on a tour. The kids were in blue and white uniforms, and of that age, twelve or so, when the girls are a head taller than the boys. Andean flute music came over the speaker system. A bit of stagecraft, suggestive of eerie rites, but nothing to do with the Maya. Beth also liked to run the lights up and down with the rheostat.

I took Louise aside and told her that Rudy was missing. She didn't collapse in tears but was only fretful. A blank stare, a delicate cough, some floating thought, a quotation from L. Ron Hubbard—I never knew what to expect from her. Maybe she saw this as a merciful release, free at last, from Rudy and his tapes.

"I knew something like this was coming," she said. "I could feel it. It's all my fault because I'm such a coward."

Louise was far from being a coward. She was largely indifferent to the ordinary hazards of life, and yet she had a fear of stinging insects, something to do with an allergy, and she seldom ventured into the deep woods. She seemed to think she was to blame because she had stayed behind.

"It's not as bad as it sounds," I said. "He's just out of touch. We'll find him. I have a friend who knows that country well."

"Do the police know about this?"

"They know in Chiapas."

"Should we notify the vice-consul?"

"It won't hurt."

"I wonder if he can do anything. That man has the pink eyes of a rabbit."

"He'll do what he can."

"What about an air search? Beth would lend me the money to charter an airplane."

"You couldn't see anything but treetops. There's really no such thing as searching the Petén jungle. Miles and miles of unbroken greenery. He hasn't gone far. We'll turn him up along the river somewhere. Tumbalá, probably."

"He may have lost his memory. Rudy may be wandering around down there with no idea of who he is or where he is."

"Has that happened before?"

"No."

I waited for an explanation. None came.

"I'm just turning things over in my mind. Various possibilities. Someone could have murdered him for his tapes."

"You have his latest tape. I brought it to you."

"Not the very latest one. He would have made others by now."

She thought he might have fallen into the hands of hostile Indians. He was lying on the ground, bound hand and foot, with the village elders squatting in a circle around him. They were chewing bitter narcotic leaves as they passed judgment on him, and took their time over it.

I assured her that the Lacondón were a peaceable enough folk. They might tease Rudy or sell him a defective souvenir but they weren't likely to knock him in the head. I asked her what he was really up to down there.

"I don't know."

"I think you do know and you better tell me if you want to see him again."

"You're the one who gave him the map to that place. It's all your fault. That place with the little houses you told him about."

"What was on the tape he sent back?"

"Nothing much."

"I want to hear it."

"Rudy has strict rules—"

"I don't care about his rules. Either I hear that tape or I'm not lifting a finger."

"All right, but there's nothing useful on it. I didn't want to mention this—not to you—but it has to be considered. He may very well have been carried away in a spacecraft."

"I don't think that's likely, Louise."

"No, you wouldn't, would you? You don't want us to make a quality contact. Rudy finally makes a quality contact and you resent it. You're jealous of him. You've always been envious of his field equipment and his City Planning degree, and for some reason I don't understand you're trying to stop him from becoming a distinguished author and lecturer. It's small-minded people like you who make it so hard for the rest of us. You're jealous of anybody and everybody who's working on the frontiers of knowledge."

"Yes, but when these visitors do snatch someone, don't they always bring him back? To pass on their warnings about pollution and atom bombs and such?"

"A simple peasant, yes, or some dumbbell off the street, sure, they would bring him back after a quick body scan, but with someone like Rudy they would want to take him onto the mother ship. They would want to go over his notes and listen to his tapes and study his brain. They must have known he was on to something down there. It was a golden opportunity for them."

"Well, no need to borrow trouble. My guess is he hasn't gone far. There's a good chance he's already walked out somewhere."

"Not if they took him back to their own planet."

"No, in that case he's sunk, but there have been no reports of any landings. Someone would have seen the lights. The nights are very dark in Chiapas."

"They don't always use lights in the visible part of the spectrum. They're so far ahead of us in lasers and fiber optics that it isn't funny."

The children trooped out with their teacher, and Beth came over to see what was up. She and Louise badgered me with suggestions, relishing the drama. Beth thought I should use my "underworld connections" to help in the hunt. I went dead silent. Usually I brighten up a bit in the company of women and am not so much the lugubrious bore, my natural and most comfortable role, but my thoughts were far away. I was thinking not of Rudy but of Dan and his tribe and the little runaway girl they called Red. Yes, that was me to a T, lugubrious and punctual and facetious, all at once, a combination I would have found tiresome in another person, if I had known one.

Louise and I went to her *casita* and listened to the tape. It was just Rudy going on and on with his descriptions and measurements at Ektún. I thought it would never end. The murdering tape thief would have been annoyed when he got back to the quiet of his room and heard this stuff and looked at the blood on his hands. I fast-forwarded some of it. Rudy made no mention of his plans. I left the Checker car with Louise and suggested she move in with Beth, who had a telephone. "Stay close and I'll let you know as soon as I find out anything."

The night had turned off cool. A *norte* must have blown in. I walked over to the Posada and got my truck. Refugio would be waiting for me at Doc's place. On the way back across town I caught a glimpse of the night dog. I checked the moon. It seemed to be in about the third quarter.

A word here about the night dog and *El Obispo*. It took me almost two years to figure out what the old man was muttering. I picked up a word here and a word there and finally pieced them all together. Then one day Jerry asked me what he was saying. I told him and he wrote it down in his anthropology notebook. I felt cheated of my time and labor.

The common belief was that The Bishop was simply going through his rosary, but no, I knew the sounds of that litany all too well, from mountain bus rides on rainy nights, with terrified passengers all around me telling their beads. No, it was a text from Mark he was reciting. I looked it up.

"*¿Ves estos grandes edificios? No quedará piedra sobre piedra, que no sea derribada.*" ("Seest thou these great buildings? There shall not be left one stone upon another, that shall not be thrown down.")

Those were *El Obispo*'s words as he marched around Mérida with his eyes cast down. That, with variations, was what he said day in and day out. At noon he sat against the shady side of the cathedral and rested and ate squash seeds. Once I stuck an ice cream cone into his curled paw. He received it passively and may or may not have eaten it. He may have been asleep. I kept moving and didn't look back. On certain nights, in his shed behind the church, he changed himself into a small reddish dog with a fox face. The animal was about eighteen inches long, exclusive of the tail, which itself was about the same length, and stiff as a new rope. It curled up and around to form a near-circle, with the tip touching his back.

At least there was such a dog, I had seen him myself many times, and Fausto and others claimed that you could never catch the two of them together, The Bishop and the night dog. He moved at a trot, a dog on pressing business, and was always just going around a corner, it seemed, out of view. He was too healthy and sleek for a scavenger.

But on what business? No one could say. As it happened, I caught a glimpse of him on this night. He was jogging into an alley. The looped tail was unmistakable. I parked the truck and got out with my flashlight.

I knew this street slightly. This was the Naroody block. The Hotel Naroody was on the corner, and next to it was Foto Naroody, a photography *estudio*, with framed pictures in the window, portraits of brides and fat babies tinted with gruesome colors. Along the way there were shops with such names as Importaciones Naroody and Curiosidades Naroody. I had never seen Naroody taking any *fotos*. The display pictures gathered dust and were never changed. Some of those falsely colored babies may have been brides themselves by now. I wasn't even sure I had seen Naroody. Whenever I spotted some likely Levantine candidate I would be told, "Him? No, that's not Naroody."

I played the light about in the alley and kicked at boxes and piles of trash. The dog was gone. I doubled back and found a chubby man waiting for me at the entrance. He too had a flashlight. His eyelids drooped. One hand was resting in the pocket of a loose smock, such as a photographer might wear in his darkroom. I asked him if he had seen the jaunty dog.

"Ah, the dog. I thought you were a burglar. Yes, I know this dog. You will never capture him."

"I'm not trying to capture him. I just thought I had found his sleeping place."

"He passes this way on his rounds but he doesn't sleep here. He never stops. Why do you wish to capture him? The little dog is not harming anyone."

"I don't wish to capture him. I don't wish to bother him in any way but I would like to get a closer look at him."

"Why?"

"I hear these stories. I'm curious."

"The stories are nonsense."

"They say he comes out at certain phases of the moon."

"I don't listen to such talk."

"You're not Naroody, are you?"

He was startled. "What? Naroody? No. I only work for him."

"I hear he's a good man to work for."

"Where do you hear this?"

"You must be the watchman."

"I keep an eye on things, yes, but I have other duties too." He looked around and drew close and his voice fell to a whisper. "May I tell you something in confidence? All his methods are out of date."

"Naroody's methods?"

"His business methods. He won't listen to anyone."

"Do you know where the dog goes from here?"

He hesitated. I gave him some money. He thanked me and apologized, saying he was not moving up as fast in the Naroody organization as he had hoped. Naroody kept him short of pocket money. He got his keep and little more. He pointed to a window above one of the shops. That was his room. He had a room of his own up there with running water, or trickling water anyway, and he ate well enough at Naroody's second table, but he saw very little cash, not nearly enough to buy fashionable clothes and take women out at night. His life was not fulfilled. There were men his age, much less deserving, who drove cars and had as many as ten pairs of pointed shoes in their closets.

"But the dog."

"They say he goes to the rail yard and later comes out of the big drain pipe behind the feed mill. After that I don't know. Who has time to listen to such foolishness? These are not good questions. You drive a fine white truck that will take you anywhere you wish to go. Do you tell me that you believe in ghost animals?"

"I believe he's a strange dog. You say yourself that I could never capture him."

"Let me say too that I am disappointed with this talk about the phases of the moon. I took you for a modern man like me."

His name was Hakim. He wanted to chat some more, but about California and career opportunities there in real estate management. I knew nothing about it. Yucatán is off the California flyway, and we didn't see many of those birds around here. There was a heavy squarish lump in his pocket. Hakim, I think, was holding a little .22 or .25 automatic in that smock pocket. He was ready to defend Naroody's property with force.

I went to the rail yard and the feed mill and even watched the round black hole of the drain pipe for a while. I crouched in the weeds like a stalking cat. It was downright cold there, though the wind had fallen off. The dog didn't show.

What we had here, according to Jerry, another modern man, was a case of conflation or confabulation. *El Obispo* and the dog, taking similar steps, made regular circuits around town. Someone had noticed this and with an imaginative leap had spun a tale combining the two elements. It was a good enough explanation except that the two gaits were not alike. The old man and the dog just didn't walk in the same way, and as far as I could see there were no points of physical resemblance whatever.

Jerry then was not above a little confabulating himself. He too dealt in fables, and this was a good name for his science, I thought, confabulation, not that Jerry ever defended his science, not with the tiniest of pistols, being trained as he was to believe in nothing. In the Anthropology Club, as I understood it, you were permitted, if not required, to despise only one thing, and that was your own culture, that of the West. Otherwise you couldn't prefer one thing over another. Of course Jerry's curiosity was no more damnable than mine, a poking, pointless, infantile curiosity, but then he got paid for his.

After cruising around the cathedral a couple of times, I gave up on the night dog and went to Doc's house to pick up Refugio. He wasn't ready to go. They were upstairs in the bedroom looking at old photographs. A little tepee of sticks was blazing away in the fireplace, so seldom used. The fat *ocote* wood was popping and there were some cedar sticks, too, some *kuche*, for the pleasant scent. How long had it been since the three of us had sat around a fire at night?

Doc said, "Look, Jimmy. See what Cuco brought me. It's by far the finest jade I ever held in my hands. This is the work of a master."

Refugio had given him the little Olmec man. Quite a gift. Quite an exchange. A $7,500 jade for a $200 pistol. Doc asked me if I would place the little *idolo* in his mouth when he died and see that he was buried with it. I refused.

Then would I just clasp his dead fingers around it? A simple grave offering. No! I wouldn't put that snarling little demon into the grave of my worst enemy and I told him so. He tried to pass it off as a joke. Refugio, looking troubled, must have turned him down, too, or more likely had hedged. It took an effort to cross the great Doctor. Or he may have been having second thoughts about his generosity—if in fact he had made a gift of the thing. Doc may have misunderstood him.

The moment passed, and we went on to other things. Doc offered advice on how to conduct the search for the missing boy in the *selva*. "Chombo is the man you want for that work." Soon it was like the old days around the campfire, with Doc toasting the soles of his big white feet and Refugio spitting at the coals. We laughed and talked foolishly for hours. We must have burned up a donkey-load of pine knots, or *ocote* wood. But then we pushed it too far, tried to make the happy occasion last, and along toward daylight our talk trailed off. Doc let his pipe go out and began heaving mighty sighs. He said, "Well, what does it matter in the long run? When you get right down to it everything is a cube." One by one we went numb. The fire died. No one stoked it. We were grainy-eyed and lost within our own heads again.

NO USE turning in now. Refugio and I had breakfast at the little café on the *zócalo* called the Louvre. The crazy black ants of Yucatán were at play on the tabletop. They never let up. From birth to death they went full out, racing about to no purpose on the oilcloth and crashing into one another like hockey players. The Louvre would do in a pinch. A cook was on duty all night and the onion soup was good, but they wouldn't give you enough crackers. They begrudged you every last *galleta*. The biggest and most modern cracker factory in Mexico was right here in Mérida, but you would have never guessed it at the Louvre, where they doled them out two at a time.

Refugio tried to sell some of his plastic pipe to a Dutch farmer, a Mennonite, who was sitting there in overalls spooning up corn flakes from a huge white bowl. He could have washed his hands in that basin. *Give them all the corn flakes and milk they want but make them beg for crackers.* What kind of policy was that? The Mennonite said nothing and missed not a beat with his spoon and yet he managed to show a kind of crafty interest in the pipe deal.

147

I was watching the jailbirds, the *degradados,* who were out early sweeping the plaza. One was a very tall American with a black goatee. It was Eli Withering. I picked up an orange from the table and walked across the street. I gave the guard a cigarette, and he allowed me to have a word with my *cuate.* My pal, that is, which was stretching it a bit.

Eli said, "They got me cold, Budro. Can you let me have $500? They got old Nordstrom too. That amber was bad news. You knew it and I didn't. I never had any luck with that stuff. Now look at me. These flat Popsicle sticks are hard to sweep up."

Yes, there was Mr. Nordstrom in the line of sweepers, working hard with a pushbroom to cover his shame, poking away, trying to get a purchase on the *paleta* sticks. He would be a model social-democratic Scandinavian prisoner. Mr. Nordstrom wouldn't bang his cup against the bars or otherwise give trouble. It was too bad, but I had told the old man not to meddle in this business.

Eli was disgusted with himself. "It was really dumb. Sauceda was tailing me and I didn't spot him."

"He would have gotten you anyway. It wasn't the amber."

I saw a third gringo in the work gang. It was Louise's friend, Wade Watson, the young man from Missouri. He was dragging a trash box along and he still seemed to be taking a dazed delight in everything. First he couldn't believe he was in Yucatán and now he couldn't believe he was a prisoner.

"That boy there," I said. "What's he in for?"

"I don't know. Sauceda grabbed him too. He was just standing there with us, asking a lot of questions. I thought he was with Nordstrom. Do you know him?"

"I've met him."

"There's something wrong with him. He won't shut up. He talked all night in the tank. Here, let me have that."

Eli grabbed my orange and ripped it apart and sucked the pulp to shreds. "I need that money today. I'm counting on you, Budro. I need to get this settled before it goes up to the Director of Investigations."

"Do you want Nardo to handle it?"

"Hell no. Bring the money to me in dollars. I'll cut my own deal. Sauceda is a man you can talk to. You know I'm good for it. I'll put my car up against it. Bring me a blanket, too, and get me a hat of some kind. Somebody stole my hat while I was sleeping."

I told him I would see what I could do. And there was poor Wade, caught hanging around the wrong people, on his first night here too. He must have been hoping to catch some sparks off the conversation of two old Maya hands. I went over to him and asked if he had any money.

"A little. Who are you? I have my credit card."

"That's no good. Here. You'll need a few pesos if you're going to eat. I may be able to get you out of this jam."

"How? I don't even know what I'm doing here."

"It's a tradeoff. I may be able to pull some strings, but first, you see, I'll have to know where the City of Dawn is."

"Oh yes, you're the curious guy from the bar. Why do you want to know?"

"I'm to meet a friend there, but she forgot to tell me where it is."

"Oh? Then she must have had her reasons for not telling you. Just as I have mine. There are good and sufficient reasons why certain people know things and others don't."

"Well, you think it over. They've got you on a pretty serious offense. Encroaching on the national patrimony. I won't be able to do anything after you're formally charged."

The guard shooed me away. I didn't want Eli's car. I didn't need a Dodge Dart with burnt valves and major oil leaks and an electrical system that shorted out every time you hit a puddle. The distributor was mounted low on the block and was readily swamped. Eli kept saying he was going to trade the Dart for a heavy car with a long trunk lid. But I did owe him for services rendered. Unclean bird that he was, he was always square with me. Or he wasn't always square but he was generous.

He had shown me the ropes in the antiquities business. It was Eli who had put me on to the job with Doc Flandin. They had worked together briefly and then fallen out over the First Fruits Rule. This was the rule whereby Doc, as boss, had the pick of the finds. It wasn't as bad as it sounds. He was no hog. Doc didn't always take the most valuable pieces. In his more swaggering moods he called this privilege his *quinto*, or royal fifth, though it was more like a half.

I felt too that I had let Eli down. I had sent Nord-strom to him. Nardo had warned me that he was in danger, and I had done nothing, sat on my hands.

So now I had to wait until the banks opened. Refugio took a nap in my room. I called Louise at Beth's place and told her about Wade. She was still in bed, her voice languid and nasal.

"You're not in Chiapas?" she said. "You haven't even started yet?"

"Not yet. If you want to help this Watson boy go to the police and carefully explain to them that he has a screw loose."

"Why do you say that? You think everybody's silly but you."

"Do you want to get him out of jail? They don't like to be bothered with crazy people. I'm telling you how to get him out, Chiquita."

"Don't call me that."

"And then I want you to find out from Wade Watson just where this City of Dawn is. You know how to talk to those people and I don't."

"What does this have to do with Rudy?"

"Nothing, but it's important. It's something else I'm working on."

"A city of dogs?"

"Dawn. The Inaccessible City of Dawn. It's some-thing your New Age friends are talking about. You must have heard of it, an insider like you."

"No, I haven't."

"Rudy didn't mention it?"

"I don't think so. Does it have another name? What is it anyway?"

"That's what I don't know. A place. That's all I know."

"He was going to Tumbalá. That's the only place he mentioned to me."

"Yes, and that's where we'll find him. All right, get up and brush your hair and go to the city jail. Tell them Wade Watson is *loco, débil* in the head, and that he has no money and will give them a lot of problems. Tell them you will put him on the next bus to the border. Then I want you to get that information out of him. I need to know where this city is. Do you understand?"

"I still don't understand why Wade is in jail. What did he do again?"

"He didn't do anything. It was a mixup."

"I've been thinking. Maybe I should go to Chiapas with you."

"No, that's not a good idea. Just do what I tell you. Ask for Sergeant Sauceda at the jail. We can't keep changing our plans. I'll be in touch."

There was a crowd outside my bank. At opening time it always looked like a run on the funds. Old Suarez was there waiting in the *cambio* line, the exchange line, a revolutionary in coat and tie and black felt hat. He was all in black, watchful, on the lookout for little signs of disrespect to his person. A big American woman had sat down on him once. She hadn't seen him on the park bench. Today he was lecturing. The leathery woman in front of him was from Winnipeg. She painted big brown landscapes.

Suarez didn't think much of Canadians either and he was setting her straight on a few things. Their nation was illegitimate. Their sovereignty had been handed to them on a platter, an outright gift, instead of having been properly won through force of arms. The birth throes had to be violent. There had to be blood. He told her too that no woman in Spain would dare to show herself in public in her underwear—a reference to her shorts. She listened in icy silence. Why didn't she slap him or claw his face? Draw some of that consecrating blood. Why didn't she forget all that dead brown topography and buy a bucket of black paint and do a portrait of the fierce little *anarquista?* I got the money in fifties. It was a big withdrawal for me, but I can't say it cleaned me out.

It would have been little enough, $500, a *gasto*, a modest business expense, back when I was selling those long tan coats and making money hand over fist and living at the Napoles. That was my first period of prosperity in Mexico, before I drifted into the relic business. I bought soft leather coats from the Escudero brothers and sold them to Rossky's in New Orleans.

Ramón Escudero had a tanning and softening process all his own, using alum and extract of oak galls and yolks from sea bird eggs and I don't know what else. Every woman in New Orleans wanted one of those coats. We couldn't deliver them fast enough. Then there was a family squabble. Ramón walked out of the workshop one day, accusing brother Rodolfo of making life unbearable for him. "The devil is in this business!" he said, and he went home and wouldn't come back. He wouldn't even come out of his house. Rodolfo, the younger brother, tried to carry on with the same workers, but the coats were never quite the same. They didn't feel right and they didn't drape right. I think I must have poisoned the lives of the Escuderos with my production demands. Anyway, the women in New Orleans stopped buying the coats and went on to newer things. Rodolfo and I were left high and dry.

It was lunchtime when I got back to the jail. I advised Eli to call in Nardo or some other lawyer. He said it would only jack up the price. We were standing in the courtyard with prisoners and visitors milling around us. This was the old municipal jail downtown, a very loose jail, nothing at all like the new one. You could keep your belt, and your shoelaces if you had shoes, and your necktie too. You were free to hang yourself. Wives and mothers and sweethearts were there with bowls of pozole, a Mexican version of grits, for their men. It was like a busy bus station. Fausto had more rules at his hotel. I gave Eli a blanket and a couple of paperback westerns and a few packs of Del Prado cigarettes. The money was taped inside a book. I didn't forget his hat. It was a cheap straw hat and of course too small. They didn't make them big enough for gringo skulls. He wanted it so he could whip it smartly off his head in the presence of Sergeant Sauceda.

I didn't see Wade Watson. Louise must have sprung him already. Say what you will, you could rely on that girl to do her job and do it right the first time. When I left Eli he was writing something in a tablet, working *zurdo*, left-handed, with his fist twisted around. A journal? Prison literature? Yes, of course, I knew about that, an old tradition, but I had no idea they started in on it so soon. Jail was a place for reflection, no doubt. Time would hang heavy. But Eli with pen in hand? Well, why not? It would make for some good reading, the confessions of *El Zopilote*. Pancho Villa himself had gone a little soft in his prison cell. He applied to a business school for a correspondence course. He would learn to use a typewriter and begin a new life, a clerical life. He would live in town and wear a clean shirt and write business letters all day. *Most Respectfully Yours, Francisco Villa, Who Kisses Your Hand*. But then after a day or two with the study materials he became annoyed, saying it was *tedioso* and all a lot of *mierda seca,* and he broke out of jail and went back to his old bloody ways on horseback.

REFUGIO WAS a good salesman, a natural closer, and he had the Dutchman right where he wanted him. They were sitting on the curb in front of my hotel. Refugio was going for the No. 3 close. This is where you feign indifference to the sale, while at the same time you put across that your patience is at an end, that you are just about to withdraw the offer. On that point you mustn't bluff. You can't run a stupid amateur bluff.

It was a little trick I had picked up in a salesmanship school at a Shreveport motel. The League of Leaders, we were called, those of us who completed the three-day course and won our League of Leaders certificates and our speckled yellow neckties. I had to learn such things, but Refugio knew them in his bones. He spit in his hand and rubbed away the figures that were written there. He was washing his hands of any further bargaining. *"Dígame,"* he said to the man. Say something. Speak to me.

The farmer saw that the moment had come. The polyvinyl chloride pipe was as cheap as it was ever going to get. He gave in, with conditions. He would have to inspect the bargain PVC pipe and he wanted the slip couplings and elbow couplings thrown in and he wanted it all delivered. Agreed, said Refugio, but no cattle and no checks. *En efectivo*—strictly cash. A rare Mexican, Refugio had no interest whatever in owning livestock, unless you count fighting poultry and short-haired dogs with pointed ears.

The Mennonite would go with us then to Chiapas, this big fellow in bib overalls, with his gray flannel shirt buttoned right up to his chin. He would take a 300-mile ride in a truck with complete strangers in order to save, maybe, a few dollars on some irrigation pipe.

Refugio jumped up and clapped his hands together. "*¡Listo!* Done then! Let us get out of this terrible place!" Mérida made him uncomfortable, as did all cities, with their busybody policemen and parking restrictions. I had my eye on all the street approaches, expecting Louise to appear any minute with news of Wade Watson, and perhaps with Beth, the two of them marching arm in arm, the league of women voters. But it was Gail who came instead, in a taxi, with her suitcase. Word of our trip had somehow reached her at the Holiday Inn, and here she was with her pink plump hands, wearing her field gear.

Would I take her back to Ektún? She had thought it over and decided that desertion in the field, no matter what the circumstances, would damage her career. It was particularly bad for a woman. She might never get another fellowship or grant unless she returned at once to her colleagues and made amends. She wouldn't have made such a rash move in the first place, she said, if I hadn't been there at the dig with my truck, offering an easy way out. "I know you were only trying to help, in your way."

Yes, all my fault, naturally, but what about Denise?

"She wanted to go back, too, but she lost her contact lenses at the motel. She flew home last night."

Then here came Doc Flandin, breathless, walking as fast as he could. "Wait up," he said, "Wait up, Jimmy." He was wearing his surgeon's cap and there was a machete in a canvas scabbard swinging from his belt. It was an old one and a good one that kept its edge, forged by the Aragon family in Oaxaca. All the other swords in the world were now dead ceremonial objects, or theatrical props, but the machete was still whacking about and smiting every day. Doc had his gourd canteen, and his pockets were bulging with what I took to be a change of underwear and socks. The machete pulled him over to the left. He missed the weight of the .45 on the other side, which would have put him back in trim.

"I'm going with you," he said. "I'll ride up front by the window."

"Going where?"

"To the *selva*. With you and Cuco. I want to see it all one more time, Jimmy. You can't refuse me that."

"It's a long run. Do you feel up to it?"

"I'm fine. Never better."

"What does Dr. Solís say?"

"He says onward. *Adelante*. St. James and at them! That's what he says. I'm not an invalid yet. Do you think I'm going to collapse?"

"Mrs. Blaney approves?"

"She knows."

"I don't want that woman coming back at me."

"I'm still responsible for my own actions, thank you."

"What about your book?"

"What about it? The book will keep. The unleavened lump. A few more days won't matter. It's not as though anyone was waiting for it."

"A lot of people are waiting for it."

"So you say. Well, perhaps. My loyal Jimmy. But you mustn't expect too much. I'll ride up front by the window. We'll stop at Salsipuedes on the way and pick up Chombo. He's just the man for our search."

It wasn't a bad idea at that except that Chombo had been dead two or three years. He was an old hunting guide who knew the rivers.

Rudy had it right all along—never reveal your travel plans. I didn't mind about the farmer or Gail—I would see that she paid for some gasoline this time—but I knew Doc could only be a burden.

I went into the Posada and called for Agustín, the boy, and sent him down the street to fetch Soledad Bravo. "Tell her it won't take long. A brief *consulta*, that's all."

We waited. "Just call me Dicky," Doc said, to one and all, and Gail took him at his word. I didn't like it much but then I thought, well, she doesn't know who he is. Over the years he had invited me to do the same. "Why don't you call me Dicky?" But I knew my place and I could no more have called him Dicky to his face than I could have called my regimental commander Shorty.

Soledad came in some haste with her heavy *curandera* bag. She was in her slippers and house dress, a loose *huipil* dress, and she was peeved a little when she saw that this was no real emergency.

I said, "Here's what it is, Soledad. Dr. Flandin wants to ride down to Palenque with me. Is he fit to travel? That's all I want to know."

"He is sick?"

Doc refused to answer. I said, "He is not well."

"He is in discomfort?"

"He says not."

"Can he button his clothes without help?"

"I think so."

Passing blood? No. Appetite? Good. Chest pains? No. Does he catch his feet in things and fall to the ground?

No, I had to admit that Doc was no stumbler. He wasn't easily tipped over.

She worked fast and Doc might have been a sick cat the way she went at it. She took him by the ears and blew into his nostrils to give him a start, then looked into his eyes to see what she had surprised there. She examined his fingernails. She ran her fingers around under his jaw. Then she pronounced.

"He can travel on the road for three days in a motorcar, God willing, *si Dios quiere*. Don't overfeed him. After three days he will need some rest in the shade." She held up three fingers.

That was good enough for me. She knew her business. It was all over before Doc could protest much, and Soledad was gone before I could pay her.

Here we were, all mustered and ready to go, but who got the third seat, up front? Doc had already staked out his place by the window. Who took precedence these days, a Mexican *patrón* or an American female anthropologist or a Dutch Mennonite deacon? I couldn't work it out and so left them to decide among themselves. Gail and Refugio deferred to the big solemn farmer. His name was Winkel and he was a senior deacon in his church, with authority to make major purchases. That was about all we could get out of him.

He sat between Doc and me and said nothing, staring straight ahead, when he wasn't sneaking looks at the speedometer. I mumbled and Doc fiddled with the radio. What a crew. Taken as individuals we were, I think, solid enough men, but there was something clownish about the three of us sitting there side by side, upright, frozen, rolling down the road. We were the Three Stooges on our way to paint some lady's house. It may have been our headgear.

Refugio and Gail had to rough it in the back of the truck, scooping out what seats they could amid all the luggage and junk. Refugio had bought an old oily Tecumseh engine in Mérida, and some other hardware. There was a heavy iron cylinder of welding gas and some used milk cans—he couldn't resist empty containers—and a little sandblasting chamber for cleaning the electrodes of spark plugs. It was no longer the custom to clean plugs in the States, the new ones were so cheap, but down here we still practiced these little economies. We still put hot patches on inner tubes and we still filed down the ridges and pits on burnt contact points. We would set the gap with a matchbook cover.

I drove fast. This racing about at my age was unseemly, but I was still impatient. Refugio and I were both forty-one years old at the time of these events. Few Mexicans passed us and no gringos. The cargo shifted about as we pulled some hard G's on the curves. The least bit of lateral tire slippage made Winkel go stiff. He said, "You must think the devil is after you."

"The devil will never catch this truck, Mr. Winkel."

Gail was thrown from side to side. Refugio kept her amused with his high jinks. He stood on his *dignidad* with Mexican women, but it was all right to be a little silly before young *gringas*. They were shallow vessels in his estimation and didn't count for much. He popped a burning cigarette in and out of his mouth with his tongue. He raised the lift-gate and fired at road signs with his .45, including the ones that said DON'T MISTREAT THE SIGNS (NO MALTRATE LAS SEÑALES). I had done the same thing as a kid. I was an old mailbox shooter from the Arklatex, no use lying, but I no longer approved of such behavior and I rapped on the window glass and made him stop.

Doc grumbled and sulked when I wouldn't turn off at the Labná ruins. He said he only wanted to take a quick look at some of the restoration work. I knew he would start pointing out architectural errors and correcting the hapless guides, and we would never get away. Farther along, I did pull over and let him buy some cut flowers from a girl at a roadside stand. He wanted a bouquet for Sula.

Winkel became more and more uneasy after the sun went down. I felt bad about frightening the man and I told him to relax, he was safe enough, that I was an old hand at these night runs. I told him about the night I had driven an FBI agent named Vance up to San Cristóbal de las Casas in the fog. These agents, who worked out of the embassy in Mexico City, were not permitted by their superiors to drive at night on Mexican roads. Strange rule, for cops. They didn't call themselves FBI agents either—their cards simply said Department of Justice.

I had found a soldier they were looking for, a warrant officer who had run off with the payroll, or a good part of it, from Fort Riley, Kansas. He had dyed his hair but was still using his own name, which was McIntire. He felt safe up on top of that mountain with all his dollars tucked away in a duffel bag. He thought he was at the end of the world in that chilly Indian town high up in the clouds, but he wasn't counting on the likes of me, with my sharp eye and my Blue Sheets. I was eager in those days. Vance identified him and called on the Mexican Judicial Police to make the arrest.

Doc said, "How much did they pay you?"

"I did well enough out of it."

"Were you proud of yourself?"

"Why not? It was a clean job."

"Jimmy, Jimmy, the things you do."

Used to do. Not so much lately. Still, it was a clean job, if I do say so myself, over and done with in two weeks and none of the usual hitches. There was no trouble at all with the extradition since he didn't have a Spanish name or a Mexican wife. He was a warrant officer, neither fish nor fowl, and his name was Gene McIntire, and he let down the people who trusted him. But there was no whimpering from the old soldier. He just said, "I'm going to miss San Cristóbal. This place is cool and pleasant the year round, a fat man's dream."

Whether Winkel followed any of this, I couldn't tell. Probably it was of no interest to him. The antics of people who were all tangled up in the world. Was it worse than he thought?

I tried to get Doc to talk a little about his so-called translation of the Maya glyphs. I couldn't draw him out. "No, not now," he said. "Not before a third party." Then he apologized to the Mennonite. "No offense, sir."

But the night ride had set him musing on other things, of his early poverty and lack of staff support as a young scholar. He talked and talked and then he sighed and said, "Well, you know, what does it really matter in the long run? When you get right down to it everything is a cube."

He had taken to saying that lately. *Everything is a cube*. I don't know what he had in mind. When you get right down to it everything is not a cube. You can look around and see that. Hardly anything in nature is a cube. Some few crystals, I suppose. Art and Mike thought it might have to do with cubic increase, geometric progression, or with some mystical notion, of life raised to the third power. Had Doc really hit on something? Who knows. Maybe he just liked the ring of the words. I made a point of not asking questions.

We stopped in Palenque to check with the police, and they had a body to show us. I knew it was going to be Rudy. A fisherman had found it bobbing about in the Usumacinta. Some loggers had brought it in on a truck.

The officer in charge, who for some reason believed Rudy to be a painter of pictures, was sympathetic. He took a flashlight, and Refugio and I followed him through the back door to a toolshed. There in the wooden tray of a wheelbarrow lay the body, wrapped in a tarpaulin. It was all very sad, the officer said, a fine artist drowned young. Even at its lower stages the big river was treacherous. There would be no more beautiful pictures form the hand of this particular young artist. But there were other artists, hundreds of them, plenty of artists, and the identification would take only a moment and then we could have some coffee in his office and deal with the various forms and fees. He was looking forward to a good long session with his rubber stamps and his stapler.

"The young man was your brother?"

"No, just a friend," I said.

"He was an unfortunate *leproso?* Your brother?"

"What? A leper? No."

He held the beam of his flashlight on the wheelbarrow. "There," he said, standing well back. He wasn't going to touch the thing. No one is more fastidious than a fastidious Mexican in uniform. It was the Chicanos in the Marine Corps who had their shirts tailored for a skin-tight fit, like those of state troopers, and who had gleaming horseshoe taps nailed to the heels of their cordovan shoes.

Refugio crossed himself, and the two of us set about unrolling the tarp. The smell wasn't so bad. The corpse hadn't gone off much because it was all leather, mummified. The eyes were two dull yellow marbles, bulging out from the face like the eyes of a Chihuahua dog. It wasn't Rudy, it was King Tut, a tiny old man, long dead, with bald head and bared teeth. It was a freak-show exhibit.

Refugio said, "This is what you call a young man? Drowned three or four days ago? This is some fine young artist you show us!" He grabbed a toe and held up one of the feet for the officer to see. It was a pitiful brown lump, badly calloused, as broad as it was long. "This is what you call the foot of a gringo? You are wasting the time of important men!"

The officer turned to me. "The man is not your brother?"

"No."

"You don't identify the person? Look carefully."

"I don't know him, no."

"They told me it was the missing artist."

"Anyone can make a mistake. We are grateful for your help."

"It was nothing, sir. Our work goes on."

The others were waiting for us out front by the truck, under a dim street light. Everyone was tired. None of these people knew Rudy Kurle. My news, that the body was not his but that of an ancient little man, caused no stir. Refugio told them it was the body of a *chaneque*. There was a dead *chaneque* back there in that shed. Here was their chance to see one of those evil dwarfs in the flesh.

Did anyone want to see the *chaneque*? They seemed not to understand what he was saying. Doc was drooping. I had gone without sleep for two days. I suggested that we stop here at Palenque for the night.

At that, Winkel suddenly became assertive. "No, no, I have no money to waste on a hotel. Let us go on to the pipe place."

Doc took a handful of paper money from his pocket. Those knots in his pockets were wads of money. "Don't worry, I'm paying. We'll put up at the Motel Barrios."

But Winkel wouldn't hear of it. "No, no, please, this was not our agreement."

So we drove on to Refugio's place.

THERE IS a lot of nonpoverty in Mexico that you don't hear about. Everybody is not destitute or filthy rich. Refugio, for example, had just bought a new Dodge truck, bright red, with V-8 engine, a fine truck. He paid cash for it. But he wouldn't use it for hard service until the new was off. He was waiting for a molded plastic bedliner to come in from Veracruz.

Knowing this, I should have seen the sandbag job that was coming my way. The pair of us were up at daybreak, and Sula was serving us breakfast in the little office, where I had slept. "The Doctor is still sleeping," she said. They had put him up in their own air-conditioned bedroom.

Refugio said, "Well, don't disturb him. Let the man have his rest. Where are those beautiful roses he brought you?"

"I have them in a bowl of water."

"Bring them in here so we can smell them and enjoy them with our coffee. You see how this great man is always thinking of other people? You have a saint sleeping in your feather bed (*colchón de plumo*). Jaime and I are coarse men of business (*hombres groseros*) but look here, how the Doctor has time to think of the pretty roses."

They weren't roses. They had no smell that I could smell, whatever they were. I think they were dahlias, national flower of Mexico, shaggy and orange, nothing at all like roses. Refugio knew his trees, he could tell you the names of all the bigger trees in the forest, the local names, but any flower at all was a *rosa* to him.

He sprang his proposal on me as we ate, calling my attention to two important points. His truck was new and mine was old. Mine was sagging. One more crumpled fender, one more busted headlight, one more rock flying through my radiator could hardly matter. The only thing to do was to use my truck for the pipe delivery. He could hook up his flatbed trailer to it, and Valentín could haul the pipe away while we went on to the *selva* to look for the young gringo. We would take the Volkswagen into the woods. This was an old salvaged delivery van that still carried the yellow markings of Sabritas potato chips.

"No, you can forget that," I said. "Valentín is not driving my truck."

"Then I myself will have to take the pipe to the *evangelistas*."

"Manolo can do it."

"Sula would never let Manolo drive to Yucatán alone."

"Valentín can go with him. Or better, Valentín can go alone in your truck."

"I don't want my trailer ball scratched up just yet."

"But it's all right to scratch mine up."

"Yours is rusty and ugly. Mine is still silver."

"Then we can switch balls. Or put a rag over yours."

"I don't want my bed exposed to the sun just yet. The sun fades red paint."

"I've been hearing about this bedliner for months. When is it going to get here?"

"God alone knows. You say all these hard things. Why can't you let me eat in peace?"

Valentín was Refugio's half brother or stepbrother. I never got it straight. I never got the relatives completely straight in my head, all these Bautistas and Peñas and Osorios and Zamúdios. Valentín was a jackleg mechanic and carpenter, fairly useful to have around, when he wasn't drunk. I didn't trust him. He was sly, with the startled eyes of a chicken. Sula didn't care for him either. She said Valentín never got his full growth because he was nursed as a baby on Coca-Cola instead of milk. She thought some of those *gaseosa* bubbles had floated up to his brain.

Winkel, of course, didn't want to impose on anybody. He had slept in the back of my truck, and then he said he wasn't hungry and Refugio had to force some breakfast on him. Winkel was up early, too, working alone, loading the pipe on the flatbed trailer. There was more than he had expected. He was delighted with his daring purchase. Small animals who had nested in the pipes scurried for new cover as they were disturbed, snakes and rats and scorpions and rabbits and lizards. Refugio showed Winkel how easy it was to cut the plastic pipe with a hacksaw. Saws with coarser teeth would splinter the ends. These were special hacksaw blades, he said, and he recommended that Winkel buy a dozen of them to insure clean cuts and no wastage. That was his advice. Winkel said he had his own *arco* blades at home.

I was walking the grounds. Gail joined me, with a mug of coffee. Dogs trailed at our heels, though not Ramos, son of Chino. Ramos didn't mix much with the yard dogs. Gail said she had slept comfortably enough in a hammock, in a small room with a great heap of red fire extinguishers bearing yellow tags that were long expired. She said, "What is that I smell? Surely they don't have an oil refinery around here."

"No, that's only the stuff in those drums out there."

"What is it?"

"Various choking and blistering agents."

"What are we waiting for now? When are we going on to Ektún?"

"First they have to stack all that white pipe on the trailer and tie it down. It won't take long after Refugio gets his people stirring."

She asked me about Doc, or Dicky, as she called him, and I told her he was a great Mayanist and a rich man who had lived in Mérida for many years.

"Great Mayanist? I've never heard of him."

I let it go but I thought she should have heard of him. If she had known her business, she would have heard of Doc.

"This coffee has cinnamon in it."

"Yes."

"What kind of business is Mr. Bautista in?"

"*Salvataje*. We're both in the *salvataje* business. *Salvamento*."

"Salvation?"

"Well, salvage."

"I heard him calling this place his *ranchita*. It doesn't look much like a ranch."

"He just says that. Anybody who lives out of town has a *ranchita*. It's a junkyard."

It was an industrial age boneyard in the jungle. It was a little kingdom. Refugio's father, the old *chiclero*, he who had gathered tree sap so we could have Juicy Fruit gum, had squatted here long ago, before there was a road. Refugio had made improvements. He kept pushing his whitewashed boundary stones outward and now claimed to own twenty-two hectares. Certainly he possessed the land. He held dominion over these fifty-odd acres, and anyone disputing his claim could expect to be threatened and called a monkey-head at the very least.

Once he had suggested that we clear the tract across the road and plant onions. Someone had told him that there was a fortune to be made in sweet red onions. But neither of us was a farmer, and besides, the soil was poor, and it seemed to me there were already enough onions in Mexico to go around, and then some, sweet or not. You pull up onions one by one and then sell them by the ton. That didn't appeal to me. We had other schemes. Now and again we talked about our kennel scheme. We would breed dogs here and train them to sniff out dope and explosives at airports. The government would pay us well. The way to get rich was on government contracts.

Or we would breed war dogs. Not to work singly, leashed, on sentry duty, but in snarling packs. We would form them into platoons and train them to assault fortified positions at night. Once loosed and engaged in the actual fighting, they would be led by their own officers, such as Ramos.

The loading went forward. Refugio brought out his box of Mayan pieces to show Gail. He held them up and quoted prices to her. She was amazed that such things should be in private hands. Why not buy three or four of these little *idolos,* he asked her, all of a similar style? She could smudge them up, claim she had found them here or there, then return to her comfortable home and write books about them. Why not? Other *arqueos* did this. He knew from experience. No one would know. The pieces were genuine. They were a good investment and would put her just that much ahead of her hated rivals.

She laughed. "Yes, but I am only a poor student, you see. I can't afford such things."

"Ah, *pobrecita.* Well then, I make you a gift."

He stuffed a small ceramic bird in her shirt pocket. She protested, he insisted, and they went back and forth until she gave in. Now then, he said, shaking his finger, I will speak to you as a father. She had her Indian toy and could return home. She had no business messing around out here in the dirt far from her comfortable home. She should be with her family at Christmas time. This filthy *arqueo* work was not suitable for young ladies.

Gail went red in the face. "I am not ready to go home yet, Señor Bautista."

At last we came to an agreement about the delivery. Manolo, sitting on a pillow, was to drive my truck and tow the load of pipe to the Mennonite farm. Valentín would go along but was not at any time to be allowed behind the wheel.

"Do you understand that, Manolo?"

"Papa knows I can do this job. How many times have I driven him to Villahermosa?"

He was swaggering and dancing about so that I had to grab his shoulder to get his attention. He had the same quick moves as his father. With a swipe of his hand he could catch a fly in midair.

"I know you can do the job, but this time you're answering to me, not your Papa. This is my truck. Do you remember when those loggers in Ocosingo jumped Flaco Peralta and me and your Papa? Do you remember what Flaco did to that Tzeltzal who called himself the Captain? Well, that's just what I'll do to you if you wreck my truck."

Manolo laughed and dropped to a crouch and began weaving about and making passes with an imaginary knife.

"No, I'm not joking now. Listen to me. I want you to show proper respect for your Uncle Valentín, but you're the one in charge. If he starts drinking, just leave him behind. Don't fool with him for one minute. Keep the tanks topped up so you won't get a lot of bad gas all at once. Don't pop the clutch and don't ride the brakes, use the gears. Keep it under sixty *millas*. Watch the heat needle. If it gets much past the halfway mark, pull over and let the engine cool down. But don't try to back up on the shoulder of the road or you'll jackknife the trailer. You'll need to add a liter of oil when you get to the Escárcega junction. Thirty-weight Ebano is good enough. Check it again in Mérida and once more on the way back. Keep your mind on your business, and remember, that trailer has no brakes and no lights. Now what did I say? Tell me what you're going to do."

You couldn't trust a sixteen-year-old kid in the States these days to look after a goldfish, and not many kids here, but I had confidence in Manolo. I wasn't really worried, for all my lecturing. He had a better feel for machinery and the flow of the road than I did, a finer touch. Still, it's just as well to have things understood.

Sula wept. Her only baby was going off into the world. "But so many leagues to Mérida!" she wailed. Valentín, in a clean white shirt, was glad of the trip, happy to be going anywhere. He appeared to take no offense at the slight—having a boy put over him. Maybe I had misjudged him. He held the truck door open for Winkel, poor man, who would have to ride in the middle again. No matter, he was taking home enough irrigation pipe to build a new Zion in the thorny scrubland of Yucatán.

At the last minute Doc came up, cap in hand, and pressed some money on him. "For your mission work, sir. Remember me in your prayers. Richard Flandin. I have always tried to do right by my fellow man. And I have gone beyond personal ambition (*aspiración*). All that is behind me now (*atrás de mé*)."

Winkel didn't understand. He couldn't follow Doc's peculiar Spanish. He held the money away from him as though a subpoena had been slapped into his hand. The Mennonites were always the first ones on the scene after a hurricane or earthquake or other disaster. They were much admired for their practical works of charity but they carried on no mission work as such around here, that I knew of. "An offering for your church," I explained to him. "Keep it."

Doc, backing away, said, "That man is much closer to God than we are."

Manolo popped the clutch and they were off with a lurch. Refugio, with Ramos at his side, was very much the *patrón* this morning. He stood apart from the rest of us, his head thrown back and his fists jammed down into the pockets of his long rubberized apron. He hadn't lifted a finger to help, as it wouldn't do to be seen performing menial labor before his people. He was proud of his son and pleased with the big sale. That PVC pipe had been a slow-moving line of goods. Saplings had sprung up around the pile. We had both known the despair of trying to sell things that nobody wanted.

ON TO Ektún in the potato chip van. The plan was that Refugio and I would drop Gail off there and then make our way down to Tumbalá along the rivers. We would catch a boat ride on the Usumacinta, as Rudy must have done. The van stood high off the ground and did well enough in the water. The hydraulic brake system was out, and Refugio had to work the hand brake and hold the wheel and shift gears, all three things, with his two hands.

Doc was glowing. "What shall we find today?" he said. He seemed to think we were off on a dig. I had tried to persuade him to stay behind at the salvage yard. He could do Refugio a real service there, sorting out his relics and appraising them, but no, he was determined to make one last venture into the forest. "My last *entrada*," as he put it. He sat up front beside Refugio, holding Ramos between his knees and calling him Chino.

Dry season or not, a shower of rain was falling when we reached the ruins. The place was deserted. Refugio fired two shots in the air. We went from tent to tent and found no one. The motorcycle was gone. Ramos barked at a wooden box in the mess tent. Refugio kicked it over and a big diamond-back *palanca* came tumbling out, or what they called a *nauyaca* around here. In any case, a fer-de-lance, who righted himself in no time. He stood his ground, with his head rolling about and his jaws flung open about 160 degrees. Don't tread on me! Ramos, still yapping, shied back, as did we all, except for Refugio. With one hand he tossed a rag over the snake's head and with the other he grabbed the tail and popped him like a whip, cracking his neck. Snakes take a good deal of killing as a rule, it's a long business, but this one was stone dead, and all at once.

Doc and Gail waited inside out of the drizzle while I went down to search along the river bank. At least the mosquitoes were grounded. I took my shotgun, slung muzzle-down from my shoulder. Soaked or dirty, the old L. C. Smith had never failed me, with its exposed hammers and double triggers. It was simple and sure. The only firing mechanism I knew of with fewer moving parts was that of a mortar, with none. Refugio looked around in the woods behind the camp. I turned up nothing. He found two Lacondón Indians hunkered down in the old steam-bath chamber. They were drinking cans of beer and smoking long cigars they had rolled themselves.

He marched them back to the mess tent and questioned them sharply in their own lingo. Why had they not shown themselves? Did they not hear us calling out? The gunshots? The dog barking?

It was raining. They were waiting out the rain.

Where was everybody? Where were all the *arqueos?*

Gone away for a time. To Palenque or some other town. It was the rain. They couldn't work in the mud.

Refugio was a little rough with them. I could see they were frightened of him, with that big pistol at his side. It was Cortez grilling the baffled *Indios* again. The thin one, the one called Bol, had some Spanish, and I got it out of him that they were here to keep an eye on things. The bearded Lund had hired them. They were to sleep here and watch things and take what food they pleased from the stores—though Bol wasn't sure about the beer. He thought we might be angry at them for drinking the beer.

"No, it's all right," I said. "The beer is yours too. Don't worry about it."

But they knew nothing about any missing gringo. Everybody had gone away to Palenque. That was about all I could get because Refugio kept breaking in with accusations and Doc was roaring around the tent, having a fit.

"Look at all this equipment! I can't believe it! Cases of canned milk and a professional drawing board and electricity to boot! Look at all the logistical support these people have! They even bring their own little secretary along! And for what! When it's all over they'll turn in some piffling report that nobody will read! That nobody *can* read! Well, these are your modern road-bound explorers! They hear the patter of rain on the leaves and what do our brave boys do? I'll tell you what they do! They down tools and head for the nearest motel!"

Bol and his friend thought this tirade was directed at them, and it took me a while to straighten things out. Doc apologized and gave them hearty handshakes. He gave them some money. He had always been a true friend of the Lacondones, he told them, even though he could not accept the claim that their cultural line went unbroken all the way back to the classic Maya. No, he was sorry, but he rather thought they were a hybrid, pariah people, descendants of runaways, drifters, outcasts and renegades, who had come together here in the forest in the not too distant past, to form a kind of tribe, and what was more, he believed he could prove it to their satisfaction. But he didn't think any the worse of them for being pariahs—he was one himself, a real outcast—and had he not always been their true friend, in thought, word and deed? Here was some more money, take it. The whole wad was theirs if they could direct him to the Lost Books. They must understand this was his last *entrada*. He would pay well for books of the *antiguos* or any fragments thereof . . .

There was a lot more of this, and they didn't take in a word of it. I explained to them that the old man was offering a reward to anyone who found the missing young man. He had yellow hair and wore army clothes. He was last seen walking down the river a few days back. Refugio went over it again in their own *idioma*, adding for good measure that the boy was rich and would buy them new motorbikes if they brought him out safely. Then, with some gifts, we sent Bol off to spread the word among his people. The other one stayed behind.

Gail didn't know which way to turn. Her boss was dead and her friend Denise had flown home and now her entire crew was gone. She had fallen in with a pair of pyramid looters, most vicious of all criminals in the anthropology book, and a loud old man who, if she could believe her ears, had just called her a little secretary. We could hardly leave her here and she couldn't drive the brakeless van out alone. Or could she? I knew so little about her. She didn't talk enough for me to get a good reading on her. Later I got a pretty good reading.

Refugio saw a good chance to jump ship. His heart had never been in this job, a lot of gringo nonsense, bound in the end to be abortive and unprofitable.

"So. I will drive the young lady back to my *ranchita,* or Palenque, wherever she likes. That is all we can do, no?"

Gail said, "You don't have to cart me around like some old lady."

Doc said, "Palenque? What are we discussing here? Weren't we just in Palenque last night?"

Refugio couldn't get the Volkswagen going again. He ground away on the starter, but the little pancake engine wouldn't catch. Gail said that was all right. She would go on with us to Tumbalá. She would like to see the big river. Refugio told her it would be a hard and dirty trip. Doc said anybody who thought he could go to Palenque in a boat was crazy as hell. More delay and confusion. It was like those last frantic days in the coat factory. Scenes such as this had driven me to working alone. It was the old Rudy situation, where I had responsibility without authority. I couldn't tell these people what to do, but if they went wrong, got hurt, I would have to answer for it.

But then I no longer cared and I said I was going off on foot, now, down the Tabí to the Usumacinta. There I would hitch a boat ride to Tumbalá, pick up Rudy Kurle and continue on down the river by way of Yoro to the rail crossing at Tenosique. It was the easiest way out. They could come along or stay here, just as they wished.

Doc began giving orders, left and right. I had to tell him again that this was not a dig, that he was not in charge this time, and that we would go and stop as I directed. He threw up his hands. "Fine, fine. Don't mind me. I don't know anything. Just tell me what to do. I'm not anybody. I'm only the man who found the big eccentric flint at Cobá."

Sula had packed some food for us, and we took some more out of the camp stores. Refugio found a square packet of delicatessen ham in an ice chest. He held up a piece and flopped it about and laughed at how thin it was sliced. Look, he said, here was this gray and sickly meat, cut to about the thinness of a cat's ear, that you can see light through, and this was what they called a piece of ham in the great land of America! No wonder the gringos couldn't win their wars anymore!

I was glad to have him along, willing or not, and I was glad to have Ramos, too, who quickly sensed the plan and led the way, jogging ahead of us down the river bank. He knew his job, which was to give notice of any trouble down the way, to scatter varmints from our path. We walked in single file and spoke little. The brush was so thick in places that we had to walk out into the water.

We came to the opening in an hour or so, a big sand-bar, where the Tabí, running deep brown, flowed into the muddy and lighter stream of the Usumacinta. The water was *café con leche*. We stopped there to rest and eat.

The rain had let up. There was a light breeze. Doc stood at the point of the sandbar with his white pantaloons fluttering. "The mingling of the waters," he said, looking across the way to the Guatemala side. Nothing was stirring over there. An unbroken line of trees, all even at the top, as though clipped with shears. "A rare day," he went on. "This is truly the Garden of the kings. *La Huerta de los Reyes*." He drew his machete and nicked an earlobe to get some blood, then flung it from his fingertips in what he called "the four world directions." Some more of his cubo-mystico business, I thought. Gail said it was an ancient rite of the lowland Maya. An act of reverence then, in its way, which was fine with me. A blood offering, the only kind of any value, according to the Suarez. Big Dan was strong on blood, too. There had to be blood.

Doc called me out on the sandbar. "A word with you in private, Jimmy, if you don't mind." I joined him, and he asked me in a confidential way if I had heard him say that this was his last *entrada*.

"Yes, I have." I had heard him say it about four times.

"Well, that's just what I mean. I mean to lie down out here and die where I was happiest. Please don't interfere. I will just lie down under the canopy of the trees. With my old empty heart. I will die and melt away and be with all the other forgotten things in the earth."

"Where? Where will you do this?"

"Anywhere. Tumbalá will do."

"What's that in your hand?"

It was the little jade man. He was going to lie down and die with that thing in his mouth. I told him there was something heathenish about this that I didn't like, and he said no, don't worry, he had already paid Father Mateo to say seventy-eight masses for him, one for each year of his life, and none too many, he thought.

"I don't know. I'll have to think it over."

"The signal will be when I give you my machete. I want you to have it. At that point you will take the others and walk away. Don't look back and don't say anything. I couldn't bear any words. This is how I want it. You can't refuse my last wish, Jimmy. And don't let Cuco interfere."

I left it at that. He was determined, and I saw no hope of reasoning with him. But I had already thought it over and I had no intention of leaving him out here. Melt away? A nice way of putting it. Doc wasn't dying. Soledad Bravo would have seen it in his eyes. It was one thing to help along an old man on his deathbed, to dispatch him with a razor blade, but this business, no. I would tie him in the boat if it came to that, and Refugio would help me.

Gail offered to make him a sandwich. "You haven't eaten anything, Dicky."

"I got a boiled egg down."

It sounded like he had poked it down his throat whole.

Refugio shaded his eyes and made a show of looking up and down the river, "I don't see no *cayucas*." He cupped his ear. "I don't hear no boats." He was going to dwell on every difficulty.

"One will be along," I said. "Let's go. It's not far to Tumbalá. A little more walking won't hurt us."

We set off downstream and the going was easier now, though we were out of the jungle twilight, into the full blaze of the sun. The river cut its way through rounded hills, with steep wooded slopes that came right down to the edge of the water, or almost to the edge. At this season there was a sandy shelf to walk on. The big river, we called it, and so it was for Mexico, but this upper middle stretch I would put at no more than a hundred yards wide. The water had not yet taken on a dark tropical look. It was just pale and lifeless ditch water coursing along.

No boat came, up or down. Gail had some good mosquito dope, the best I had ever used. The trick is to keep them out of your face, from swarming in your face, which can't be endured. We drank from springs and small feeder streams, after I had poured the water through a paper cone, a coffee filter. It trapped all the bigger parasites, or so I told myself.

Refugio stopped to look at a hairy object washing about in an eddy. Then he jumped back and cried out, "Mother of God! Another *chaneque!*" Another little brown man, that is, of the kind we had been shown at the Palenque police station. These small woodland creatures took sick and died, just as we did, and their bodies were always committed to flowing waters, according to Sula. Fair enough, but I didn't expect to see two of them in two days. They were washing up like sick whales.

This thing was vaguely childlike, a torso with something like a tiny arm flung out. It was just hide and bones, a headless, decaying mess of no very definite shape. Doc said it was a dog. Gail thought it might be a howler monkey. Ramos showed no interest. Much too hairy for a humanoid, I said, knowing nothing about humanoids.

Refugio snapped back at me. "Do you say I don't know a *chaneque* when I see one?"

"It's not like the one at Palenque."

Later, farther down the trail, he said, "Some *chaneques* are hairy. The older males have much body hair."

I might have believed that, coming from Sula, but Refugio knew no more about *chaneques* than I did.

He stopped us again when we reached Tumbalá. He raised his hand. "*¡Escuche!* Listen up!" Ramos was doing some furious barking around the bend. I was certain he had found Rudy. Refugio and I ran on ahead, across the ruins and up into a ravine, where Ramos had cornered something in a hole. It was a small cave in the hillside. I called out to Rudy. No answer. Then I thought it might be a jaguar. Yes, a *tigre*, I was sure of it, though real *tigrero* dogs are stalkers and don't bark at all. After all these years of going up and down in the woods, I was at last going to behold a jaguar at bay, in whose wonderful coat the Mayas saw a map of the starry heavens. Refugio said no, it was no *gato*, more likely a pig. This was pig madness. Ramos hated pigs.

Chino would have charged the hole. Ramos was content to race about in a frenzy before the entrance. Nor would Refugio, brave man that he was, enter a cave. Close places didn't bother him, or man-made holes. You could grab his ankles and hold him head down in a *chultún*, a kind of bottle-shaped underground Mayan cistern, and he would work calmly away with a flashlight in his mouth, scratching about for artifacts with one hand while swatting at snakes and scorpions with the other. But he wouldn't go into a natural cave. Unquiet spirits still lingered there from the old days, far back in the darkness where virgin water dripped. You could go in and never come out. I was no spelunker myself. It was Doc who liked to prowl caverns, where one day the cache of lost books would be found. That was his firm belief.

Refugio fired a shot into the cave. I set fire to a dried palm frond and tossed it inside, more for illumination than with any hope of driving the animal out. There was movement. Then we heard voices.

"¡Vale! ¡Vale! No te alteres! Okay, hold it! Take it easy!"

Two scraggly young men came out with a small chain saw and a .22 rifle. They were laughing, their eyes smarting from the smoke. I went inside with another blazing frond to make sure there were no others. There was a nest of bedding where they slept, and some scanty baggage. I poked around in it. If these two *chamacos* had done away with Rudy, they would have kept some of his fine equipment and his fine army clothes. I found nothing in that line, only three lumpy sacks hidden under a pile of brush. They were sisal sacks filled with sawed-off fragments of inscribed stone. I dragged them out into the light.

These boys were commercial pot hunters, and they had hidden here, they said, when they heard us coming, thinking we might be an army patrol. One of them had a bad arm wound, a ragged *cuchillazo*, gone purple along the edges. The chain saw had kicked back on him and ripped a long gash in his forearm. They had packed the wound with sugar and poured gasoline over it and tied it up with two pieces of rope. I got some antibiotic capsules from my shoulder bag and told him to take one every few hours. Leave it to me to have some antilife pills tucked away somewhere. He swallowed the lot, which hardly mattered, as the stuff was old and probably inert anyway. Doc and Gail came up. She gave the boy some aspirins, and he gobbled those down too.

I questioned them. They laughed and jabbered. The long and the short of it was that they hadn't seen Rudy. They had seen no one for four days.

Doc looked over the cave. He had a good eye and a good feel for these places. He pronounced this one a dud. It was barren, sterile, he said. And yet all around us were the tiny temples of Tumbalá, doll houses of stone and scaled-down shrines that stood no higher than your waist, a wonderland for flying saucer theorists. I don't know how Doc could tell so quickly, but he was always decisive. He kicked at the sacks of carved stone and asked the boys if they had come across any *libros*. He made a show with his hands, as of someone unfolding a road map, not an easy idea to put across. He gave them some money.

But of course they had found no books. Were there any left to find? There were only three Maya manuscripts or codices extant, and none dating back to the classic period. All three had turned up in Europe many years ago, with no back trail, no provenance, as they say. No one knew where they were written or where they were originally found.

Not around here, I would bet. Somewhere up in dry Yucatán perhaps, or in the high mountains of Guatemala. Not even bones survived in this sour soil. They were soon leached away to nothing. I had heard a lot about bones, too much about bones, from people who called us ghouls and grave-robbers and other hard names. Their idea was that we trampled about ankle-deep in old bones, crunching skulls and femurs heedlessly underfoot and raising great clouds of unhealthy bone dust in our bonemad search for treasure. In fact, there were no bones. We came across a tooth now and then but never a human bone, not one. I had never disturbed anyone's bones, that I knew of, which was more than the *arqueos* could say.

I told the boys we wanted to hire their boat.

"*No barca.*"

They had no boat and had seen no boat for days. They had not heard motors on the river since yesterday morning. But those sacks of stone would collapse a mule, I pointed out, let alone a man. How did they propose to carry them out of here if not by boat? They laughed some more. No, no, I didn't understand. A friend was coming up from Yoro tomorrow to pick them up in his dugout. A couple of nuts, Refugio called them, a pair of *chiflados*. He didn't trust them, didn't like them. They were poaching in his private valley. Their mindless laughter annoyed him. He refused to answer when they asked if he would sell his .45. Instead, he climbed a tree and came down with a yellow orchid for Gail. "A pretty rose for your hair." She stuck it in her khaki hat. It would go on living up there, disembodied. These strange flowers lived off the air, if my information was correct, in the way of Dan and his people. Again the two *chiflados* asked about the pistol. Refugio said they would never have enough money to buy this gun. "This is a man's gun!" What business did a pair of monkeys have with a man's gun? They couldn't even handle a baby chain saw with a short bar!

Then he turned on me. "You say the boy will be in Tumbalá and then our work is done. Well, where is he?"

I had no idea. Rudy had left no camping evidence here. It was all a bust. I knew the smell of failure. I was chasing after a shadow. In any case, the thing now was to get Doc away from this place, keep him moving. He hadn't gone for his machete belt yet but I was worried. I was afraid to meet his eyes. The time has come, they would say to me. Without a boat we would have to take him by the heels and drag him out of the forest against his will, with his arms folded across his chest and his head scraping a little furrow across Chiapas.

"The boy is dead," said Refugio. "That is what I think. Now we can go back to our homes."

"Not yet. Somebody must have seen him. And we may as well go on down to Yoro now. There are bound to be boats at Yoro."

The gloomy Refugio said Yoro was far, far away and that we could not possibly walk there before dark.

"It's still the easiest way out. It's better than going back. A night on the river won't kill us. And a boat may come along yet."

Gail was naturally curious about Yoro. "What is it, a town? A ruin?"

"It's a river terminal where you can buy gasoline. Just a little village with some hens pecking around in the mud. Or it used to be. I don't know. They may have a yacht club there now."

I hadn't been to Yoro in years. The first time there I nearly starved to death on a 500-peso note. Nobody could change it. The widow woman who served meals wouldn't accept my *tortuga* note and she wouldn't feed me on credit. They used to call that note a turtle because it moved so slowly. Now you could just about buy a pack of cigarettes with 500 pesos.

Doc, to my surprise, said, "Yes, Yoro is a wonderful idea, Jimmy. Why didn't I think of that? Yes, Yoro and Yorito. We can go up on the bluff and see the great old city of Likín again. We can drink from the hidden spring of water. Is it still flowing, I wonder? What's wrong with me? I had forgotten all about Likín."

So had I. It was a sprawling hilltop ruin across the river in Guatemala. I had also forgotten, if I had ever known, that "Likín" was the Yucatec Maya word for "east" and "sunrise." An important word, as it turned out, though it wasn't until the next day that I made the connection, what with so many things on my mind. Had Doc then decided against lying down and giving up the spirit, or was he only putting it off? Best not to ask. He may have feared that the two *chiflados* would disturb him after he had arranged himself on the ground here. They might stand over him and look down on him with disgust and talk over his condition, in the way of medical students.

I got the party moving again and picked up the pace a little. At least our way was downhill. A night on the river wouldn't be so bad, if it didn't rain, and if Gail's mosquito dope held out. Strong stuff, though I believe my powder bag—a knotted sock filled with sulfur—was more effective against the ticks. Where were all the boats? Doc was holding up well, his little cap now dark with sweat. He wanted to keep those vapors in his head. Everybody else in Mexico was trying to keep them out. Straggling behind a bit, he and Gail were lost in a lively chat. He told her about the panoramic view from atop the great *Castillo* at Likín.

Refugio glanced back at them over his shoulder. "This Gail," he said to me. "She will make you a good enough wife, Jaime." *Esposa regular*.

"You think so?"

"Look how round and fat her arms are. She is quiet, too, and dedicated to bennee."

"Yes, well, Gail is all right."

But I wasn't interested in her in that way, nor she in me.

Around each bend we foolishly expected to see something new, and it was always the same line of trees and another stretch of brown water leading to another bend. A thousand years ago this valley was inhabited with stone cities every few miles. Now it was an empty quarter. No one lived here now except for a sprinkling of drifters and outpost people. We saw none of them, a shifty lot on the whole, not much given to the planning or building of cities. We saw no animals other than bugs and snakes and circling eagles.

The low-water trail was too good to last. At a gap where the river cut between two hills, we came up against a thick and impassable stand of bamboo. Not even Ramos could penetrate that canebrake. I went to borrow Doc's machete, only to find that he had given it to Gail. What was this? She had taken up the web belt a notch or two and strapped on the whole business. Something significant here? The passing on of the Aragon machete? Or had she only relieved him of the weight? Neither of them offered an explanation, and I asked no questions.

Refugio and I hacked away and cleared a narrow path along the edge of the water. It was hot work. Colonies of ticks showered down on us. They swarmed all down Ramos' haunches. He made for the river and took a quick dip and then well and truly shook himself off. When everyone had passed around the thicket, we stopped to beat each other with branches, trying to brush off the teeming *garrapatas*. I pounded at them with my sulfur bomb. Then, right in the middle of this whipping and dusting dance, and very much startled, we were hailed from across the river by three Guatemalan soldiers.

One was a young officer, a military policeman, with a red PM brassard on his sleeve. The other two were even younger, mere boys, carrying old American carbines with long banana clips, which made me suspect they were the fully automatic models. You can't really tell at any distance. The officer had drawn his pistol, and all three weapons were at the ready, if not quite pointed at us.

The water was turbulent at this narrow cut, and the officer had to shout. "What is your business here? I want to know your business!"

"*¡Pescadores!*" Refugio called out to him. "We are fishermen who lost our boat! Do you have a boat? We need a ride to Yoro! We lost our boat and one of our people! A gringo! Have you found a young gringo?"

The soldiers consulted among themselves. Then the PM came back to us. "What, will you shoot the fish? No, I don't believe you are fishermen!"

"Yes, can't you see? Look for yourself! A party of gringos! Their *equipaje* went down with the boat! They come to catch the fish and shoot the birds! You are brave soldiers serving on the *frontera!* We are nothing but fishermen and gentlemen shooters! *¡Escopetas blancas!* Don't you have a power boat?"

Another consultation. The young PM pointed downstream with his revolver and fired off a round, for the joy of it, I think. "*¡Mas abajo!* On down! At the *ruinas!* The *arqueos* have a boat! At Chupá!"

"How far?" I shouted.

"Not far!"

"Have you seen a young gringo?"

No answer.

"The young man is lost! He may be in your country! Will you make a report to your *comandante?*"

No answer. Policemen, lawyers, soldiers, doctors—they hate to tell you anything.

"Then with your permission we will be on our way!"

Again they said nothing. The parley was over. We moved off warily, unlikely communists, and they watched us, not altogether satisfied with our story. We were in Mexico, the Colossus of the North, and didn't need their permission. They would have been lucky to hit us at that range with those pieces. Still, it's just as well to step lightly around teenage boys in uniform carrying automatic weapons. I had been one myself and I had known, too, with my heart knocking against my ribs and my finger on the trigger of that BAR, that there was nothing sweeter than cutting down the enemies of your country.

Doc said, "An important lesson back there for all of us."

We waited. What lesson? It pays to be courteous to the army? Something to do with the ticks? What? No, the lesson was to be careful with chain saws. Doc's thoughts had drifted back to the cave of the two laughing *chiflados*.

"That poor boy could very easily have lost his arm. A chain saw is a very tricky customer, and if you don't know what you're doing, leave it alone. You must always grasp it firmly with both hands and never, never raise it above your head."

Refugio didn't know Chupá. Doc, calling it Shupá, claimed he had been there once, around 1946, and knew it like the back of his hand. Gail was familiar with the name. The ruin was on the Guatemala side, she said, and some Mormons were reported to be digging there. I had never heard of it, though it was situated on the river. You can float right by some of those old cities, walk right through them in the jungle and never notice a thing. The trees and roots strangle them, the humus accumulates and the temples lose their sharp edges, become rounded hills, little wooded *cerritos* that appear natural.

"We're coming up on it now," Doc said, time and again. "Over there . . . in the shade of that headland. . . . No, that can't be it . . ."

Probably he had been to Chupá, just as he had been to hundreds of these sites, but now they all ran together in his head. Not far, the officer had said, which could mean anything. If the *arqueos* had hidden their boat and set up their camp back from the river, we might well miss the place. We might already have missed it. The red sun was almost down. I was looking for a good place to hole up for the night, some hillside depression with a nice overhang.

"Two boats! There!" Refugio saw them first. We could just make them out in the shadows, a *cayuca* and a green plastic boat on the far shore, tied up in the mouth of a creek. A thin line of white smoke rose from the forest. It was a camp, all right. We shouted across the river in Spanish and English. Out of the trees came a tall bearded man in a baseball cap. He looked us over with his binoculars in the failing light.

Here is how fast night fell. We watched the man climbing into the green boat and starting the engine, and then as he came to us across the river we lost sight of him. We could see the boat and then we couldn't see it. He pulled up short of the bank and turned a spotlight on us, still not sure of us.

"We're looking for someone," I said. "We're making our way down the river. Can you put us up for the night?"

"Do you have papers for Guatemala?"

"No, but we'll be off in the morning. We'd like to hire your boat. Can you run us down to Yoro?"

"There is a sweet young lady here with us," said Doc. "Otherwise we wouldn't bother you. I appeal to your gallantry."

The man laughed in the darkness behind his bright light. "Okay."

Roland was his name, and he ferried us across and took us up the hill to a green tent and fed us well. Mashed potatoes are all the better for a few lumps, in my opinion, and gravy too for that matter. Roland was our solitary host. There were three other gringos in this Chupá crew that we didn't see, all laid up sick in their cots. Roland himself was healthy enough, a big strapping fellow with a clean beard and clear eyes, a walking tribute to the Mormon dietary laws. So many *arqueos* are sallow, bony little men with leg ulcers and bad skin rashes on their hands and arms.

It was a fine supper, with fresh peaches for dessert, out here where no peaches grew. "Might as well finish them off," he said, and so we did, piggishly, downy skins and all. We ate everything but the pits. It didn't occur to this decent man to hide the peaches until the plague of guests had blown over. After the meal, with a playful wink, he said he was sorry but he had no "highballs" to offer us. "Gentiles" of our type, he knew, just barely made it from one drink to the next.

I had served with some Mormons in Korea and they were good Marines to a man, if untypical ones. They didn't smoke, drink, swear, malinger or complain, except occasionally, about the P for Protestant that was stamped on their dog tags. They claimed to be some third thing in Christendom, neither Protestant nor Catholic, or rather some unique thing, but the point was too fine for the Marine Corps to grasp.

What they called themselves down here, in this work, was the New World Archaeological Foundation, their aim being to find evidence of early settlement by the "Jaredites" and Hebrews. All the Indian civilizations, they believed, were founded by these people, who came here by boat from the Middle East in two separate waves, the "Jaredites" or Sumerians in 2800 B.C., and the Hebrews around 600 B.C. It was a variation on the Lost Tribes of Israel theme, with certain strange Mormon wrinkles— strange to me—such as that Quetzalcoatl, the Toltec man-god from Tula, known to the Maya as Kukulcán, was the same person as Jesus. There was a tradition, they said, that Quetzalcoatl, the crested serpent, was crucified.

Not that they pushed the belief on anyone, far from it, for all their missionary work elsewhere. They were reluctant to discuss it with outsiders, or with me anyway, no doubt fearing that it would be hopelessly misunderstood, a religious quest mixed up with practical field work. It was all I could do to drag it out of Dr. Norbee, bit by bit, when I was hauling freight for him at a New World dig in Belize. Once I asked him outright—had they found any evidence to support the theory? Dr. Norbee, leery of casting pearls, put me off with a nonarchaeological example. There was a town in Honduras called Lamana, he told me, and Laman was one of the early Israelite chiefs here, chief of the Lamanites in fact. Laman of the Lamanites. Lamana. He left me to think that over. Pretty thin soup, but then the secular *arqueos,* always going on about the scientific purity of their motives, were usually out to prove some case or other themselves. From all I heard, the Mormon diggers were honest men who refused to fake or stretch the evidence. No more than anyone else, that is.

Roland knew Dr. Norbee and gave me news of him in Utah. He had heard nothing of any American boy being lost or found in these parts. Still no sighting. But he had seen a lot of gringos coming downstream in powered dugouts. Some had stopped here to stretch their legs. Hippies, they were, who had put in, most of them, at a place called Sayache, on the Pasión River, which is the upper Usumacinta. They were on their way to Yorito, or actually to the ancient city of Likín, for some sort of hippie jamboree. This accounted for the absence of boats. The boatmen were all lingering down at Yoro and Yorito, ferrying the hippies back and forth across the river and making a killing.

Yes, if you're going to Likín, Sayache would be the place to put in. It was one of the few towns on the upper part of this river system that you could reach by car or bus. You drove to Belize, then over to Flores in Guatemala, then down to Sayache, end of the road. Rudy, of course, wouldn't want to do it that way, the easy way, but why would he do it at all? Could he be part of this? Rudy was no hippie.

I asked Roland what the occasion was. "What are these people gathering for?"

"The annihilation of the world. Tomorrow, on the stroke of midnight."

"They're celebrating that?"

"Well, they say they're trying to stop it, with a blood sacrifice. There's supposed to be another group doing the same thing down at Machu Picchu in Peru. They seem to think this is the end of the thirteenth *baktun*. The end of time. Unless their sacrifice proves acceptable. They're expecting to meet someone there called *El Mago*."

Doc had gone all heavy and slumped from the big feeding, which Soledad Bravo had advised against. Now he was roused. "What's that? *Baktuns?* The completion of the *baktuns* doesn't come around until the year 2011."

"Yes sir, but they don't go by the Thompson correlation. They have some reckoning of their own. I couldn't follow it. They've tied it all in somehow with New Year's Day."

"What nonsense. Our January one, Gregorian, is in no way related to the beginning of the Mayan year."

"Unless by chance."

"No, not even then, if you mean the approximate year. It was in summer that the Mayan year began, and certainly not at midnight. They must be thinking of the Aztecs."

Gail said she didn't see how the Incas could be involved. "What does Machu Picchu have to do with it?"

Roland said he didn't know. "I couldn't follow that either."

"And the Spinden correlation is·out." She took a small calculator from her shoulder bag and punched around on the keys. "It's not the Weitzal correlation . . . or the Escalona Ramos correlation . . . I can't imagine what system they're using . . . wait . . . let me try the day itself against the heliacal rising of Venus . . ."

"Try it against all four phases."

She and Roland and Doc continued to wrestle with the problem, surely knowing it to be an empty exercise. The hippies knew nothing about the Mayas and their *baktuns*—400-year periods—or the Incas, or the planetary movements, much less the end of the world, certainly nothing that could be worked out on a calculator. Rudy carried one, too, in his shirt pocket. He was fond of decimal points. He would add up his guesses and rough estimates in an exact way on the thing and come out with falsely precise figures, which looked like hard-won data, very pleasing to the eye. Still—Doomsday at hand. The prophecy never fails to pull you up short. You stop a bit, before going on. No one knows and so anyone might hit on it.

It got worse, embarrassing. Doc went on to repay Roland's hospitality by trying to provoke a quarrel, telling him bluntly that he was all wrong with his Hebrews wading ashore at Veracruz. It was the Chinese who had settled this country. The Meso-Americans could not possibly have come from the Mediterranean, because there, as in Europe, the snake was a symbol of evil. No, it was in the Far East, in China, where you found benign reptiles, holy lizards, celestial dragons, and such, as you also found here with the iguana god and the cult of the mighty plumed serpent. The same lotus theme too. Just as it was here, as in China, that jade was believed to have divine properties.

And was not every Indian baby born with the Mongolian Spot at the base of his spine?

Roland took all this in a good-natured way, deferring to the old man, calling him Sir, saying he made some good points, that the jury was still out on so many things down here.

Gail was drowsy, and I was nodding too. Ramos moved about impatiently under the table, nudging my leg for more scraps. Doc tried again. He asked Roland where he stood on carbon-14 dating. Roland said it was a useful tool, but he said it with no confidence, sensing he was going to be on the wrong end of this argument too. Doc informed him that carbon dating was a colossal hoax, perhaps the greatest scientific scandal of the twentieth century. "You can get any date you like. If you don't like the reading, you just say the sample was too small or it was contaminated. You keep running the stuff through the lab till you get a reading you do like. Look at what they did to Spinden. First they said he was right, and then they said he was wrong. Off by 260 years. Of course he *was* wrong, but they had to keep cooking their numbers to show it. You boys are easily taken in, if I may say so."

We put up for the night in a temple chamber with thick walls of glittering crystalline limestone. It was the camp storeroom. The ceiling was high and at least fifteen feet across, about as wide a free span as you will see in this land of the false arch. Most of the chambers in these great structures were no bigger than closets, and Art and Mike maintained that the Maya were not really architects at all but essentially sculptors. Their purpose was to throw up solid white platforms against the sky, and only incidentally to enclose space. There was a single doorway. Roland took pains to close it off with a double thickness of mosquito netting. He wished us goodnight.

"Nice boy but a mere technician," said Doc. "He has no comprehensive vision." We settled in against boxes and lumpy sacks. Ramos did two or three tight little dog turns in place before dropping down at Refugio's feet. Doc prowled around with a citronella candle. He looked in corners and ran his hands over niches in the wall. "The ceremonial vesting room, I think. Yes, it seems we have been assigned to the vesting room." He was never at a loss to explain the function of ancient things. Show him a rough, wedge-shaped rock, and he would identify it as a *coup-de-poing*, or hand axe. Show him a smooth one and he would say, "Ah yes, a nice votive axe." Sometimes it *was* a votive axe, and for all I knew this was an old vesting room. These dead cities still lived and sparkled for him in the distance as they did not for me. This room had no message for me.

We slept. Doc woke us in the night. He came to us with his yellow candle and a scrap of paper. It was headed "Xupáh [as he spelled it] Guatemala," and dated. Underneath that he had written, "I swear or affirm that I accept without reservation Dr. Richard Flandin's theory of direct trans-Pacific Chinese settlement of Meso-America."

"Would you look this over and then sign it, please? Take your time. I don't like to disturb you but I might forget this in the morning. I'm not a hard man to work for. I do however insist on staff loyalty. If we're not all pulling together then how in the world can we ever hope to accomplish anything?"

Refugio and I signed, he, writing with a flourish, "Refugio Bautista O." We had done it before, though these chits usually ran to vows of silence about particular finds.

"I can't sign this," Gail whispered to me.

"Why not? Just put something down."

She signed Denise's name by the light of the candle.

"And I thank you very much," said Doc, simpering over the paper, all but rubbing his hands together. He was a salesman closing out on a big and unexpected order. "A formal gesture like that gives the pledge more weight, I think. I say 'theory' and that will do for our purposes here, but it's much more than that. It's more than a theoretical construct, it's a hard fact."

Later he woke us again. "Excuse me, but I forgot to mention that this loyalty business goes both ways. It must come down from the top too. I'm fully aware of that. Here is a token of my trust in you."

He set fire to the scrap of paper, watched it burn, and then left us alone. No word about lying down here and not getting up again.

ON TO Yoro. It was still dark when Roland came and said the boat was ready. I couldn't blame him for speeding us on our way. He stood to lose his digging permit, so hard to come by these days, if Guatemalan soldiers found us here with no papers. I offered to pay him for his trouble, and he said no, just tip the boatman when we reached Yoro.

He, the skipper, was a shirtless little river rat, proud of his *cayuca*, this being a dugout canoe fashioned from a mahogany log. It was a good sturdy hull about thirty feet long, well shaped and finished. The hacking marks of the axe and the adze were sanded down. The sides were damp and had a nappy, velvet feel from long use. He pushed off from shore with his sounding pole and started the engine, and we slipped away into a fog bank. Roland trudged back up the hill to search for traces of Lamanites in the rubble of Chupá. A comprehensive vision, it seemed to me, was the very thing he did have.

Our man knew the channel well. There were no lights on the boat, but he ran his engine full out. He couldn't even see the front of the *cayuca*. A heavy night bird swooped, came flapping right over our heads, confused by the fog, perhaps still looking for something small and live to eat. After that we had the river to ourselves. Doc lost his little Chinaman's cap, and he looked better, more dignified, with his white hair loose and blowing. Then he lost his wristwatch trailing his hand in the water. Refugio said, "You never know what the day will bring."

The morning light came slow and the sun was well up before we could see it through the vapor, a pale disk. Surely it would rise again tomorrow. Gail passed around some cheese and tortillas and mashed cake. Soggy cake is bad but mashed cake is not so bad. Ramos clambered from one end of the boat to the other. He couldn't find a good place to settle. The river rat had nothing to say to us. He kept his hand on the tiller and held his head high and sucked on a dip of snuff. The cud was packed under his lower lip, and it appeared to be a satisfying snuff of the very finest quality. My guess was that he was silent at home, too, if he had one. Gliding up and down the river in your own boat, knowing you had plenty of snuff in reserve, was better than yapping all the time, and being yapped at.

The engine sputtered out three or four times, and we lost half the day drifting, wiping oil off the fouled spark plug, blowing through the fuel line, yanking on the starter rope. Good mechanics that they are, and for all their Latin delicacy in other matters, Mexicans are not much troubled by a firing miss in an engine. Almost every taxicab has an ignition skip or a faulty carburetor. The missed beat doesn't gnaw at them. Time enough to fix the thing when it goes out altogether.

We arrived in the afternoon. Some of the hippies had fallen sick here at Yoro and were lying about in the shade or just sitting on the riverbank hugging their knees. Others had moved on to Likín for the big event. Nothing was moving on the river. Most of the *cayucas* were beached across the way on the Yorito side. A late afternoon stillness. No women washing clothes in the shallows.

I went to pay our boatman, and Doc said, "Here, no, I'm taking care of this. Give the fellow some money, Gail." He had turned over all his money to her.

There was a new and bigger gasoline storage tank at the landing. It seemed there were more children about, and the tire swing had been introduced here since my last visit. Otherwise Yoro looked much the same. A dirt track ran up from the landing through two rows of shacks and then petered out against the forest wall. A *ranchería,* they called it, and you could take it all in at a glance. It was still a sad little outpost.

The restaurant was the same, too, known only as the widow woman's place. The woman prepared food in her house and brought it out back to a small *ramada* open on all sides. There were four tables under a palm-thatched arbor. It was this same woman, now scowling at us, somewhat fatter but not looking much older, who had refused to take my *tortuga* note years ago.

We had disturbed her nap. It was nap time in Yoro. All the food was gone, she told us, there was nothing to be had here, the young gringo beasts had eaten everything as fast as she could cook it. They had frightened her cat Emiliano away, and look how they had trampled down her morning glory vines and her tomato plants, her fine *jitomates*—in the season of the Nativity!—bringing their social diseases and their foreign eye diseases! There was a place in Hell for them, for dirty *gorristas* like that one there!

She pointed to a hippie who was stretched out on the ground with a hat over his face. It was a touristy hat made from green palmetto blades. I thought he was asleep, but he must have been watching us through the weave cracks. "There's not a single Pepsi left in town," he said. "They're all out of bread, too, and ice."

Refugio told the woman that we were forest rangers and that she would do better to show more respect for the government. Was she blind? Couldn't she see that we were important captains from the *forestal* and not young *viciosos*? "Now go to your pots and bring us what you have." She served up some black beans and fried plantains and coffee. We had our own tortillas. Refugio said she could put on a new red dress and red shoes, do whatever she liked, crawl on her knees to the Shrine of Guadalupe, and still she would never find another husband, a scolding woman like that.

The hippie spoke up again. "My car doors are frozen shut in Chicago. All the ice you want up there." His jeans were pressed, and if anything he was cleaner and more presentable than we were. But then he really wasn't a hippie and he was quick to set us straight on that point. Right off the bat he showed me his new Visa credit card. His name was Vincent. He and his sweetheart, Tonya Barge or Burge, had flown down here to celebrate the end of his apprenticeship. He had just won his "electrician's ticket"— which I took to mean a union card or some kind of professional certification. And it was true, he had come down the big river with this wandering tribe, but he wasn't one of them.

"I thought we were going to the beach. Christmas on the beach, that was our plan, see, just the two of us, staying in bargain hotels and eating bargain food. Like bananas, you know, and tacos, and those real big Cokes? Then we ran into these interesting people, or anyway Tonya thought they were interesting, with all their talk about cosmic energy. I'm not into pyramids myself and I can't buy the mind science these people are putting out. Forget it. I like the beach. What's wrong with that? There's plenty of cosmic energy coming down on the beach."

I said, "You need to keep better company, Vincent."

"Hey, don't I know it! I mean, come on, all these potheads giving out their bum information! This big brownout they're talking about? The death of the sun? Who wants to hear that? Who needs it! And this *El Mago* that nobody knows who he is? With all his strange powers? Nobody has ever seen him here yet but oh yeah he's going to work wonders! Dark forces are gathering! Signs and wonders! Give me a break, will you! I don't like to hear stuff like that and I don't go for this sleeping dirty either and all their weird baloney about the mystery of the underground colonies! Don't get me started on that! Am I talking too loud? It's a bad habit I got to watch."

"No, don't let it get a foothold."

"Say, I been meaning to ask you. What are all the guns for?"

"Songbirds. We're hunters. Trophy kills."

"Well, hey, that's your business, not mine! I don't know one bird from another except for robin redbreast! I'm no sportsman, I'm just passing through! I'm not even supposed to be here! I mean the country is green and beautiful but all these bugs. We didn't see any alligators yet, just snakes so far and those iguanas with the ugly spines on their backs. The boat ride was fun though, I got to admit that, and last night we watched a falling star all the way down. Wait, did I dream that? No, what am I saying, everybody saw it. They were all talking about it. They said it fell out there in the water somewhere. Don't tell me you people live around here."

"I live in Mérida."

"Mérida, right, I've heard of it. And you live there! With your dog! And the old man and the girl with the machete, they're after these little birds too?"

"No, I was only playing around with you a little bit there, Vincent. We're just making our way down the river. We're looking for someone."

He put up his hands in surrender. "Hey, don't worry, I can handle that! No problem! I'm not offended! I can take a joke! You think I don't know decent people when I see them? So let me see now if I understand this. You're taking your river trip and the chunky Mexican guy, he's not a policeman or anything like that with his big pistol?"

"No, he's not a policeman."

"Then let me ask your advice on something. Should I be waiting on the other side of the river? I know this is Mexico and I don't have my Mexican papers."

"You're okay. Nobody in Yoro is going to bother you about papers."

"The last thing I want down here is trouble with my papers. Know what I mean? I don't like to break the law. That's just the way I am. I mean it's there for a purpose, right? But there's nothing to do over in Yorito, and those boat guys won't talk to you. Let me tell you what Tonya did. When we got out of the boat at Yorito. This is a great story. She went right on up the hill to that old pyramid city— in her sandals! Right off into the woods I'm telling you! With all those nuts! A long line of marching nuts and bums not saying anything! No way I'm walking into that jungle in my jogging shoes. It's so dark and shady you can't see where you're stepping and you just know the place is full of snakes and these marching ants that can bite right through canvas! Do you think I was cowardly? Tell me the truth."

"No, it makes sense to me. I wouldn't go out there without boots."

"Tonya wouldn't listen to me. I told her not to go. Are you saying I was right not to go? Just what are you saying?"

"I'm saying you were right and Tonya Barge was wrong."

"So you seem to think I can live with my decision then."

"She'll be back. I wouldn't worry about it."

"They got to her head with their mind science. She went right on up the hill in her sandals. Some of those people are barefooted. I still can't believe it. Women should be cleaner than men, right? Well, let me tell you, some of those old gals could use a bath."

"How many are up there?"

"A lot."

"Fifty? A hundred?"

"More than that. Sometimes you can hear them chanting."

I listened but couldn't hear them. Maybe the wind was wrong. You couldn't see the ruin itself from here, just the green mass of the hill downstream at the bend. Ramos came to his feet. A yellow tomcat was looking at him from a patch of weeds. They looked at each other. It was a stare-down. Then the cat, who must have been Emiliano, with-drew, but in no haste. It just wasn't time to come back yet. Ramos did his dog turn and settled down again. Emiliano wasn't even worth a growl.

Doc spoke to me with his eyes shut. White stubble glittered on his face. "When are we going over to Likín, Jimmy? I want a long cool drink from the spring. Gail does too. I hope it's not silted up." She had him lying on the ground in the shade of the *ramada*, with his head on her bag. She was fanning him. One panting old man had already died before her eyes, at another dinner table.

"We'll be going soon," I said. "After we've rested a little."

"Can we stay there overnight?"

"What for?"

"I want to take Gail up to the top of the *Castillo* and show her the Temple of Dawn. How the first beams of the day strike through that little aperture. With blinding splendor."

"It's a steep climb."

"We'll take our time going up."

"Yes, well, it's okay with me. It's just that all those people are over there now. We'll see how things work out."

A white vapor trail stretched halfway across the arch of the sky, so high that we couldn't see the airplane that was spinning it out, or hear it.

Vincent said, "That's the only way to cross this jungle if you ask me. They're up there in their seats and we're down here without any Pepsis."

He had seen some young men wearing odds and ends of military garb but no one quite like Rudy. I went around to the villagers with my questions, hoping the women wouldn't snatch up their babies and run from me. In one hut I interrupted some men hanging green tobacco leaves over the roof stringer poles. They were polite but of no help. My description of Rudy meant nothing to them. Gringos were phantoms. A few more minutes and I too would be gone from their memory. Down on the river bank I woke up a pair of hippies who had fallen asleep fully clothed and all locked together in a tight embrace, like that petrified couple they found at Herculaneum. The boy was surly, not feeling well. The girl blinked at me through her hair and said she had seen a blond fellow in army clothes back at the lake town of Flores. No, not my man. I thought not. Wrong way. He wouldn't have gone upstream. I spoke to all the sick stragglers, and, I think, to every adult resident of Yoro. None of them had seen Rudy Kurle, planner of cities. I was convinced of that, unless someone was lying. Even in this flock of migrant cockatoos he would have stood out. In khaki or blaze orange Rudy would have made an impression. He would have been noticed, pointed out, discussed and remembered.

I would have to investigate the others across the river, go through the motions at least, but not now. I was drained. All these futile questions. I went back to the *ramada* muttering a little and lay down. Doc and Gail and Vincent were talking about art. What a subject. A girl with a round belly came by. Refugio shielded his face with his hands and shouted, "*¡Ay!* Look out! God help us! She's about to pop!" The pregnant girl made a face at him and he laughed and said, "Be brave! It won't be long now! You won't regret it when you see that little wet rat!" The girl laughed too and waddled off with her plastic buckets. The women of Yoro were carriers of water.

It was Vincent's souvenir, a lacquered gourd, that had set off the art talk. Black monkeys were painted on it, under a clear coat of lacquer. Very poor workmanship, said Doc, who was drinking something from a bottle. The monkeys looked like squirrels, he said, and sick squirrels or dead squirrels at that. It was nothing, *basura,* trash. This was the only part of Mexico where the people had no gift for the graphic arts. There was no vigor or joy in their work. They lacked a sure hand. They had no more art in their bones than—he looked at me—than the people of Caddo Parish, Louisiana. Vincent defended his gourd.

The monkeys looked okay to him. This art was okay. What he couldn't appreciate was diamonds and rubies and such. "I mean, why all the fuss?" What he couldn't understand was the point at which pretty stones became precious gems, worth millions of dollars, that people gloated over. Gail said she had a similar problem with the mystery that surrounded the serpent. As a child, of course, she had feared snakes and gone in awe of them, as of some fabulous beasts. Now, of course, she knew better. She knew now—they had explained it all to her in college— that snakes were neither horrible nor magnificent, but only creeping digestive tracts. And in many cases they destroyed harmful rodents and other agricultural pests. Yet the myth persisted! She and Vincent both were from Illinois but nothing was made of it. Some social gap there. Doc said that Humboldt, usually so wise, had denied that there was any art in ancient Meso-America. Carvings, paintings, sculpture, ceramic pieces, funeral masks—all very nice in their way but only proto-art. It was just something on the long road that leads to art.

I was trying to think of some Shreveport artists. We had some, I had seen their huge swirling works hanging in bank lobbies, but I could hardly be expected to know their names. Who was Humboldt anyway and how was it that the pre-Columbian stuff fell short in his eyes? No soul? Too cluttered? Too stiff? What? You wonder what people have in mind when they speak with confidence on such tricky matters. Old Suarez had his doubts about it, too, because it wasn't socialist art. Only the royalty and the soldiers were glorified. We needed him here for this seminar, and Beth and Professor Camacho Puut and Louise and Nardo and Eli and Art and Mike. Bollard too; he could give us the very latest line out of New York, or fake it plausibly enough.

The orchid on Gail's hat had gone brown along the edges. My information was wrong. Air alone wasn't enough to keep the blossom going. They didn't feed off wind after all.

"Well, Mr. Humboldt never saw anything like this," she said. "This is art. You can tell right away. Look how it jumps out at you. Look how—*strong* it is."

Ugly was the word she wanted. She was showing us the little Olmec figure with the demonic face. So now our Dicky had given that thing to her, too. What was going on here? She rubbed around on it, the way you do with jade, then buttoned it up again in her shirt pocket. No questions about the ownership, the way she patted that pocket. The ceramic bird, the jade man. Everything buttoned away there was hers.

But now Doc was off art and onto famous men he had known. Morley, Thompson, Stirling, Caso, Ruz Lhullier—they had all come to him for advice and consultation, to hear him tell it. Great Mayanists all! He too stood in that apostolic chain, nor was he the least of them! But what could he not have done with a proper staff and a little recognition now and then! From these low-life professors who controlled everything with their petty politics! These very little men! These gray mice! Who pretended not to know him while all the time they were stealing his ideas!

Purple drops ran down through the stubble on his chin. Gail had found a cold bottle of grape soda somewhere, and she was sharing it with him. The old lizard still had a way with the ladies. She hung on his every boastful word. Refugio, too, he loved the hot words and the bluster. This was the way a man should speak, out of the abundance of the heart. Vincent was poking away at embedded ticks on his legs with the burning end of a cigarette. But Refugio stopped him, grabbing his wrist and saying, "No, don't do that while the Doctor is speaking." He said to Gail, "My name is in his book. Refugio Bautista Osorio."

Doc lay back on Gail's pack and closed his eyes again. "Oh, my vindication will come, all right, but much too late for me. You will live to see it. You will hear the acclaim. You can tell your children that you were with Flandin on his last *entrada* into the Garden of the Kings. Or call it the Valley of the Kings if you like, the pharaohs be damned. Don't forget, this was a great empire, too. You can say, 'Yes, I was with the poor old fellow shortly before he died of malicious neglect.' A victim of envy, too. A man literally murdered by the envy of cunning and hateful mice."

He paused there on the *mice*, which was just as well, and I saw a chance to get a word in. I took off my boots and directed this crew of mine in perfectly clear language to wake me in an hour. That would give me time to cross the river and climb the hill and look over that pack of hippies before sundown. I dozed. The chatter went on and on under the arbor, though a bit subdued now. It didn't bother me. There was no moving about. No one seemed able to move. We were in the grip of a curious Yoro paralysis. Refugio said to me, whispering, that, seriously now and all joking aside, the mature *chaneques* could grow hair all over their bodies whenever they pleased, at will, through their sorceries. "All the world knows this to be true, Jaime." He would be telling me next that the little men had furry paws. *Chaneques* didn't interest me at the moment. Vincent's falling star was still on my mind. I was thinking of a fiery pebble blazing out of the night and striking the river with a faint hiss, then settling with the side-to-side motion of a falling leaf to the mud at the bottom, journey's end. Down there with Doc's watch and other forgotten things, and that little jade *idolo,* too, if I could get my hands on it.

OF COURSE they didn't wake me and how could they, being asleep themselves, all sprawled together in a pile like a litter of puppies, not knowing or caring that sleeping on watch is a terrible offense. Night had come. An oil lamp was burning in the widow woman's house. There was sheet lightning to the west, far off in the mountains. It must have been the thunder that woke me. I gave Refugio a shake, and we slipped away with Ramos down to the landing.

Two boatmen were there squatting before a fire. One of them had a fighting cock tied by the leg. They were roasting river mussels in the coals. I wished them a prosperous new year. They flipped a coin to see who got our business.

"Yorito?"

"*Sí.*"

But I changed my mind when we were launched out into the river and I told the man to take us downstream, around the bend, to the foot of the bluff. We wouldn't have to walk so far. The old city of Likín would be directly above us. Yes, Rudy might well be up there observing the hippies. There seemed to be no point in taking notes on the end of the world, but he would probably feel the need to make some record of it. I was curious myself, and besides, I wanted to drink from the old spring again. I would press my face into the pool and open my eyes underwater and clarify my thoughts. It might help. For Doc everything came down to a cube. One night at Camp Pendleton I heard Colonel Raikes say that the key to it all was "frequent inspections." How right he was too. You had only to look at my unconscious crew to feel the force of that truth. But I had not yet worked out any such master principle of my own, to guide my steps. It wouldn't hurt to try the spring. I would gulp the water and clear my muddled head.

The man shut off his engine, and we could hear singing up there on the hilltop. We could see the red glow of a fire. It was an old song they were singing, something jolly like "Oh Susannah," only that wasn't it. I had expected wailing. The *cayuca* slid into the sand and went aground. I knocked against a bush in getting out, and mosquitoes rose from the branches in a cloud like blackbirds. Ramos was trembling, keen. He must have thought we were on a pig hunt. One whiff from the musk gland of a peccary and he would be off like a shot. But not all dogs hunt by scent. The greyhound must catch sight of his quarry, just as I did, and the night was black here in Chiapas, or rather Guatemala. There was no moon. Monkeys were screaming back and forth at one another across the river. The lunatic monkeys knew something was up.

I led the way with my flashlight along the bank till we came to a gully that was cut by the runoff water from the spring. Then up we went, straight up the gully, grabbing at bushes and slipping on wet moss. The spring, little used now, was about halfway up the cliff, enclosed in a circular revetment of ancient masonry. I was afraid the hippies might have found it and fouled it in some way, but no, the water was clear, with a few leaves floating in it and some bugs skittering across the surface. I pushed the head of my plastic flashlight beneath the surface. At the bottom, farther away than it appeared, grains of sand tumbled about where a jet of water surged out of the earth. I couldn't fix the exact point. The source, the *ojo de agua,* the eye of water itself, was a mystery under the whirling sand. It was a small shifting turbulence, nothing more, a spirit.

We drank and then washed our faces, saying nothing. My dripping head was perhaps a little clearer than before. It was hard to say. My bad knee was a good deal worse for the climb. There was a smooth outcropping of rock here about the size and shape of a bus. We sat on the ledge and had a smoke.

Refugio said, "The boy is up there then? With the *tóxicos?*"

"I don't know. We'll see."

"I think he is dead."

"You may be right."

"The two *chiflados* killed him and threw his body into the river. All that laughing didn't fool me."

"They would have kept his equipment and his clothes."

"It was hidden. With their boat. They had a *barca* somewhere. Or a raft, a *balsa.* They won't need a motor to go back downstream to Yoro."

"No, they would have forgotten something. Some little something of Rudy's. I don't miss much when I'm looking hard."

"You will die out here, too, a fool, with no money in your pocket and no wife at home and no pretty little child of your own."

"Not me. I have my plans."

"*Qué va.* You don't have no plans."

"I have long-range plans that I never talk about."

"*Qué va. Poco probable.* . . . Do you know what I am doing, Jaime? I am praying for my baby. Sula was right. I should be with Manolo on his long drive to Yucatán and you take me out here on your foolish *paseo.*"

The *opresión* was on him. It was a terrible thought, that he might have to put up one of those little roadside crosses for his dead and mangled son.

"Your Manolito is all right. He's a better driver than you are. Manolo is in Mérida right now. He's in some game room playing a *futbolista* machine."

"I should have listened to her. Sula is never wrong. You must drag the Doctor out here, too, and he is old and sick."

"We'll have a quick look around the *ruinas.* If the boy is there we're done and if he's not there we're done. We'll go home."

He sighed. Not a word of concern about my truck. From here to the top, about 300 feet above the river, a flight of steps had been cut into the rock, still useful though overgrown and eroded. We were huffing and puffing as we came over the crest, two blowing men out of the night with guns and a dog. We appeared suddenly before a ring of hippies around a fire. There were open cans of food in the embers. A hobo jungle, you might think, if hoboes sang. They stopped singing and looked at us. Someone was always breaking in on their fun. In the heart of the Petén forest they still couldn't get away from the likes of me.

I saw other watchfires here and there in the clearing. The place was a campground. There were beach towels and little orange tents and coconut shells and a stalk of bananas and pickle jars and bread wrappers and water jugs and sleeping bags and colorful serapes and pitiful shelters made of plastic raincoats. There was a girl with lightning bugs in her hair. One brave boy had made it up here on aluminum crutches. He supported himself on those half-crutches called forearm canes.

Many others must have dropped out along the way. These were the hardy ones. There may have been a hundred people scattered about on the plateau but no more. Vincent had led me astray there. I was expecting I don't know what, a shrieking mob, the last hours of Gomorrah, a good deal of eye-rolling, but in fact the crowd was thin and listless, such as you might see at a track meet. Nothing of a ceremonial nature was going on. There was no apparent focus to the thing. No one seemed to be in charge. It was just one more herd of hippies milling around in a pasture. Had something gone wrong? Maybe the frolic was to start later.

A pasture, I call it, this long plaza or courtyard of the old city of Likín, which the people of Yorito kept cleared for their single milk cow to graze on. It was a rectangle bounded on the long sides by a series of mounds, with temples underneath the dirt and greenery. The Mayas had flattened the hilltop and built their City of Dawn here high above the jungle roof, where they could get a breeze now and then. This end of the plaza was open, overlooking the river, and at the far end there was a partially excavated pyramid, known as the *Castillo*. Most of the digging had been done there, at the pyramid complex. The grand staircase was exposed, leading to a shrine at the top, a stone box, and on top of that, capping the whole thing, was a decorative bit of stone fretwork, what they call a roof comb. No one was moving about on the *Castillo* stairway. It was odd. When travelers come upon a pyramid, they must climb it and crawl all over it and wave from the top.

I spoke a bit loud to the hippies. It was my experience that their attention wandered. "We're not here to bother you," I said. "We're not going to interfere with your— program. I'm looking for a friend. An emergency has come up at home. His wife is sick, and I know you'll want to help me. His name is Rudy. Can everybody hear me? Rudy Kurle is the name. From Pennsylvania. He's a big blond fellow in army gear. A brown army outfit and heavy boots. Does that ring a bell? You may have seen him speaking into a tape recorder. He carries a lot of stuff on his belt. How about it? If you've seen him, please tell me. You'll be doing him and his wife both a big favor."

Someone said in a very low voice, "He may have his reasons for staying away from home."

A Scandinavian girl with hairy legs said, "I am not even listening to you. Your words have no more significance

to me than the buzzing of flies. I am no longer hearing all
these dead words floating around in the air."

Not a bad policy on the whole. "Suit yourself," I
said. "But we're not leaving here till we find him. I think
he's around here somewhere. The sooner we find him the
sooner we'll be gone."

The others had nothing at all to say to me. They
weren't so much defiant as puzzled and annoyed. Tired
too, no doubt, from their long trek. It was hopeless.
I would need a bullhorn to get through to these people.
I went about my old business of looking them over one
by one. I put my light into the faces of those in the shadows. Some took this indignity better than others. I interrupted their feeding. I lifted the flaps of their little tents.
We moved from campfire to campfire. Refugio walked
behind me, grumbling. Ramos drew back and bared his
teeth at those who tried to pet him. They took him for
a Frisbee-catching pal, a great mistake. The girl with the
lightning bugs followed me around too, saying the same
thing over and over again.

"Share the wonder, bring a friend."

"I did bring one."

"Share the wonder, bring a friend."

"Most people wouldn't want bugs in their hair."

"Share the wonder, bring a friend."

The bugs were tied to her hair with thread, and they
flashed on in ragged sequence with a cool green light.
Refugio said we should have brought along something to
sell. We could have coiled great long ropes of sausages
around our necks and sold them here at monopoly prices.

I agreed, we should have thought to bring sausages and a megaphone. The *arqueos* or some other looters had been here since my last visit. All the inscribed stelae had been uprooted and carried away, leaving only the blank ones. They looked like blank tombstones. They were memorials to nothing, or perhaps some daring artistic gesture.

The Yorito milk cow, of a stunted breed unknown to me, stood very still in a sunken place, a walled-in arena where the Maya once played a game with a rubber ball. She was ivory-colored with drooping ears and a pink deflated udder not much bigger than a goat udder. The weeds looked tough and wiry there in the ball court, but it was a quiet place to wait out the siege. All this vegetation and you could see her ribs. I wished I could have given her an armful of sweet alfalfa.

They weren't all young dopers at this *congreso*, as Refugio called it. A middle-aged man with bangs came up to me. He wore a baggy shirt with a dazzling floral pattern, and of course sandals. Feet are all the better for a good airing out, and I would be the last one to deny it, but I think these people had something more than ventilation in mind. They were downright aggressive about displaying their feet to the world. The man came up to me, hesitant and polite, and asked if I might by any chance be *El Mago*.

"Who? No."

"No, I didn't think so. Excuse me. I didn't really expect *El Mago* to be armed, though they do say he is a complex and unpredictable brute. The thing is, I don't know what he looks like. He could very well be right here among us."

So, they were waiting for this *El Mago* fellow to appear. He, The Wizard, was overdue and there was growing fear that he might not show. Just who was he? What would he do? No one seemed to know. The only *El Mago* I knew was a very old man who lived in the town of Valladolid, if indeed he still lived. He was a famous *brujo,* a witch, who could read the future from the flopping throes of a decapitated turkey, and who was credited with forty-four sons out of a long series of wives and mistresses. The daughters went unnumbered. I knew of him, that is, from newspaper articles and photographs. I had never actually seen him give a reading. But that scrawny old bird could hardly be described as a complex brute, nor at his age would he be fit to make the hard journey to Likín. Unless they had lashed him to a chair and borne him in here on shoulder poles, with his old head lolling from side to side. I put nothing past them.

I wondered about their theory and what part *El Mago* would play and how they saw the end coming. Why gather at this place? Why gather at all? Was there to be a spectacle or just lights out? No wrath? I couldn't get a feel for the mechanics of the thing or for the shape of it. I was curious but too proud to show much interest. The line I took was one of indifference—no lofty contempt, just that I couldn't be bothered. In fact I was uneasy. These lost sheep knew nothing. I was pretty sure of that. They simply wanted to be on stage for the dramatic finish. It must all wind down with them and nobody else. The thought of the world going on and on without them, much as usual, and they forgotten, was unbearable. Nothing important was going to happen here. The burning light from heaven might indeed fail one day, but not, I thought, tomorrow. And yet I was uncomfortable. I didn't like meddling in such things.

Down the way from the ball court, a dead woman lay stretched out on a striped blanket. Two girls were sitting there fanning the body. The dead woman's name was Jan, I was relieved to hear, and not Tonya Barge. Then I saw that she was probably too old anyway to be Vincent's sweetheart. One leg of her shiny black slacks was cut off, exposing a black swelling on her calf. Boots might or might not have helped. The snake had struck her a few inches below the knee, a *palanca* I had no doubt. By way of treatment someone had squeezed lime juice over the wound and poked around in it with a knife—a red-hot knife, the girls said. They didn't know the woman's last name or where she was from. She wore a white blouse and braided gold belt. The metallic strands gleamed under my light. No watch, no finger rings, one silver bracelet. It was my habit to note such things in case the description turned up on a Blue Sheet. The girls said she had passed out at once from the shock of the bite and never came around, never opened her eyes again. They were fanning her with branches to keep the flies off. The male fanners had already slipped away, if they had ever been here. You couldn't count on men to stick with a thankless job like that.

A gust of raindrops came and went. The lightning drew closer. Sula had told me that you can only see a person's true face in the glare of lightning. Refugio was disturbed by the way these *congreso* people walked, or he pretended to be. Youngsters should show more spirit, he said, more gaiety, *mas alegría*. It was a shame the way they moped around. They should stand up straight and carry themselves through life with a manly bearing—like Refugio, that is, who strode about like the Prince of Asturias. With that carriage and that air, he had no real need for elevated loafers. Now he dropped into a slouch and imitated the hippie movements. He went into a creeping shuffle and then did a kind of slow chicken walk. I was limping myself. The rain came back in a scattering of fat drops. The *congreso* people said various things to me.

"I have styes on my eyelids and ulcers on my tongue because I haven't been eating right."

"*El Mago* feeds on human hearts."

"Just what is your authority?"

"This is the landscape of my dreams."

"There are food thieves in this camp."

"*El Mago* is worth a hundred of you."

"They told me there was going to be a golden pavilion here with plenty of good food for everybody. They said you could pick grapes right off the trees."

"*El Mago* is waiting in his great house. You must know the right word before you can see him."

"It's early yet."

"Why don't you set your own house in order?"

"*El Mago* can see the hidden relation between things."

"I almost didn't come."

"I can't get anything on my radio but static."

"Touch *El Mago* and your hand will curl up and wither into a claw."

"When *El Mago* needs something he always finds it."

But there was no Rudy news and not much about the sun and nothing at all to the point. Some of these folk were pale and shaky, barely able to stand. These, the fasters, had eaten nothing for days, so as to make themselves light-headed, the better to see visions. Only one of the entire lot had anything to say about the Maya, and he told me that they had invented soap and "wireless telegraphy."

Refugio said, "What is it they say? I can't hear. Do they speak well?"

"No, they don't. They make a poor showing there, too."

Art and Mike in one of their flights once claimed that, given some plague or holocaust, our little gang at Shep's In-Between Club, an ordinary lot at best, was quite capable of reestablishing Western civilization, over time, with the help of a Bible and a dictionary and Simcoe's old broken set of encyclopedias. They didn't say how much time. But could it all spring anew from the crowd on this hilltop? I thought not. Better that a band of guerillas out here in the woods should survive, or an army patrol, with their camp women. Or a single lodge of the Elks Club. An Elk culture. My knee was blazing. I vowed never again to set foot outside Mérida.

Refugio turned up his hands. "*¿Listo?*"

"Yes, I've seen enough. Let's go."

All at once rain came sweeping across the plaza in dense curtains that quenched the campfires and raised clouds of steam. There was a scramble for cover. In the hurrying confusion, I thought I caught a glimpse of my hotel neighbors, Chuck and Diane, if that was their names. In the lightning glare, I thought I saw them running together hand in hand, and then they were gone. Refugio and I ducked through a doorway into a narrow stone chamber. Ramos, too, and with each clap of thunder he barked at the heavens. Chino would have tucked his tail. I turned my light about to see if we had guests. I smelled sour clothes. No, it was us. We reeked. On the back wall there was a small black handprint and the words A KOBOLD FEB 1941. Old Alma had been here, in this very room! Perhaps waiting out a rain herself, or just getting away from Karl for a bit. She had left her mark in the way of the Mayan architects, who sometimes signed their monumental projects with a red handprint. *All that you see here is the work of this hand.* My flashlight filament was getting redder and weaker. I turned it off, and we waited in darkness with the mosquitoes.

It was a black night again in the old city of Likín. Others had found shelter across the way in cubbyholes like this one. Here and there through the rainy blear, I could see feeble points of candlelight. Then we did get a guest, a young man in dripping jeans and a sailor's blue woolen jumper, who asked if we had room for him. He had been running. We made way and he came in breathing hard. His sleeve cuffs were folded back one lap, and I almost ordered him to turn them down and button them properly. When I was on gate duty at the Bremerton Navy Yard, I made the sailors button their sleeves and square away their caps, among other things. It was for their own good, a kindness really. We couldn't let them get jaunty. It was their great weakness in those outfits they wore. They liked to turn their cuffs back to show the golden dragons embroidered there, which meant they had served in the China Sea or some such thing. They hated us and we loved it. We cherished our power at Marine Barracks. Nobody could get to us. We even had our own bakery. I should have stayed there in the guard shack, imposing a petty bit of order on the world.

The boy wiped off his glasses, which were of the utopian communard model, with small round lenses and earpieces of the very thinnest wire. He had to raise his voice over the roar of the storm. "I got caught out there in the woods behind the big pyramid," he said. "It's really tough going out there without a machete. There must be a trail to the top, but I couldn't find it."

I said, "Why not go up the front way? The staircase is cleared."

"They won't let anybody on those steps. They'll run you off. They won't let you up there unless you know the right words."

"Who won't?"

"The two baldheaded guys. They pushed some people down earlier with their forked poles. It's like they own the place. I don't know who they are or what words they're talking about. You can take a bad fall down that thing."

"There are people up there now?"

"Yes, in that square chapel or whatever it is on top."

"How many?"

"I'm not sure. They have a goat. All I've seen is the goat and the two bald thugs, but there are some others moving around inside. *El Mago* himself could be in there."

He was a sensible kid and you could talk to him. Here was a piece of news. Yes, now I could make out a yellow light up there on top of the *Castillo*. Of course, that's where Rudy would be, at the heart of it all, at the citadel, taking useless measurements and perhaps chatting with the temple bullies. I would have to drag my inflamed knee all the way to the top, step by step. We waited. Rain this hard couldn't last. On summer afternoons we got these pounding showers in Mérida, and in five minutes the sun was shining again. And when it didn't rain, Fausto would run a hose on the sidewalk and let the water pool up in hollow places so the birds and the town dogs could get a drink.

We shared our dank closet with mosquitoes. They had done their worst to Refugio and me years ago, infecting us for life with malaria and dengue bugs, all the various fever bugs they carried. But in their numbers here and their agitated state, these big black Petén *bichos* were driving us crazy. They had only one raving thought and that was to get at our blood. They swarmed in our eyes and clogged our nostrils and our ears and finally drove us out into the rain.

Refugio thought we were making for Yorito, and I had to grab his soaked and flapping shirttail. "No! Up there! The *templo!* We'll have to check it out!"

"You say we are done! *¡Término!*"

"We've come this far! We can't get any wetter! A quick look and we're done!"

The pyramid was tilted slightly, with water coursing down one side of the staircase in a hundred little cataracts.

The thing had not been designed for easy ascent, certainly not for the Maya themselves, who stood five feet high at most. The pitch was too steep, the stone risers too high, and the stone treads too narrow. You couldn't get into a comfortable stride no matter how long your legs or how sound your knees. We struck off up the higher side, away from the falling water. The incline must have been close to sixty degrees, and the wet lichen on the stone was slippery. It was like climbing a ladder without using your hands. We could have tacked, gone up in prudent zigzag fashion, but no, it was straight up to the top for us in one go, with Refugio leading the way. He was angry. I hobbled along behind using my old Smith shotgun as a support stick. Ramos followed me, advancing in awkward hops, until, just short of the crest, he stopped and froze in place, spooked, like a frightened housecat up a tree. His hair, wet and heavy though it was, stuck up in a spiky ruff around his neck from all the lightning in the air.

Let him wait there and ponder the glyphs carved on the riser faces. We could pick him up on the way down. I knew, looking at those strange symbols, that Doc could no more read them than Ramos could. Probably he would "interpret" them, not translate them. But that was all right with me, he was still a formidable man and in his own way a great man.

I knew too, suddenly, and so late, that we were dealing here with Big Dan and his people. This was the sunrise city, Likín, the City of Dawn. And now the two bald boys. But my poor head was so muddled that I didn't work it out until that moment on the pyramid steps. It came to me all at once. I stopped dead in my tracks and took off my hat in this driving rain and offered up a prayer of my own. I asked God to let me find the little girl, LaJoye Mishell Teeter, promising not to let her out of my hands this time. I promised not to take any money for her recovery. The wind was fierce up here above the forest canopy. The rain came sideways. Down there in the treetops the monkeys must have been hanging on for their lives.

The little temple was oblong rather than square, and it took up the entire summit platform, except for a narrow bit of deck space on each side. There was a single doorway, or so I thought, in the front. A male figure stood there in the opening with a faint light behind him. I could smell the burning wax of candles.

He didn't see us until we had stepped up onto the platform, and then he gave a start. "Hey, that's far enough!" He came forward holding a six-foot length of trimmed sapling that was forked at the slender end. "Hold it right there! Let's have the words! Do you know the words?"

I put my light on him. There were colored stripes painted front to back across his shaved head. He was one of Dan's Jumping Jacks.

"The password tonight is L. C. Smith," I said.

"What?"

"Put that pole down and get out of the way. I don't want to hear any more out of you."

He must have seen the shotgun leveled at him, and still he made a lunge. He came at us like a pole vaulter, with the pole held low. Refugio was a small barrel of a man standing on two stumpy and bowed legs, but he was fast on those legs. He sidestepped and grabbed the middle of the sapling and jerked the boy off his feet, and then with a kick sent him tumbling down the stairway. The boy didn't cry out. He fell on his back with a grunt and was gone, just like that. Ramos yelped down below. He came hopping up to join us, barking away, all fight again now, as though he had stopped back there only to take a leak or look at an ant. Now he was Ramos again of the 1st War Dog Platoon.

I moved fast on the others, who had crowded into the doorway to watch. "Back inside! Let's go!" I wanted to get in there out of the night so they could all see the gun. No need for any more trouble. It was a smoky, high-vaulted room. I drove them into a corner and made them sit. Their faces too were painted with vertical stripes. They looked sick and hungry. Each one held a sprig of something green. But I had bagged only five Jumping Jacks and these were the lesser, dimmer ones. Dan wasn't here, nor was LaJoye Mishell Teeter, nor the big woman, Beany Girl, nor the second skinhead. There was no goat. Rudy Kurle wasn't here either.

"Where is Dan?" I said. "Listen to me now. I don't have time to fool around with you people. Where is the little girl you call Red? Where is Dan?"

"*El Mago* is biding his time."

"His knife is keen and yet it gives life."

"He is one set apart. He is no longer Dan."

"*El Mago* is our father. You will never enjoy his favor and intimacy."

"He used to give us doughnuts sometimes when he was Dan."

They went into their group hum and said nothing more. I had given them time to recover. I should have struck faster and harder. I should have knocked one of them down right away and got in his face. But the moment had passed, and to compound my foolishness I said, "Dan is the false *El Mago*. I was sent here to tell you that Dan is a false teacher. Look at me when I'm talking to you! Can you at least understand what I'm saying?" All a waste of breath. They sat there droning away with their mandrill faces cast down. Their hymn had one disagreeable note and no words. They had tuned me out. Old Alma had a word for this. It was *urdummheit*, primitive stupidity, which she used freely with servants, and with me as well when I let the wheels of her chair drop down hard off a curb. *Urdummheit!*

"Such people!" Refugio kept saying. "What a mess! . . . *¡Qué gente! ¡Qué embrollo!*" He had his .45 out and the hammer was pulled back. Mine was cocked too. L. C. Smith was known for his "hammerless" shotguns (and for his typewriters, later to be called Smith-Corona), but this old fowling piece had two big upright S-curved hammers like they don't make anymore, and when drawn all the way back under tension, they gave you some sense of the detonation to come.

A few candles burned in wall niches. At this end of the room there was a small campfire on the floor, with the flames jumping and falling. The gusts of air should have told me there was another big opening somewhere. This was the east end, where two wall slits in the shape of a T caught the first rays of the morning sun. Those dawn rays were said to light up the shrine for an instant in some striking way. I had never taken the trouble to see this flare effect for myself, perhaps a mistake, though such sights are often disappointing. A tau-window, it was called. Now a dead toad was stuffed there at the intersection of the slits, with his belly cut open and a length of red yarn tied around his neck in a bow. I pulled the bloody slimy thing out of the crevice and flung it into the lap of a Jumping Jack. He didn't move. The girl next to him was twisting something in her hands, a greasy rag. She pressed it to her face and kissed it and moaned. It was Dan's old head covering, the knotted blue bandanna, in decayed tatters. I noticed too that she and the others had smears of blood around their lips. They were off doughnuts now and on toad blood.

"Here's our rathole," said Refugio, at the far end. "This is the way he left, all right. You can see. But why should the boy run from you?" He had found the other opening behind a partition wall. There were two walls, with a wide space between them, and a passage, and the outer wall was split from top to bottom. The crack had spread and eroded into a hole at floor level. It was a bolt-hole big enough even for Dan to crawl through.

"No, it's not the boy," I said. "We're not looking for the boy now. We're looking for a dangerous fat man and a little girl." I snatched the rotten bandanna from the hippie girl's hands and took Ramos by the scruff of the neck and rubbed his nose around in it and spoke soft and unusual words to him. I could always talk to dogs, certain dogs, if not to people very well. It was a gift; the words just came to me.

We made a quick circuit around the outside deck and then struck off down the backslope. This side was uncleared but not nearly as steep. There were trees and earth and tangled undergrowth and rushing water madly seeking an ever lower place. Ramos was in the lead, taking us below and off to the right. He knew what was wanted, and even with the rain there was still a good smelly trail to follow. That bandanna was strong, and Dan himself would be pretty ripe by now. There was the goat, too. Refugio said, "What a night!" I told him to be careful.

Our path was littered with yellow blossoms which the rain had beaten off the *palo blanco* trees. I lost my hat in the vines. Down to our right there was a complex of structures, still half buried, called the acropolis, though it was by no means the high point of the place. It was a maze of galleries and chambers, most of them roofless shells, set at different levels on terraces. We broke out of the woods onto the topmost terrace, and Ramos was off at a lope and into the maze. We lost sight of him. We had to follow his barking through twists and turns, up and down. Diggers had been here recently. They had cleared one corridor and put up marker ribbons along the way. Strange looters though, to leave the artworks behind. I saw a fine stucco mask of the long-nosed rain god, with the fragile nose intact, a rare find. There were wooden door lintels, untouched. That carved sapodilla wood had endured tropical heat, rain and insects for a thousand years, and it was still in place and still bearing a load. Iron would have crumbled away centuries ago.

We passed through a small forest of derelict stone columns, supporting nothing, and then we were suddenly out in the open once more on a bare terrace. It was good to get on level ground again. I thought we would catch up with Dan somewhere in the woods, crashing through the brush, but there he was standing in the rain at the very edge of the terrace, he and three others and a dead goat. A kerosene lantern burned at their feet. Ramos was running about before them in a fury. The second baldheaded boy was keeping him at bay with a forked pole.

I didn't see the tall woman. Dan wore a white headband and a long white or tan smock over his old outfit, nothing very priestly, more like something from the early days of motoring. There were dark splotches down the front. The skinhead made a swipe at us with his sapling, and we stopped just outside his range. I had never known anyone so crazy that he couldn't understand a 12-gauge shotgun, and here we had run into two of them in one night, or three. They had courage. Raindrops sizzled on the hot lantern. I could see the dead goat, a brown and white billy goat, with a red string around his neck and the black lump beside him that had been his heart. Dan had just cut his heart out. It was still bleeding—I won't say smoking.

Big Dan was lifting one foot and then the other about an inch off the ground. He was rocking from side to side like an old bull elephant. He had a crude knife of chipped flint or obsidian in one hand. In the other he held a lead rope loosely at his side, with LaJoye Mishell Teeter and a small Mexican boy in tow. The two children were bound wrist to wrist with baling wire, and the rope was tied to the wire. The girl now wore an outsize football jersey that drooped below her knees. She was number 34, a little mite of a fullback. A bow of red yarn was tied at her throat. The Mexican boy had one too. I thought at first that his face was painted. The face paint on the others, if any, had washed away. The boy was about six years old and he was in a torn white shirt and some pathetic little blue trousers. They were dress trousers with cuffs and creases. Dan must have grabbed him on a Sunday.

I said, "What's all this about the sun, Dan?"

"Who is that? Where is Harvey? What do you want with me?"

"We came for the kids. Tell your boy to put the pole down,"

"Who gave you permission to approach me? You don't belong here."

"No, we don't. So we'll just take the kids and be on our way. I want you to drop that rope and move away from them. Okay? None of your crap now. Just do what I say and we'll get this over with."

"You can't interfere with me in my own city. It wasn't easy getting here at the appointed time. You don't know the kind of people I've had to work with. Even *El Mago* let me down."

"Yes, but it's all over now, Dan. Those folks out there want their money back. I told them you were a fake."

"This is the City of Dawn. You don't have no business here."

"Our business won't take long."

"Wait. I know that stupid sharecropper voice. You're the one who broke my staff. And my car windows. How did you get here? Beany Girl had a disturbing dream about you."

"I don't want to hear about your dreams."

"A prophetic dream. 'We're not through with Curtis yet.' That's what she said. I didn't believe her. All right. A sign then. But that's all you are. You can't touch me. You don't have no power over the *Balam.* Do you know who I am? I have three yards of fine linen wrapped around my head."

"No, we're not going to talk about your wrappings. You can save that stuff for somebody else."

"Where is Harvey? Who is that with you?"

"He's a policeman from Guatemala City. He has some questions for you. Let go of the rope now and step aside. And you better get your boy here under control pretty fast. The other one is dead. Harvey is dead and you better get this loco son of a bitch out of my way before you lose him too."

Dan looked bad. There were inflamed swellings on his face and knots on the side of his head the size of hickory nuts. The bridge of his nose was bruised and puffy, perhaps broken. One ear was flopped over at the top with the cartilage crushed. All this from the police beating, I supposed, but it was more than that. I think he had been fasting. He was still a big round man, the belly undiminished, but his face had gone slack. There were sagging yellow pouches under his eyes like folds of chicken fat. The mosquitoes had been at him too. He was breathing hard through his mouth, gasping. Two or three buttons were missing from the smock, and I could see a bit of his hairy white belly and the expando waistband of his pajamas.

Refugio said, "What a fine gringo circus this is!" I touched his arm, the one holding the pistol. "Don't spook the big one," I said. "Keep your eye on the boy with the pole."

"If he strikes Ramos I will choot him."

"No, not until we have the *niños*."

There was a drop of about forty feet behind them, and I didn't know what Dan might do with that demon in him. Would he go over the side and take the children with him? Just how crazy was he? Then there was the knife, a stubby double-edged thing. No Mayan priest had ever used it to tear open a human breast. It was a cheap souvenir letter-opener from a curio shop but no less a sharp ripper for that. I put my light on the Mexican boy and spoke to him in Spanish, with a bit of English for Dan's benefit. "Don't worry son. Dan has thought this over and he's going to let you go. It's all he can do. He's not dumb. Everything will be all right. Can you tell me your name?" He was crying and too terrified to speak. I could see now that the little fellow had *mal del pinto,* a skin disease that left pink and blue patches on his face, like the markings you see on piebald Negroes back home. The rain was letting up. I spoke to the girl. "LaJoye Mishell? I know your name and I came here to see you. I have a cold Coca-Cola here for you. Can you just step over here a minute? You and the boy. Come on, the dog won't hurt you. He does just what

we say. His name is Ramos. Come on, Dan is all finished
with you now." She didn't respond at all. Wet strands of
hair lay stuck across her face.

Dan jerked the rope tight and pulled the two small
bodies up against him. He said, "My offerings are blemished, as you see. A spotted toad and a spotted goat and
a spotted boy and a speckled girl with vile red hair. It was
the best I could do. You don't know how hard it's been.
Finding the correct path. People like you can't never
understand anything. I had to take the hard road. I could
have been a famous musician. I could have cut an album
and rocketed to stardom and won awards on TV if it wasn't
for people like you controlling everything."

Now I was the master sharecropper in control of
things. There was nothing else left to do. I put the shotgun
to my shoulder. "You're all done now anyway, Dan."

"Why do you call me that? Dan died long ago. There
is no more Dan. Some call me *El Mago* but my true name
is *Balam Akab*. I am the Jaguar of the Night."

"No, I tell you we're not going to have any more of
that. Here's how it is. We're all wet and tired and hungry.
We're a long way from home. You're not thinking straight.
Now listen to what I'm saying. I won't say it again. Turn
loose of that rope or I'm going to send you back to the Gulf
of Molo."

His voice changed a bit. He stopped being crazy for
just a moment. "All right then. Take the boy and go. He's
no good to me anyway. I can't let you have Red. We've
come too far. She is prepared. I have my instructions. And
now I have the final sign. Which is you. I have my work to

finish here on this rainswept promontory. Even you can understand that, Curtis."

"No, I can't."

"I deny that you have any power over me."

Rainswept promontory. Blemished offerings. Rocketed to stardom. This was what came of reading a lot of books and magazines in prison. The tireless baldheaded boy irritated me with his jabbing and dancing about. Ramos had had enough, too, and he made a dash under the swinging pole and went for a leg. The boy kicked him. Dan tried to change hands for some reason, switching the knife and rope about, to get the knife into his right hand, I think, for a quick thrust at the girl. Refugio fired once at the skinhead and killed him. I let go of both barrels at Dan. There were two sheets of flame and his headband and the top of his head went away. The girl squealed. I gave Dan both barrels up high of No. 2 shot, goose shot, which scalped him and blinded him and shattered his teeth and all but severed his thick neck. He was a dead man on his feet. The knife slipped from his fingers. His knees buckled and he fell backwards over the side, still holding the rope with a feeble grip. I went for the *niños,* slipping on the wet stone, knocking the lantern over and grabbing at the wire that joined their wrists. They were both howling as I dragged them back from the edge.

Then something struck me across the back, not very hard. It was the other skinhead, the one we thought was dead. It was the faithful Harvey, all crippled up, come back from his long tumble. I couldn't believe it. He held a short stick in one hand and beat at me with it and spit blood on me. The other arm hung broken and useless. The dome of his head was bleeding. Refugio shot him twice. Harvey was just as tough as whitleather but he could take no more. He dropped the stick and broke away in a stumbling run. Ramos was right behind him, and then Refugio, who fired again. The boy had at least two .45 *balas* in him—they don't make handgun balls any bigger—and he was still on his feet when I saw him last.

"Let him go!" I called out. "That's enough! We don't have time for that! Get Ramos back here!" One time you smash a bug with no mercy. Another time you find one helpless on his back with his legs flailing the air, and you flip him over and let him go on his way. The struggle that touches the heart. Refugio rightly paid no attention to me. I broke the breech of my gun and re-loaded quickly out of habit. The girl wanted to know where her Coke was. I tore the red string from her neck and the one from the boy's neck.

The thing now was to get back across the river, out of Guatemala and into Mexico. It wasn't such a serious matter as all that, one gringo killing another in Latin America, and when the dead one needed killing to boot. Down here too you could always plead that you had acted from motives of honor. I could say that the *cabrón* had insulted me. But sorting out the mess would be a long and expensive business, and I wanted to be many miles away in another country when the military police came, if they came.

Not far off in the darkness I heard two more booming shots, the *golpes de gracia*. Ramos came back and ran around in mad circles, eager for more of this sport. Then here was Refugio shouting in my face. "You can't stop in the middle of a bloody *fregado* like this! You have to finish it off!"

"All right! It's done now!"

"You have to finish it! Ramos knows that much! In the name of God! What's wrong with you!"

"You're right. But we're wasting time! Let's go!"

"You can't just stop in the middle of a stinking business like this!"

"I said all right! Can't you hear! But now we're done!"

"So now you say it! Now you say we're done!"

"Yes, I say we're done! Does that suit you! *Término!*"

We were yelling at each other face to face, and I was never one to do that much, even when provoked.

THE MEXICAN boy was so weak from hunger that he could barely walk. Refugio carried him down the hill on his back. Not a single light burned in Yorito. The rain came back in a soft drizzle, and I had the devil of a time rousting out two boatmen from their dry hammocks. I had to pay through the nose for this rainy night emergency service. It was no time for haggling. We would need two *cayucas* to carry this growing flock of mine downstream to the railroad bridge near Tenosique. There we could flag a train to Mérida.

All four of us made the crossing to Yoro in the lead boat. The river was up. Our skipper wore a knitted cap pulled down over his ears to keep the malignant *aires* out of his head. LaJoye Mishell told me that she had been given nothing to eat for two days. I fell to muttering and then realized that Refugio was speaking to me.

"Who was that *hipopótamo?* Who was that big lop-eared *pagano?*"

"His name was Dan. That's all I know. Some wandering *cabrón*. He tampered with my truck once at Tuxpan.
A jailbird, I think. Some *preso* from the States."

"But all the same a *mago*? He could cast spells?"

"Just on certain people. Not on us."

"What was it all about?"

"I don't know. But we'll keep it to ourselves. The less
said about this the better."

"His neck was bloated with poison."

"Yes."

"Did you see his breath? It was green."

"I didn't notice that."

"The two boys were drugged."

"No, I don't think so."

"Yes, a pair of *tóxicos*. Didn't you see their ugly naked
heads? Like baby heads! Not a natural thing! It was dope
that turned them into beasts! And not one but two! Who
would expect to see two of them!"

"Harvey was the hard one. That first one who came
back."

"But the dead goat. What was that for?"

"I don't know. Some *pagano* stuff about blood."

"Ay, then they get all they want, no? We show them
plenty of blood! Maybe they get just a little more *sangre*
than they want! We teach those animals some Mexican
manners, no?"

I told the boatmen to keep their engines running,
and we left them at the landing with the props churning
the muddy water. The widow woman's *ramada* had
collapsed into a heap of sticks and fronds. Her morning

glories had been stripped clean by the storm and her fine *jitomate* plants battered down in the mud. Yoro was if anything darker than Yorito. We found our people and the stragglers huddled together in a storage shed behind the big fuel tank. Vincent was grumbling about the fleas. The dirt floor was infested with them. I had to wake Doc and Gail. She thought the little Mexican boy, Serafín, thirty-two inches high, was Rudy Kurle. "You found him!" she said.

"No, but we're leaving anyway. Where's the food sack? Let's get a move on."

Only a few tortillas were left, curled leather flaps now. The two children chewed on them greedily and ate them without salt. I assured Vincent that Tonya Barge was fine, not really knowing. "She'll be back by daylight. They'll all be back. The show was a bust. It was a complete washout." He said he wished now he had taken his chances with the storm rather than suffer here in this nest of fleas. Doc advised him to eat brewer's yeast and plenty of it. "It comes out in your sweat, don't you see, and repels them." I promised Vincent that his sweetheart would appear very soon out of the mist, and I left him there with my knotted sock sulfur bomb and my earnest good wishes.

So now there were seven of us in two *cayucas*, not counting the boatmen—Doc, Gail, Refugio, me, the two children, and Ramos, and we were off on another night ride in these mahogany dugouts. We could have used some name tags. Doc asked why we were traveling in the rain and when would we reach Likín.

"We've already been to Likín," I said. "We're going home now. We're leaving this garden."

"But I wanted to show Gail how the sun strikes the tau-cross window. The radiance."

"We'll do that another time."

"But she wants to see the House of the Consecrated Bats and the hieroglyphic stairway. She is particularly interested in that. I promised to show her how easily you can read the dynastic information with my key. How it all flows down in a connected way in columns of twos."

"Maybe another time. We're going home now."

"You won't give us time to see anything! All these boats! You're just a terrible person to travel with, Jimmy! All this mindless movement! It's a sickness with you! I think you positively enjoy driving helpless people about!"

We spoke in darkness above the engine noise, our faces unreadable. I explained that we had to get in ahead of the hippie brigade, who would be departing now and taking all the boats. Then there were the two children. They were homesick runaways who had been traveling with the hippies, and I knew that he, Doc, would want them restored to their families without delay. He said nothing more. I let it go at that.

LaJoye Mishell didn't know where she was or where she had been. Her lips were cracked and her skin was peeling and her arms and legs were criss-crossed with red scratches. She was numb. It was all the same to her whether Dan cut her heart out or she went back to Perry, Florida. The boy could tell us little more than his name, Serafín. Mostly he slept. Dan had picked him up, the girl told me, in a city with a long main street that led to a pretty little seaside park. The Mexican port town of Chetumál was my guess. She said it was later when the big woman, Beany Girl, left them, deserted the Jumping Jacks, she didn't know why, at an island town on a clear green lake. That could only have been Flores, in Lake Petén Itzá in Guatemala.

The storm had passed, but the river was still choppy. These *cayuca* boys had only one speed and that was flat out, which suited me. We were well sprayed. As the morning light came, I saw sparklets of gummy blood stuck to the hairs on my arms, from Dan's face, and from Harvey, who had spit blood on me. I sloshed my arms about in the rushing water and washed my face too for good measure. But you can't get those stains out of a cotton shirt. There was no fog on this first day of the new year. It was a day like other days. The sun came up full and warm. The greater light that rules the day. It would never scorch Dan again or dazzle his eyes. Wrong about so many things, he did get the terminal day right. Jan, too, and Harvey, and the other hairless thug. For them it was truly the end of this world.

Yes, a strange business back there on that high terrace, and over so fast too. Shotgun blast or not at close range, I was still surprised at how fast and clean Dan had gone down. It was like dropping a Cape buffalo in his tracks at one go. I wasn't used to seeing my will so little resisted, having been in sales for so long. We passed more ruins and a village here and there, but they were all on the Guatemala side.

Everyone was hungry. Doc said, "Now you won't even let us eat!" I didn't permit a stop until we came to a settlement called Punta de Arenas, or Sandy Point, on the Mexico shore. It was a smaller Yorito, a Yoritito, an old *chiclero* camp, with the shacks now occupied by a few fishermen and squatters. In the woods behind it there was a minor ruin of four or five mounds, well picked over and too small even to have a name.

The skippers nosed the boats in around a jam of floating trees, brought downstream by the high water and stuck here at the point with a lot of dirty foam. The resident fishermen were at breakfast and made a hospitable fuss over us. There is always room for unexpected guests at a Mexican feed. We sat on a log and joined them for black coffee and some rice with scraps of pork mixed in, and peppers on the side. No fish. They trafficked in fish the way I trafficked in art. It was for other people. All the talk was about the storm, the big *tronada,* so unseasonable. The trees here were still dripping. Doc asked if they had come across any writings of the old ones, but they couldn't understand a word he said. Refugio asked if any *ídolos* had been turned up lately from the mounds here. They laughed. "No, no, no. *No hay nada aquí." There ain't nothing here*. They had only three coffee cups, and we passed them back and forth. An old man, too old to work, just hanging around now, showed us he could still crack nuts with his teeth.

Gail bathed the kids in the backwater and scraped up some clean clothes for them, shabby adult garments but dry enough. She found a jar of yellow salve in the camp and rubbed it on their sores. Poor little LaJoye Mishell had taken the worst of it. Her scalp was spotted with scabs where Dan had pecked her with his stick when she displeased him. She couldn't learn how to answer him properly. Whatever she said was wrong.

I could hardly keep my eyes open. This was the green and wet part of Mexico, and I liked it and this place in particular, Sandy Point. I liked the old man and the bushes covered with white blossoms like snow and the way the clearing opened up to the sky, some happy combination of things. I marked it down in my head as a good place to come back to for an extended stay. But then I liked the brown parts of Mexico, too, and I had marked down so many places, never to see them again. Refugio shook me awake and said we had best not linger here. He had just been told there was a soldier prowling about. The big *soldado* had come down the river a few days ago, a lone passenger in a *cayuca*. "They say he is a big clean fellow in fine boots with many badges on his fine uniform." An officer then. He would want to see our papers. He would be curious. What was our business here on the *frontera?* We were an odd enough party, worthy of a report, and he would remember our guns and our faces if not our names. It was indeed time to leave this sandy hook.

Refugio rounded up the crew. Doc was no longer speaking to me. We were already in the boats when the lone *soldado* appeared. It was Rudy Kurle in his military rig. I hadn't even bothered to ask about him here. He and three local boys came out of the woods with a plastic dishpan full of dark honey, all clotted up with leaves and sticks and dead bees. They had robbed a bee tree. Rudy was chewing on a sticky comb. A gleaming strand of honey hung from his chin and swayed. Something new was attached to his belt. I thought I was familiar with all his field gear, but the pedometer was new to me.

"Hey, Burns!" he said. "Is that you? What in the world are you doing here? Look! Do you know what this is? Nature's most perfect food! A field expedient! Living off the land!"

"I've been looking all over for you, Rudy."

"Yeah, why?"

"You've had everybody out beating the bushes for you."

"What for? You should see how these little guys can climb. They don't speak a word of English."

"You've put a lot of people to a lot of trouble. Did you know that? Why did you have to sneak off like that from Ektún? Can you tell me what you're doing here?"

"I'm here for an international conference if it's any of your business, which I doubt. Now I'll ask you a question. Do you have any idea of where you are?"

"Yes, I do."

He laughed. "I mean where you really are. Right back there, Burns, is the site of an ancient city that you never heard of, known in our modern language as the Inaccessible City of Dawn. I've had it all to myself. There's not much to see, you think, and then you realize that this is just the tip of an extensive conurbation. It goes back for miles in the jungle. Other people will be coming along soon, but I can't discuss that. I can't talk about our agenda.

I can tell you that a compass needle does some very crazy things here. Mine won't even move. There's a powerful magnetic force field here and it's highly localized. It's an entry window. You've always underestimated me, Burns. You never dreamed that I would find an entry window all on my own. Did you know I was the first one to arrive? But I think now I may have gotten the day wrong."

"All right, get your stuff together. We're going downstream to catch a train. We're going back to Mérida."

"Oh, no. The other delegates will be along soon. I've already made a rough map of the central court, what I am calling the Promenade, and I've dug two latrines. A lot of these conference chumps won't know the first thing about field sanitation. Right now I'm trying to clear some separated areas so we can have several workshops going on at once. It's the hardest work I've ever done in my life. The brush is too wet and green to burn. We killed two snakes just this morning."

"Nobody's coming, Rudy. They called it off. This is the wrong place anyway."

He finished off the honeycomb and licked his fingers. There were bee stings on his face. "Oh? Is that a fact? And just how would you know?"

"The City of Dawn is a long way upstream on the other side of the river. You got the day right but you came down too far and you're in the wrong country on top of that."

"How would you know? Who invited you?"

"We just came from there. Ask any of these people. It's all over. Your conference got rained out."

"You're not a trained observer."

"No, but I could see that much. I was there."

"It's odd how you keep turning up. Anyway I'm not going downstream. I left my trailer and my Checker Marathon back at Ektún."

"Your car is in Mérida. There's nobody at Ektún. They're all gone. Now get your things and let's go. Louise is worried about you."

"Louise sent you out here?"

"She thought you were lost."

"Me lost?"

"Yes."

"It's funny how she keeps running to you with every little thing. You never even went to college. What's that on your head? Who are all those people with you?"

They were prisoners. I was dealing with prisoners, and here was one more. All I could think of was to keep my head count straight and get them back to the brig intact and sign them over to the turnkey and be done with them. As for my headgear, it was one of Doc's gift handkerchiefs with the corners knotted, a skullcap, a Dan cap.

Finally I got Rudy into the boat, after telling him about the shriveled corpse at Palenque. It was a mystery. I could make nothing of the thing and the police too were baffled. My friend Refugio believed it to be a kind of woodland elf, or in any case something less than human, or more. He, Rudy, might want to investigate the matter before other writers got wind of it, or before the remains were buried. I couldn't promise anything. This might or might not be a quality contact. No wreckage was found near the body, as far as I knew, no melted fragments of an unknown alloy. But it seemed worth looking into, a little man with spindly limbs and yellow eyes and a great swelling globe of a head. I exaggerated the size of the head. Refugio confirmed my story, showing with his hands just how wide the creature's feet were. He confirmed too that the yellow car was in Mérida. He himself had driven it there.

How about it then? The body was there at Palenque to be claimed. Rudy only half believed us, and the big feet weren't a selling point, as space aliens were known to be the daintiest of steppers. And yet he couldn't take a chance. There might be something in this, and if so he would have to move fast. Other writers were pigs, to be sure, but worse, there were government agents to fear, so efficient in their neat business suits and gray Plymouths. They would spirit the body away to a hangar at some remote air base and then deny all knowledge of it with their fixed smiles.

On the way back he made a nuisance of himself in the boat with his calisthenics. He flapped his arms and shook his fingers and twisted his head about and bicycled his legs up in the air. From now on I would work alone and travel alone. Once again I made that vow. He showed me some shiny black pebbles, vitrified, he said, from exposure to extremely high temperatures, as from rocket exhaust gases. I asked him how many miles he had registered on his pedometer. He said it had stopped working, as had the drive gear in his tape recorder. Humidity and rust and dirt, I suggested, but he said no, it was the magnetic blast that had jammed so much of his equipment. And somewhere up the river he had lost his signalling mirror and his giant naval binoculars.

Rudy knew about the City of Dawn but not about the death of the sun. He thought he was coming to a high-level UFO convention at a reported landing site. He wouldn't tell me how he knew about it or who was behind it, and I suspected he really didn't know. Some of the people at Likín thought the event had to do with seed crystals or pyramid power or harmonic solar resonance, and for a few it was the end of the Mayan calendar, the end of the fifth creation, the end of time. Others were ignorant of the last-days theme and saw it as nothing more than a hippie festival in the jungle. They had come, one and all, I gathered, on the strength of rumor. Such information as they had about *El Mago* appeared to be hearsay too. It was just something going around, a buzz of magical words in the air, of big doings on the Usumacinta.

For Dan it was to be a blood ceremony to appease the sun or something along that line, but then it seemed Dan was not the principal either. There was another *El Mago* behind him, according to LaJoye Mishell. She had never seen the other man but said she had heard Dan speaking to him on the telephone, or pretending to speak to someone. But all that came later, the *El Mago* business. They had been knocking around in Texas and New Mexico, these Jumping Jacks, stealing cars and running over dogs and peeping in windows at night and humming together. Then one day Dan told them that the correct path led through the deserts of Mexico. There they would clarify their thoughts. He said he had received an urgent long distance telephone call from the Gulf of Molo, with orders to go directly to Mexico and seek out a particular white goat. They made their way south, and it was at a hippie campground near a tropical river town (Tuxpan, perhaps) that they first heard of *El Mago*. There was something written about him in a paper or magazine that they were passing around, and all the hippies were talking about him. Dan became excited and said that he was now being directed by this *El Mago*. He had new orders. They were to proceed without delay to a coastal town called Progreso, where *El Mago* would meet them and lead them to a place called the City of Dawn. So they went to Yucatán. Along the way Dan made telephone calls, to this same *El Mago*, he claimed. But *El Mago* didn't show on the beach at Progreso. They waited and waited. Someone stole their belongings, their plastic garbage bags. Dan then declared that he himself was *El Mago*, it had come to him in a dream. He himself would lead them to the City of Dawn with three yards of fine linen wrapped around his head. They would live there for a time under the roots of a giant tree called Ogon or Agon, with a white goat. It would be a time of fasting and purification. Then he would complete his historic mission.

Well and good, but *was* there another *El Mago?* Who? Where? Had Dan killed him? LaJoye Mishell thought so. She said Beany Girl had dropped hints to that effect, this being their tiresome way of communicating. The Jumping Jacks didn't go in much for plain talk, not even among themselves. But LaJoye Mishell couldn't be sure and she admitted that Big Dan may simply have broken with his master and struck off on his own. If in fact there were a master. What was I to make of that truly long distance call from the Gulf of Molo? Who was at the other end? A diabolist? A joker? An insane alcoholic mother? Anyone at all? It was hard to know how much of the story to credit. I got it from a dazed little girl who thought she was traveling with a rock and roll band for the first few days after the Jumping Jacks picked her up. That was what she yearned for, a life on the road with rock musicians, though she had no wish to sing herself or otherwise make music. She just wanted to live with them and do their laundry and fetch and carry for them and pick bits of trash out of their hair, and so she ran away from home and jumped into the first old car she could find that was packed to the roof with hoodlums.

IT WAS the first time Ramos had ever ridden on a train. Emmett was dead when we got back, and Alma was in the hospital. Art and Mike and Coney and McNeese had been turned out of their rooms by Señora Limón, their landlady, who said she was tired of looking at their faces. They had stayed on too long. She wanted to paint her walls a bright new color and put down some new linoleum with new geometric patterns and get an altogether fresh set of roomers to go with the other improvements. It was a reverse revolution, with the dictator kicking the people out. Louise had seen Wade Watson off on a flight to the States, or so she said. Eli and Mr. Nordstrom had been deported. The city of Mérida had swung big new green signs across the entrance highways, with new words of welcome and a new and greater population figure. The rush of events wasn't quite over. There was another letter waiting for me from my secret enemy, and this one was shorter and sweeter than ever. "Just looking at you makes me want to vomit up all my food," the message read, and it was signed "Alvarado." A strangely feeble performance.

I thought the writer must be growing bored with the game, or perhaps was simply too tired to think up any more really wounding words. A falling off in any case. Señora Limón? Was she weary of my face as well? Even sickened by it? Possibly, but I couldn't see her taking the trouble to write this stuff and mail it. I hardly knew the woman.

Nardo drove me down to Chetumál to return the boy Serafín to his family. He was pretty sure he could keep the Judicial Police out of it. Nardo knew the ropes. He was well connected. For a modest fee he could get your tourist visa renewed, saving you a trip to the border every six months. He worked it through some *coyote* in faraway Guadalajara, which I never understood—why the fixer should be there instead of in Mexico City. He told me again at some length about his football days at Bonar College, how the opposing teams would laugh and jeer at the Bonar boys when they pulled up to the stadium in two yellow school buses, with the coaches driving the buses. "But they didn't laugh long. We went twenty-eight and two in three years."

We bought Serafín some toys. He rode in the back seat and blew bubbles into the air, nonstop, all the way to Chetumál, with his wire loop and his bottle of pink viscous stuff. Quivering pink transparent bubbles floated about inside Nardo's car and broke against our ears.

Serafín knew his city when he saw it, though he still couldn't call the name. Nor did he know the name of his street. We drove back and forth around the downtown blocks, and he knew it when he saw it. The familiar buildings made him laugh. "*¡Allí! ¡Allí!* There!" He pointed to the dark doorway of a home tailor shop.

That was where he lived. I saw two women inside, with the older one pumping away on the treadle of an ancient sewing machine. The floor was earth. Many straight pins must have fallen there and been lost forever.

I left Nardo to handle it from there, leaving it to him, the *licenciado*, the lawyer, to cook up a convincing lie, advising him only to keep it vague and leave me and Refugio out of it. He said he would blame it on gypsies. This would be readily understood. A band of *gitanos* had taken the child away, deep into a wet forest, where, weeping bitter tears but unharmed, he was found by some kind hunters and rescued from a life of thievery and certain spiritual ruin.

I waited. I walked up and down the main street of the old smuggling port, so different with its salty maritime air from Mérida, which itself was only twenty miles from the sea and might as well have been 200. Downtown I came across a Presbyterian church, which I had not noticed on previous visits. Some kind of Anglo-Scotto cultural overlap from nearby Belize, I supposed. You never know what you'll run into in Mexico, John Knox in a guayabera shirt, or a rain of tadpoles in the desert, or a strangely empty plaza in the heart of a teeming city with not even a bird to be seen. Once in Mazatlán I rounded a corner and literally ran into an old American movie actor I would have thought long dead. He was a big man who had played the boss crook in hundreds of cheap Westerns, the only character in coat and tie, directing all his dirty work out of the back room of a saloon. His name was usually Slade or Larkin. I apologized to the old crook. "One of these fast-walking guys, huh?" he said to me, in the old Larkin snarl. Here in

Chetumál the traffic police, unlike other police in Mexico, were fitted out in U.S. Marine undress blues, but with a deep Latino swoop in the wire frames of their white hats. They were hard little *Indios* with no body fat. The air trembled with heat. I was dripping. They stood buttoned up under the sun all day in a cloud of engine fumes, and their starched cotton shirts remained crisp and dry.

Someone was haranguing a crowd behind the bus station. There were gasps and cheers and applause. Surely the revolution wasn't starting here in Chetumál. So far east? The straw catching fire at last? I shouldered my way in to get a look at this fellow who was inciting the people. What I found was a fast-talking young man in a T-shirt selling cake decorators. They were soft plastic tubes with adjustable nozzles. He squeezed pink icing onto white strips of cardboard, showing how you could make little rosettes and stars and hearts, and spell out birthday greetings. He was an artist with a sure hand, and a funny speaker, too, a fine salesman. "Add a personal touch to *all* your cakes!" he kept shouting at us, and he meant right down to our very smallest muffins.

Nardo reported that all had gone well. The boy lived in the tailor shop with his mother and two older sisters, who had fallen upon him with kisses and thanks to God. They feared that Serafín had gone wading off the municipal beach and been swept away by the undertow or taken by sharks. The sea had swallowed up so many young ones. Nardo said the women were too overcome to ask many questions but that they did offer him money, whatever they had, which he refused. He told them it was nothing, *de guagua*. The kind hunters were only too glad to oblige, as was he, a representative of the PRI, the party of all the people. He made me wish I had been there to see them hugging brave little Serafín, loved all the more for his *mal del pinto*. So often I missed things, hanging back, always expecting the worst.

Back in Mérida I did get to see the reunion of LaJoye Mishell and her father, Dorsey Teeter, a bony man of about my age in a pale blue suit made of some spongy looking cloth. He was a logging contractor. I had telephoned him in Florida, bypassing Gilbert, at the Blue Sheet office, and now here he was at the airport. I stood aside and looked away as he and his daughter came together in an embrace. He wept. "Your mama and them thought you was dead but I never did give up." LaJoye Mishell was pleased enough to see him, too, but in no way upset or remorseful. She still held her sprig of Jumping Jack greenery. It was acacia, she said, though she didn't know what acacia was. I didn't either. She wore a new orange dress and a flattop Zorro hat with little balls swinging from the brim, and some big earrings, silver-plated hoops, bought with a little money I had given her. Dorsey was uncomfortable with me. In his eyes I was guilty of something, too. "What do you do down here anyway?" He asked me that two or three times. He was eager to get the business over with, just as I was, and so I spared him the details. I simply told him, again, that his daughter had been traveling around with a pack of hippies, more or less against her will, in a spotted station wagon.

"No," she said. "Not the first one. The first car was a blue four-door Oldsmobile Regency Brougham with a moon roof and dual glass-pack mufflers and blue velour seats.

But Dan rolled the Regency in Texas, totalled it out, and that's when Harvey stole the Country Squire wagon. Then we came down here to Old Mexico to clarify our thoughts. Dan kept saying he was going to put us all in white coveralls, but we never did get our white coveralls. He told us we were going to live far away from everybody under the roots of a giant tree called Ogon. Every night he said the same thing to us. He said, 'Death is lighter than a feather.'"

So, it was worse even than rockers; his daughter had run off with some nasty poet, but Dorsey had little interest in the man and his remote burrow. A little of this stuff went a long way with Dorsey. He cut down pine trees by the thousand, like weeds, and not one of them had a name of its own. He didn't want to linger in this country and he wouldn't even set foot outside the terminal. There was a general smell of flyspray, as with all Latin American airports, and long dim corridors that led nowhere, with empty offices along the way. The ones here had a quiet yellowish Mexican vacancy all their own. We went to the cafeteria. Dorsey had a Coke, not wanting to eat whatever kind of food it was they had here. He laid two booklets of travelers' checks on the table and got out his pen to countersign them. I explained once again that there was no fee, that I was in the woods on other business when I found the girl, and so was really out nothing in the way of expenses.

"But what about the Blue Sheet man?"

"I'll square it with Gilbert. You don't have to worry about that. There won't be any bill."

"Don't I need to see the police about anything? Sign some papers?"

"No. Unless you want to hang around here for two or three weeks."

"LaJoye Mishell is a good girl."

"Yes, and she's had a hard time of it, too. You're not going to whip her, are you?"

"Naw, I'm not."

"She's too old for that now."

"I never taken a switch to her in her life but two or three times. She never did have a smart mouth."

"Just go easy on her for a while. She'll be all right."

"Well. I feel like I ought to give you something for your trouble."

"It's all taken care of, thanks anyway. We do a free one every now and then for tax purposes. You can pay for the Cokes."

"I'll tell everybody what a good job ya'll done for us."

"You tell them we deliver the goods."

Dorsey was still looking for the catch. He couldn't size me up except that he was pretty sure I didn't report to work every morning. The back of his neck, a web of cracks, was burnt to the color and texture of red brick from much honest labor in the sun. A badge of honor, you might think, but no, it was the mark of the beast. The thanks Dorsey and his people got for all their noonday sweat was to be called a contemptuous name. Few rednecks actually had red necks these days, but Dorsey Teeter had one that glowed. At least he had come here personally to pick up his lost child, which was more than his betters could find the time to do. Usually I had to turn these kids over to the protection officer at the embassy in Mexico City.

I said my goodbyes and got up from the table, and my head went light and strange for a moment. The dengue fever was coming on again. I thought it might go away this time without really taking hold. I gave everything a good chance to go away before seeing a doctor, and then I saw Soledad Bravo. But what a relief, to get to the end of this mess, this custodial care. It had been a problem, keeping watch on LaJoye Mishell. She could say what she liked in Florida, but I didn't want her talking around here about Dan and how he came to a bad end, and I could hardly stuff a sock in her mouth and lead her around wired to my wrist, not here in town. She had already told Fausto that I had blown her master's head off with a bazooka.

Dorsey called out a parting word as I reached the glass doors. "I appreciate it," he said, and Little Red said, "Bye," with her hat balls in agitation and the heavy hoops swaying from her peeling red ears. She was still clutching her weeds. Was she going to press them in a book? It galled me that Dorsey seemed to think I was a hippie of some kind myself—why did I need his approval?—but no matter, I was done with all the Teeters of Teeterville, and I thought I had seen the last of the Jumping Jacks.

Neither of Emmett's sons came down from the States for the funeral. They must have written him off long ago. He said to me once, "I love my children but I don't rejoice in them." We buried him in Doc's mahogany coffin, and it was all I could do to hold up my end of it, what with the bad knee and the fever coming on. Old Suarez was a pallbearer, too, for the first time ever, he told me, in a long friendless life. He couldn't lift much weight at his age, and then there was hunchback Coney, in no shape for this work, and Professor Camacho Puut, frail and thin, flicking his head to one side, like a swimmer trying to clear an ear. The others were sturdy enough.

Huerta's coffin was a fine piece of work, though the copper fittings showed to no advantage, being the same color as the wood. Ulises' shallow carvings were hard to make out, too. More art to be buried. Doc said he wouldn't need the coffin now that he had some decent staff support and wasn't going to die. He said cancer was all in your mind. You couldn't let your body cells give way to cubic replication. Gail had moved into the big house on the Paseo Montejo and was helping him with his book. There was no more talk about lying down in the forest and melting away. But Doc wouldn't come to the service because he couldn't bear to see a person he knew let down heavily into the earth, hand over hand on the two ropes. He said Emmett had no one but himself to blame, guzzling all that pure cane alcohol day after day. Only two women came. Louise was there with her ringlets brushed out soft, and one of Emmett's former wives, an American widow he had met on a bus. It was one of the later, shorter marriages, and this woman, Geneva, who had some retirement income of her own, still lived here in town somewhere.

Father Mateo, good man that he was, came boldly to the graveside wearing his cassock, in defiance of the anti-clerical laws. He said what words he could over the remains of a non-Catholic. After the prayer, Harold Bolus sang "Let Me Be Your Salty Dog," a lively bluegrass tune.

He stood leaning on his canes in a cream-colored coat and sang:

> *Let me be your salty dog*
> *Or I won't be your man at all*
> *Honey, let me be your salty dog . . .*

I don't know whose idea that was, but it fell flat. At the proper time and place, yes, by all means, let us have a song from Bolus, give us "The Orange Blossom Special" on the harmonica, but here it didn't work at all. Supposedly it was Emmett's favorite song, which was news to me, and the idea was that we would make merry in the presence of death, take it lightly in our stride, raffish crowd that we were, in fitting remembrance of our old friend. But it was forced, we couldn't bring it off, and the appearance was that we were meanly and nervously celebrating our own survival. Bolus himself admitted as much later. And how could that be anyone's favorite song, least of all Emmett's, he who was never known to dance the two-step, or any other step? Otherwise the service went off well. Suarez addressed the *padre* as *Señor Cuervo*, Mr. Black Crow, but otherwise behaved himself. Father Mateo called Suarez a *godo* (Goth) and said he should learn to curb his evil tongue, that other unruly member.

Emmett left his money, what little remained of the family fortune, to be distributed among blind street musicians, with Shep to control the share-out. An odd choice for a steward. Emmett had some odd ideas. He left me the trailer and that was odd, too, quite a surprise. I had done him a few trifling favors over the years but nothing to justify this gesture. He meant Louise to have it, I think, and just never got around to changing his will. But I took it and gladly, and it was unseemly the way I moved into the Mobile Star so fast, ahead of the legal process and with the fill dirt still loose on his grave. I found hundreds of brown paper sacks stuffed under the bed and crammed into the cabinets and closets. "So, he saved sacks," I said aloud to myself. In a drawer I found a stack of newsletters from a foreign matrimonial agency called *Asian Gals Seeking U.S. Pals*. There were small photographs of the gals with a few lines underneath listing their hobbies and telling of their sunny natures and other good points. But it seems Emmett was only browsing here, thumbing idly through a mail order catalogue of women, window shopping, as none of the pictures had been circled or checked off in any way.

Fausto said I would soon be back downtown asking for my old room, that he knew me too well, that I would not stay long confined in a tin box on the edge of town. It was just one step up from a tent. It would be an oven and there would be no maid service and a storm would blow it away and the beds and toilet seats in those things were less than full size and trailer air was unhealthy and so on. He had already tacked up a photograph of Frau Kobold in the hotel lobby. She was still alive, barely, but there was her face, that of a younger Alma, but with the bloom off, already gone hard, up on the wall in the company of Mr. Rumpler, who had taken a heart walk every morning to no avail, and the Pedrell woman from Cuba, and other deceased guests. Fausto put up pictures of all the people who died in his hotel, or who had been residents near the time of their deaths. There was also in this gallery a newspaper clipping showing the inky, murky likeness of a young boy, not a guest, who had been struck and killed by a speeding motorcycle in front of the hotel. Fausto claimed him too.

I saw Alma once more before I collapsed into my own bed. This time I had no stale cakes for her. She was all doped up with an intravenous tube in her arm but she knew me. She was waiting for me. "Ah, *der schatzgraber*. You took your time getting here. I have an urgent commission for you." She lay in a high bed in an open hospital ward. A bowl of tomato soup had gone cold on her table. *No Fumar*, the sign said, but I lit a Faros cigarette for her, with the sweet-tasting paper, and she polished it off with three deep drags. The commission wasn't so urgent that she couldn't tell me again about the time she and Karl were filmed by the Fox Movietone newsreel crew. "They showed it in theaters all over the world. 'Bringing an Ancient Civilization to Light.' With march music in the background. Did you see it?"

"Everybody saw it."

I told her about finding her handprint at the Likín ruin. Likín? She had never heard of the place. Then she said wait, yes, she did remember it, high on a bluff, Late Classic, with the medial moldings and the high roof combs, though not the business about pressing her blackened hand to the stone. "What a goose I must have been in those days. Writing my name on walls. Well, I'm properly ashamed. Fools' names and fools' faces are often seen in public places."

"The City of Dawn," I said. "That's what some people call it."

She looked at me in an odd way and said something I didn't understand at the time. "Yes, of course they do. With the tau-cross window. My mind is going. They've got me on all this dope. Well, well, the City of Dawn. Mercy me. Hee hee. The young gringos at their foolery. Were there many fools there? Besides you?"

"A few."

Then she got down to business. Night was gathering fast and there were things to be done. Fausto was the beneficiary of her small insurance policy. What she wanted me to do was clear out her room, load all the boxes of relics and photographs into my white truck with great care, and deliver them to Terry Teremoto, the crank sculptor of Japanese descent, in Veracruz. Terry had once worked with Karl Kobold in some way and had shown Alma many kindnesses in her long widowhood. Well and good. The problem was that Terry was dead, along with all his works. I had to stop and think but I was pretty sure of it. At this point I, too, was confusing the living and the dead in the moist folds of my brain. My eyes hurt. The chills would come next.

"Take special care with the glass negatives," she said. "They will make Karl immortal if you don't break them."

She feared that the Kobold collection would fall into the hands of some university or museum, hated institutions, or that "the old chinch bug Flandin" with his influence might wangle possession. She disliked Doc because he posed as the scorned outsider while all the time he lived like a king. I was to move fast, before she died, intestate. Otherwise the vice-consul would seal her room and take inventory, and, there being no immediate kin, dispose of her things to all the wrong people, the tired old official gang of committee sitters, funded scholars, and the like, who so enjoyed clipping the wings of genuine artists like Karl Kobold.

I agreed to do it if she would sign a note spelling out these instructions. A writ of removal, or was it conveyance. It took me some little time to compose the thing, in my pitiful hand. Writing is hard—it's a form of punishment in school, and rightly so—and I stood paralyzed before all the different ways this simple message might be put. I called over a nurse to witness Alma's signature. In the note, however, I named Professor Camacho Puut as the recipient instead of Terry Teremoto. The Professor was a good old man, a retired Mérida high school teacher, certainly a poor outsider, an amateur Mayanist, something of a crank himself with his snake cult theories and his shabby pamphlets, held in thorough contempt by Mexican and American scholars alike, and so, I thought, just the man to get these goods, and all in keeping with the spirit of Alma's wishes.

That was how I handled it, taking only her Spanish typewriter for myself, and some detective books, and her oscillating fan and the heavy San Cristóbal blanket and an electric Crock-Pot, like new, still in the box, for carefree bachelor cooking, and a small Mixtec piece that caught my eye, a jaguar carved from some speckled stone, sitting up on his haunches like a house cat, and one or two other items. I threw out all her magazines, including the *Gamma Bulletins*. The pasteboard boxes packed with loot fell apart, and I had to get new ones. Many of the prints and the glass negative plates were ruined, all stuck together with blue mold. Still, there was enough that hadn't gone bad. It was a treasure. The Professor couldn't believe his good fortune. "All these amazing *retratos!*" he said. "Look at the clarity and the force!" They were truly amazing, different in some important way from photographs that other people took of the same things. Sick though I was, I had to stop and look at them, too. After you had seen Kobold's work, everything else was just Foto Naroody. "Spiritualized artifacts," the Professor called these brownish prints, this being his definition of art. I knew we should have had the old man at our Yoro art clinic on the bank of the river.

My white truck. I had forgotten to tell Manolo about the sticking gas gauge needle and how you had to thump it, and about how the first gear, granny low, was nonsynchronized, and about how the steering would be light and dangerous with all that tongue weight on the back, but I needn't have worried. What a fine capable boy Manolo was. A true-bred Bautista. He had made his long delivery run and collected his father's money with no other mishap than a blown tire. My old Chevrolet came back in good shape. I parked it beside the trailer where I could see it when I sat up in bed. When I was able to lift my head from the pillow. You forget how heavy your head is.

For almost two weeks I lay tangled in wet sheets. About all you can do with breakbone fever is ride it out.

Soledad Bravo treated the symptoms with sea salt and sour red wine and tar-water and some yellow powders. The skin peeled off the palms of my hands. Louise sat with me. She put blankets on me and then whipped them off again five minutes later. I kept her hopping, poor girl, peevish invalid that I was. It was in this same scaled-down bed that Emmett had died. She had sat with him, too. Toward the end he spoke of how the years had flown, and at the very end, she said, he was hearing things. Someone was inside his head shouting nautical commands. At other times there were some children in his head singing a spirited song with many verses. Louise thought it might have been their school song. She sat there beside me drinking limeade from a big glass and writing letters and reading a book called *Famous Travelling Women*.

Beth came by with some fruit and a piece of news to cheer the sickbay. She said Bollard was putting us all into a new novel he was writing—without our permission, of course. He would make lifelike puppets of us and contrive dim adventures for us with his hard-lead pencil on yellow legal pads. Alma had made it into Movietone News while the rest of us were to be buried alive in one of Bollard's books. Beth said it was going to be a modern allegory, with me representing Avarice. This was pretty good coming from a short-faced bear who ate four or five full meals each day and who talked of nothing but the fat profits he expected to reap from his Mexican telephone bonds. Beth deserved something better, but what can you do, you can't stop women from chasing after these artistic bozos. Look at LaJoye Mishell. Look at Alma. Still, I was pleased that

Beth had at last broken the series of ever paler poets. Bollard had his points. She could have done worse.

Louise brought out the shoebox and unrolled Emmett's Jaina figurine from the towel. We had decided that Beth should have it for the *niños* museum. She touched her fingertips to the nose and lips of the terra-cotta woman. She was delighted. "Such a delicate face. It looks like the portrait of a real person. Is this genuine?"

"Yes, and extremely valuable," I said. "Don't leave it out at night."

"What do I put on the card?"

"Put down 'Royal Lady. Island of Jaina, off Campeche. A.D., say, 722.' And put down that it was a gift from Emmett."

"I believe you're feeling better."

"Much better, yes, thanks to Soledad and Louise."

It was Art and Mike who called Bollard the short-faced bear. They knew all about the book, of course, you couldn't spring anything like that on them, and besides, they had more interesting news of their own. Rudy had left town, for good, they believed. He had pulled stakes and was off on a lecture tour in his Checker Marathon, minus the camping trailer, which Refugio was still holding against the fee for his search services. I had heard not one word about this from Louise.

They showed me a clipping from a Mexico City newspaper telling about a speech Rudy had given at the big federal prison there. The report identified him as "a well-known explorer and *científico* and authority on *platillos voladores*, from Penasilvana E.U.A." He had displayed "the well-preserved corpse of an unfortunate invader from the stars," and had brought to his audience *"una relación de alegría y llenura."* A message of joy and fullness, that is. The landing site in Chiapas, he had told the Mexican convicts, was marked by a spot of scorched vegetation and a circular arrangement of white pebbles and black pebbles, which he believed to be a form of digital computer. One or two crew members of the space-craft had died there, perhaps choked by toxic earth air, and all that remained of them was "a cheese-like residue," this matter being on display as well, in a glass jar.

Rudy then had lost no time in making a run to Palenque and claiming the pygmoid cadaver in the police shed. Art and Mike said the tiny old man was now wrapped in aluminum foil and wearing a tight-fitting sil-very rubber cap, something like a girl's bathing cap, with a strap under the chin, and that Rudy was carrying him around in something like a trombone case, with the head nesting neatly in the bell end. They knew nothing about the big feet and couldn't tell me how he had managed to pack them. His first speech, his first public showing of the invader, had gone off well before an assembly of students here at the University in Mérida. Professor Camacho Puut had introduced him in a guarded way. Art and Mike were there and they said Rudy had good stage presence, made a good appearance in his belted safari jacket, that the lecture was no worse than other lectures and didn't go on too long—not too much fullness. But they wondered at this foolish desire of his to distinguish himself in the world.

I was pleased for him myself. Erich von Däniken had never found the least bit of extraterrestrial flesh, as far as I knew, and here was Rudy Kurle with a complete captain all his own, if a small and very old one, unless it was an old *Indio*, or the king of the elves. Rudy was well launched on the career he had dreamed of, a life at the lectern, of captive listeners in jails and schools, of long days and nights spent hanging around the hallways of public buildings, radio stations and television studios, a life of confabulation. But why had Louise, such a ready talker, been mum about all this? Weren't they a team? Why had she not gone with him?

"Because I didn't want to go," she said.

There had been a row. She refused to give details, other than to say Rudy had gone off with all their papers and tapes. She took up an actress-like pose at the window with her back to me, not very effective, theatrically, here in the trailer, and I thought she was going to say something like, "My marriage is on the rocks, Jimmy." But she just stood there in unusual silence. That night I told her I was deeply grateful for all the nursing care and that I knew she must have a lot of things to catch up on back at her own place, back at the Casitas Lola.

"I don't live there now," she said. "This trailer is just as much mine as it is yours. More mine really. I have a moral right to it and yours is merely legal. On three separate occasions Emmett promised me that I was to have the Mobile Star. I've already moved out of the Casitas and got my deposit back. This is where I live now."

She held up a spare key Emmett had given her, to our one and only door.

CHARLES PORTIS

"Well, I don't see how you can do that, Louise. I mean you're welcome but I don't see how you can *live* here. A married woman."

"Rudy is not my husband, he's my brother. Everybody in town knows that now but you. Beth has known it all along. Emmett knew it. I can't believe you're so dense."

I hadn't seen this coming but I knew it to be true at once. I could see the faint but real resemblance now, something about the sunken blue eyes. She wore no ring on her finger, and I had seen no photograph of bride and groom stuffing hunks of wedding cake into each other's mouths, with their arms linked and their eyes goggling at the camera. The wedlock pretense was Rudy's idea, she said. He had important stenographic work for her to do at home, and with this arrangement she wouldn't be distracted from her duties by male callers. It would offer too a kind of flimsy protection against all those flirting Mexicans who would be inflamed by her sandy ringlets and make wet kissing noises at her on the street. I wondered how she got her deposit back from Lola. Other questions came to mind. What would become of my privacy?

"Your brother then. Well. I wouldn't have guessed that."

"No, of course not. You can't see things right under your nose. You never listen to what people are saying. You think you're so smart and you don't know what's going on half the time. You call yourself a salesman and it takes you two years to find out what anybody's name is. You won't confide in anybody. You won't tell people anything and that's why they don't tell you things."

"We'll talk about this later. When I'm feeling stronger."

"I'd rather talk about it now and get it settled."

"We'll see how it works out. We'll sit down and have a long talk about it when I'm feeling better."

"No, I'd rather not put it off. I've thought this over, and it can only work out in one of two ways. You can pack your things and go back to Fausto's place or you can stay here. But if you stay on here with me, it will have to be marriage. I'm not interested in setting up light housekeeping with you. Not with you healthy. Now there it is and you'll just have to make up your mind. You're badly mistaken if you think we're going to live here together in some common-law arrangement."

Here was another grenade, blinding white phosphorus this time. Until this moment the thought of marrying into the Kurle family had not entered my head. Rudy would be my brother-in-law, and there was another one back in Pennsylvania named Glenn Ford Kurle. Why would she pick me? What was this weakness Louise had for older men with red faces? Or was it that she saw me as going with the trailer, like the butane bottle? I had expected marriage to arrive in a different way, not so suddenly, and yet here we were together, already settled in at home with our Crock-Pot and our sectional plastic plates, trisected with little dividers to dam off the gravy from the peas, and already we were having a domestic scene of the kind I had heard about but which I thought came later. She wanted to talk about it some more. Louise enjoyed extended discussion. She had dropped out of the Textile Arts Club because they didn't have enough staff meetings to suit her, and the ones they had were too short. I told her we would see how it worked out and have a long talk about it at another time.

In a day or two I was on my feet again and able to creep about. Doc sent a boy over with a message, a command. *Bring my field notes back right away.* His dusty notebooks that I never wanted in the first place. Louise helped me get the box into the truck and we set off for Izamál. As we turned onto the Naroody block, I saw a white-haired old man unlocking the door at Foto Naroody.

"Look, there's Naroody."

Louise said, "That's not Naroody."

"Who is it then?"

"I don't know but it's not Naroody. Some cousin or employee. He's nothing at all like Naroody."

She claimed she had spoken to Naroody on several occasions and had even gotten money out of him for some charity or other. She claimed further that she was on these same familiar terms with yet another old man, *El Obispo,* who responded to no one. They had chatted. She had given him a pocket knife. His name was Arturo. This irritated me, being told of such things here on my own ground by a relative newcomer. But she knew nothing of how he changed himself into a dog at night. She thought I was making it up.

Already she had suggestions about home improvements. Would it be possible to get a telephone installed in the trailer? How about putting up a patio awning and buying some lawn chairs? Or how about putting wheels back on the trailer and going off on a trip to Costa Rica together? There was a thought. In my mind the Mobile Star was part of the landscape, a rooted object, and it hadn't occurred to me that the thing might be set rolling again. It hadn't occurred to me that Louise might have some good ideas. I had been unfair to her, unless this was the only one she was ever going to have. She had called me a bum and a vandal and an enemy of the human race. I thought she was slightly insane, and of a bone-deep lunacy not likely to be corrected by age. And yet we were comfortable enough together. We didn't get on each other's nerves in close confinement.

Doc said I could keep the twenty-two handkerchiefs but he wanted Gail to go over the notebooks and transcribe them, put them in order. "It was providential the way that girl was sent to me. She is perhaps my greatest find. Working is fun again. We have a lot of fun working together in the radio. Do you know what I'm going to do? I'm going to buy Gail a pretty red car to drive around town in. She wants an open car."

"Working in the radio?"

"In the studio, I mean." He dipped his hands into the box and stirred the notebooks about. "A lot of gold here. A good part of my life. How far did you get? Toward consolidating my notes?"

"Not very far."

He treated us to lunch, if that's the word, outdoors by the pool with Gail and Mrs. Blaney. Lorena the maid served some vegetable mess. Doc was on a new health program and so everybody else had to eat stewed weeds too. There was no meat on the table and no bread and butter and no *salsa,* red or green, and nothing to drink but mineral water. We could no longer smoke in his presence. He had thrown away his pipes. It was like eating with Hitler. Mrs. Blaney was watchful. She had her position to think of and she was still trying to take the measure of this plump Gail person who had moved into Don Ricardo's house and who dared to call him Dicky. Mrs. Blaney was wary, smiling, very quick to pass the salt and pepper to Gail. She no longer had the upper hand, and I felt sorry for her.

Doc pestered me with questions. He had heard some things about Dan from Refugio, though not the part about the shooting and killing. He thought that Danny, as he called him, had grudgingly turned the two kids over to us after a bit of palaver. But who was the fellow? What was he up to? What were his teachings?

"I don't know. I have no idea."

"But what are you saying? A prophet with no teachings? Look at what you're saying. Cuco has informed me that the fellow preys on children. A corrupter of children. A man with no regard or respect for innocence. All right. Then you go on to say that he has followers of a sort. Now I don't know about you but to me that implies teachings of some kind."

"I'm not saying he didn't have any teachings, I'm just saying I don't know what his teachings were."

"Excuse me, maybe I'm stupid today, but I fail to see how he can lead people around like that without some kind of teachings. Tell me this. Does he wear magnificent robes?"

"No."

"Just what was his business at Likín? Why should he go there, of all places?"

"I don't know that either."

"Can you tell us anything about his ritual? Were there lowland Mayan elements, for instance?"

"As far as I could see, no, none."

"To the best of your limited knowledge, that is."

"Very limited."

"Yes, that's the difference between us, you see. The complacent mind and the inquiring mind. You couldn't trouble yourself to ask a few simple questions. I would have given this Danny a grilling he wouldn't soon forget. I would have held his feet to the fire and shown him up for what he is. I would have dealt with him. You couldn't be bothered."

"We were in a hurry and I really didn't care what his teachings were."

"Too lazy to get involved," said Louise. "Character flaw."

"Exactly," said Doc. "Here's what it boils down to then. You want us to believe that this fellow has no natural gifts. A brute without the least trace of nobility in his features. A man with no winning ways, no message, no teachings whatsoever. And yet somehow he manages to gain ascendancy over these people. Correct me if I'm wrong."

He couldn't get a rise out of me and so he did the next best thing. What better way to annoy all the guests than to lecture them on ancient Indian ritual, on *Hunab Ku* or *Itzam*, the great lizard god, on the *Chacs* and the

Bacabs and the red goddess. Soon he was lost in that thicket himself, trying to describe a forgotten religion that was thought to be formless, creedless and without moral content. It was worse than a pottery talk. Even those who professed an interest in the subject were finally stupefied by it. It was a teeming and confused throng, the Maya pantheon, and no one had ever sorted it out in a very convincing way. Doc certainly wasn't going to do it here over lunch. Art and Mike had given up on it long ago. Their current theory was that everything about pre-Columbian America was completely misunderstood.

I took Gail aside after lunch and asked her about the Olmec jade. As long as we were calling in gifts I thought I would have a go at it. The little green *idolo* was worth several thousand dollars, I told her, and it wasn't Doc's to give away. There had been a misunderstanding. It was on loan. The piece really belonged to Refugio, and I knew she would want to see it returned.

But she no longer had it, or so she said. The thing had disappeared. She had last seen it in the hands of LaJoye Mishell Teeter. Perhaps the girl had stolen it. "I've looked and I've looked. Such a beautiful work too. I'm so sorry."

I said it didn't matter. Good riddance. Let it remain in the piney woods of Florida. Art and Mike thought all the virtue had probably gone out of it anyway, the spirit fled, as with objects in museums. I said to her that Doc still had a bad gray look, for all his sparkle and new plans, and I urged her to press on with the big book and get it done *de prisa*. Time was short. Get on with it. That was my advice to Gail.

"It's going to be quite a job," she said.

Quite a job. This peculiar girl gave out even less information than I did. She was humoring me, almost defying me to make some comment on the new situation here. The water in the pool was still and no leaf trembled on the bushes. It was a warm day in January. She wore a loose flowery housedress to show that she was at home, that she was receiving guests at her home. She was at perfect ease. I suspected that she still had the jade. I couldn't be sure. This pool and this big house would soon be hers, too. A clean sweep for Gail. While I wound up with the handkerchiefs and the trailer. She was dedicated to bennee, all right. Well, she had her way to make in the world, too, just like the rest of us, but I thought she was lying through her teeth and still had Refugio's jade man. I was pretty sure of it, if not absolutely sure, and now I wondered too about Denise's lost contact lenses at the Holiday Inn and how they came to be lost.

"Yes, but I believe you can handle the job, Gail, if you put your mind to it."

"Do you think so?"

"I know you can. By the way, you owe me some money for gasoline."

"What? Oh, I see, you're charging me for the ride. I didn't realize. How much does it come to?"

"Let's say twenty dollars."

"So much? And you want it now? This minute?"

"If it's convenient."

"My purse is upstairs in our bedroom. But I tell you what. Maybe this will do. That should cover all expenses, don't you think?"

The loose dress had two pockets and from one of them she had taken a heavy silver coin, badly out of round and worn down smooth as a river pebble. It was an old Spanish dollar, a piece of eight. She had found the trunk in the attic. Already she had been into Doc's coin hoard with her plump little starfish hands.

"Yes, this will settle it."

"I should think so. Eight reales. It will make a nice memento for you, too, from Dicky's last *entrada.*"

I was sure of it now—she still had the jade. LaJoye Mishell was no thief. Well, let Gail keep the thing and much good may it do her. Or maybe I would speak to Doc about it later. Refugio came out of it well enough anyhow, with his big pipe sale and the pop-top trailer that he claimed as a forfeit. The shooting out in the woods became a pivotal date for him, replacing another memorable occasion— *That time we changed out the ring-and-pinion gears.* It made him laugh every time he thought of it. What a filthy knuckle-busting job. I wouldn't do that again if you gave me the bus. We were repairing the differential of an old school bus. The shop manual said it was a six-hour job for one man and it took Refugio and Valentín and me three days. But now the ring-and-pinion comedy had given way to—*That time we killed the pagans.* Now Refugio would place some event by saying, "It was before that time we killed the pagans," or, "It wasn't long after that night we killed the pagans in the rain."

Louise had me stop at the In-Between Club on the way back. She wanted to check up on Shep and see what he was doing with Emmett's money, which wasn't a bad idea.

The place was darker in the afternoon than it was at night. Cribbs was standing alone at the near end of the bar, away from the strangers. Louise warned him that this day drinking would kill him, just as it had killed Emmett, and not only that but he never gave blood to the Red Cross either. "You old barflies never do anything for anybody and you never do anything to promote international understanding." Cribbs told her that a bottle of beer or two in the afternoon wouldn't hurt a baby. He told Cosme to bring me one and he said let us all drink to better days. Louise went to confer with Shep in the office.

Back in the shadows the strangers were talking about UFO's. Some new blood in town. It didn't take long for arriving gringos to nose out this place. One of the voices, a high-pitched drone, overrode the others and made me think of Wade Watson, but I knew he was gone. This fellow had the floor. He spoke with the insistence of an expert and he kept interrupting the others, who made themselves out to be sensible, judicious men, open-minded but no fools. They deferred to him. It wasn't enough, their good will. They were out of their depth, and the scornful expert wanted to show up their ignorance. He had them reeling with his command of detail. They could have used some tips from Art and Mike, who had refined the position of having it both ways right down to a fare-thee-well. Art and Mike conceded the existence of flying saucers as a general proposition but refused to believe in any particular sighting or landing.

The strangers began to drift away. A small fire erupted on the bar back there. Cosme beat it out with a wet rag. The droning fellow came edging up toward me.

"Sir? Sir? Excuse me? Sir? May I relate a personal experience?"

I saw him in the light now. It *was* Wade, dirty and smelly and rumpled. The police had let him go, poor Wade, into Louise's care, on the condition that she get him out of the country. She thought she had done so, having taken him to the airport and put him on his honor, if not actually on a plane. He missed the flight and had been hanging about town ever since.

He recognized me. "Oh yes, you. Burns, isn't it? The nosey one with all the questions. Are you very busy right now? May I relate an interesting personal experience?"

I couldn't get anything out of him before. Now there was no shutting him up. Cribbs knocked back the rest of his beer and stumbled away in haste, but it seems to me you must let a haunted man make his report.

"All right. Sure."

"Thank you. First, who am I? I am a payroll programmer for the state of Missouri and I wear nice shirts and nice suits when I'm at home. I live in a garage apartment, which suits me, though I could afford something much, much nicer. It's comfortable enough and very private. I sleep upstairs, alone, needless to say, and my bedroom window faces southwest. At a little after 11 o'clock on the night of August third I was awakened by an expiring rush of air. Then there came a pulsing light and a low-frequency hum, or a sort of throbbing. There really is no name for this disturbance I heard, and felt more than heard. Now it is important for you to understand, Mr. Burns, that I am not a repeater. Get that through your head. This was my first and only contact. I am a professional man with a peptic ulcer and chronic scalp problems. Otherwise I enjoy normal good health. In my spare time I write stories of a speculative nature, if you want to hold that against me. People like you would call them fantasy or science fiction. Other hobbies? Well, I enjoy certain light operas. I play polka tunes on the concertina for my own amusement and for the entertainment of my friends. And yes, I am a student of the great Maya civilization, but that is not invariably a sign of madness. In my room the light rose and fell, in phase with the hum. There was sharp pressure on my chest. . . ."

He made a smooth story of it. Two shining androids one meter tall came through his window and stood at the foot of his bed. They wore white coveralls. They spoke a guttural, synthesized English and put it across to him that he must go soon to the ancient home of "the old earth mutants," which was Mayaland in Mexico, there to await— "something incommunicable." Always that. I was waiting for it, the point at which things go blurred. Wade said he had written a long account of his bedroom contact and that it was published in a UFO newsletter called *Gamma Bulletin*, out of Tempe, Arizona. The October edition was given over entirely to his story, an unprecedented event. No other contributor had ever been so honored.

Then, in the November issue, there came further instructions for him, via the mail this time, in the form of a letter to the editor from the city of Mérida, in Mexico. It was dated "End of the Fifth Creation," and in this letter Wade was told that he must come to the eastern beach of a small seaside town called Progreso, in Yucatán. He must wait there "near the turn of the year" and be patient. After a brief period of observation he would be met there and led to an ancient city in the heart of the Petén forest. This was the City of Dawn. Certain things would be revealed to him there. The letter was signed "*El Mago.*" Underneath it, Wade said, the editor of *Gamma Bulletin* had appended a note stating that while he personally could not vouch for the authenticity of this *El Mago*, he could say that the Petén jungle was known with certainty to be an ancient mutation center. Furthermore, it was reported to be active again, in current and quite heavy use as an entry window.

So Wade came to Mérida, but then he began to lose heart and stall around. He couldn't be sure of the appointed day. He was afraid it had passed with the coming of the new year. The day had come and gone, and he had hesitated out of fear. He couldn't bring himself to leave town. He felt safe enough in Mérida but the countryside of Mexico was an unknown place of terror to him. He feared bandits, strange hot food, stinging plants, unsanitary pillows, transport breakdown. He was afraid to get on a bus or take a taxicab to Progreso, twenty miles away on a perfectly good paved highway. Now he was broke and had lost his suitcase and his credit card.

As it happened, I said, some friends and I had visited this same City of Dawn just a few weeks back.

"What? You? Not the real city in the jungle?"

"The Likín ruin, yes."

"But you weren't there at the first of the year."

"We were, yes."

"I don't understand. Why would you be there?"

"No special reason. We were just going down the river at the time."

"This is amazing. You were actually on ground zero. What happened?"

"Nothing much. Some hippies were there."

"*El Mago?* You saw him?"

"No, I don't believe he showed."

"But I wonder if you would even recognize him. Was there a faint smell of ammonia in the air?"

"Not that I noticed."

"Muriatic acid?"

"I wouldn't know that smell."

"Any animal panic?"

"The monkeys were howling."

"Monkeys! I hadn't counted on monkeys! Did you see anyone collecting leaves or soil samples? Usually these creatures work in pairs. But only one carries the sample bag. Two busy little shining men."

"I didn't see anything like that."

"Any aerial phenomena?"

"No. Well, yes, it rained. That's about it. Some hippies were there and had a kind of party."

"Wearing white coveralls? Calling themselves the Children of the Sun?"

"Not in so many words. I don't remember hearing those exact words. They did talk some about the sun. A few of them were wearing coveralls."

"You say the monkeys were howling."

"Yes, but that's what they do. They're howler monkeys."

"Likín. I've seen it often in my dreams but the light is so poor in my dreams. It must have been a hard trip."

"Not all that hard. It takes a few days to get there, but it's accessible enough. Once you reach the river it's nothing more than a boat ride."

"I wonder. The rain. The monkeys. Not much in that. But something may have happened and you didn't recognize it for what it was. Some small thing. Something arbitrary—something—of grace. A tiny pressure surge or some slight shift in the balance of things. The significance may have escaped you."

"That's possible."

"What are people here whispering about me behind my back?"

"I don't believe I've heard anything."

"I see. You're going to be polite. I wouldn't have expected that. Most of the Americans here are of a very crude type. The kind who would fire .22 shorts at superior beings, the way those barnyard louts did in Texas last May. Never mind, let me tell you what they're saying." He stuck his thumbs in his belt, in what he took to be barroom swagger, and spoke in what he took to be our comical lingo. "'That there feller? Why I reckon he's plumb loco, Clem!' Well, you can just inform your pals that their ignorant remarks don't bother me in the least. I merely consider the source."

He had nothing to say about his jail time. I gave him my opinion that it was less dangerous in the countryside than in the cities. I asked if he had ever heard of a place called the Gulf of Molo, but he was no longer listening to me or talking to me. Cosme told me that Wade had been here most of the day and had set little fires here and there, on the tables and the bar. He would tear paper napkins into strips and make mounds of them and set fire to them.

"We can't have that, *Señor Jaime. No le hace asi.* It won't do."

"No, it won't."

I sent over to the Bugambilia Cafe for a chicken sandwich on toast, always good. Wade ate it in silence, and then Louise and I took him back to the airport. She told him that he had let her down and that he really must go home this time.

"I can't get you out of jail again. If the police find you here they're going to lock you up. You don't want that, do you?"

"No."

"This will all blow over. You can come back another time when you're feeling better and go to the Forbidden City."

"The City of Dawn."

"That's what I meant to say."

"Too late for me now. I had my chance. I didn't measure up."

Wade was agreeable enough in his distracted way. He went where we pointed him and stopped when we stopped. He stood perfectly still, but rigid, like a dog being washed, as I turned out his pockets and removed all matches. There was no luggage—he had lost that on the first go-round. The woman at the Mexicana counter rolled her eyes and groaned and in the end agreed to honor his expired ticket. Louise thought we should take our leave of him in the departure lounge. To linger on and hover would be insulting. We had his word. But that wasn't my idea of seeing Wade off. I said no, we would wait here until he was boarded and the hatch dogged down behind him and the plane airborne, until wheels up at the very earliest. We waited, behind tinted glass. We watched from a distance as the passengers straggled across the hot concrete, and I thought I saw Chip and Diane in identical red knit shirts going up the boarding stairway, if that was their names. They carried matching green duffel bags and disappeared into the belly of the plane before I could be certain. Then Wade Watson taking his mechanical man steps. He was embarked. We didn't see him again.

It was now late afternoon and Louise had another errand, which was to give *El Obispo* his $50. She had talked Shep out of it, though strictly speaking the old man didn't meet the conditions of Emmett's will, being neither blind, nor, as far as anyone knew, musical. It couldn't have been easy, getting money out of Shep. She had kept after him. "He knew somewhere in his false heart that I was right."

I dropped her off downtown and then went to the zoo for a quick look at the fine new jaguar. It was embarrassing. I had traveled all up and down the south and east of Mexico, and over into Belize and Guatemala, much of it on foot, and still I had to go to the zoo like everybody else to see this wonderful beast. He was a big fellow, built low to the ground, all rounded muscle, a heavy cat, nothing at all like the bony puma with his long legs and lank folds of skin. He paced about behind the bars taking no notice of us. Some children stood there with me and spoke in whispers. His coat was a light orange. The spots were black rosettes and broken black rings, and in the center of the rings there were black dots. It was a map of the starry night sky, but I couldn't read it. People here were right to call him *the* tiger.

A quick look and out for me. The place was fairly well kept, but I could never stay long. My mother didn't approve of zoos. She took things as they came, and it was always startling when she expressed some strong opinion like that. We would stop and look at each other, startled members of the Burns family, when she came out with something like that. She didn't approve of circus clowns. They were only making fun of tramps, she said, and poor fun it was. I wondered if in fact I had missed something back there at Likín. I couldn't read that pattern either. The surge, the slippage, the convergence, the vibrations, the whiff of ammonia, the design—all was lost on me. Rudy had said, correctly, that I was an untrained observer, and Wade thought I was incapable of recognizing any sign or portent short of a crack in the earth. Wade, of course, may have gotten his instructions wrong, or the androids may have lied to him, though you don't expect such radiant creatures to be jokers, swooping down on Jefferson City with their light show to have some fun with Wade Watson. You don't raise the point. You never question the veracity of the invaders.

Louise was talking to *El Obispo,* or Arturo, as she called him, on the shady side of the cathedral. Always he came back to this sanctuary. He was slumped against the wall. Did he ever go inside? Take communion? I waited by the truck, eating popcorn from a sack, thinking she should leave him alone. *Born to Meddle*. She should have had that tattooed across her forehead, to give people notice. It was a one-way chat. She had lied to me about getting a response out of the ragged old man. I was learning more about her day by day. She had a heavy tread for such a small person, coming down harder on her heels than I would have liked. Floor joists creaked under her step. I would come to recognize it at a distance, that smart little step, if I went blind, and take comfort in it, knowing my soup was on the way. Here was another thing. Where I spoke to myself, properly, in the second person, she used the third. If she dropped a coin, for instance, she would put her fists on her hips and say, "Well! Look at Louise! Just throwing her money away!" She wanted me to buy some new shirts and stop wearing boxer shorts and rearrange my hair, let it grow out into a bush and fluff it up in some way. She wanted me to confide in her and tell her my long-range plans that I couldn't bear to disclose. She wanted me to start reading nature books. We were both early risers. That had worked out well enough. She made a good meatloaf, with a nice crust, the way I like it. She knew how to make deviled eggs. She wasn't a bad cook and she didn't mind cooking.

But no, she hadn't lied. Here was *El Obispo* on his feet all of a sudden, chattering away at her, and this time about something other than the doomed towers of man. "*¡Izquierda!*" he said, flinging one hand around and around. "*¡Siempre a la izquierda!* Always to the left!"

What had roused him was her mention of the night dog. He held the dollars she had given him in one claw and made wild gestures with the other. Still he spoke with his head down. The people of Mérida, he said, were wrong to associate him with the dog, just as they were wrong and profane to call him The Bishop. He had nothing to do with the animal. He, Arturo, went one way and the dog went another. The courses they took around town were entirely different. The little dog was far too proud, like his master, a sly man, but there was no mystery about him. He was a *pelón*, a hairless *xolo* or *sholo* dog, with cropped ears, owned by a rich man, proud and sly, who turned him out every night, as with a cat. The dog made a patrol around town, stopping for nothing, going always at a trot to the left, in a diminishing spiral, until he fetched up back home in the early hours. That was his way. That was his habit, his daily exercise. Nothing more. This was the true story of the night dog, and the ignorant people of Mérida were wrong to say otherwise, to say that he, Arturo, was possessed and in demonic league with the proud little dog. They told other lies about him, too! They said that he, Arturo, stole milk! And lapped it up like a dog! That he ate no more than a snake! Just gobbled down a rat or a frog every two or three weeks! One day they would answer for their lies! And for every idle word they spoke!

He was worried that Louise might go away with the wrong idea. She might go away foolishly thinking that the dog sometimes turned to the right on his circuit, "*¡Izquierda!*" he shouted at her, making a loop with his gnarled hand. "*¡A la izquierda!*"

What a word. A truly sinister mouthful for so simple an idea as *left*. Louise found it all convincing enough. The mystery was dispelled. So much for me and my unnatural dog. I let it go without argument but I didn't believe a word of it. The night dog had a sleek red coat and a curling tail with a bit of fringe. His tail was a kind of plume. His ears were uncropped. A *sholo,* on the other hand, is naked as a jaybird, with shiny black skin, and with sweat glands, too, unlike other dogs, and with the tail of a rat. I knew my *sholo* dogs. *El Obispo* had cooked up the story. He was sly, like his invented rich man, and proud too in his rags. I offered him what was left of my popcorn, my *palomitas de maíz*, my little doves of corn, but he had already dropped down to his resting place against the thick yellow masonry and was safely back inside his own head again.

A few hippies were passing through town, not so many as before. I looked them over, half expecting to see some of the Jumping Jack stragglers. Sometimes I thought I saw one. There were days, certain hot afternoons, when the sightings were frequent. It was like watching a wave of alarm running through a prairie dog village, the way I saw their Jumping Jack heads jumping up here and there before me. But it was always someone else. Louise wanted me to stop looking these people over. She thought I should put away my Blue Sheets and my flashlight and stop working for Gilbert. I said I would have to think about it. We had to have some money from somewhere. There were no remittances coming in. I knew I would miss going out at night and putting my light in their faces.

LOUISE WAS addicted to dramatic gestures, and I had the feeling she would wake up some morning and announce that she was going to law school, or that she had decided to open up a metaphysical bookshop, some such bolt from the blue as that. She knew that my conversation, no bargain now, must soon be that of an old coot, all complaint and gloomy prophecy. We went ahead with the marriage all the same. Soledad Bravo said the auspices were fair, good enough, *bastante*, if not entirely favorable. She had seen a spider laying eggs in a dark closet. But then she had seen worse omens in January. It was surprising how fast I moved on the thing, at my age, with so few reservations, how quickly I became a husband, and an indulgent one at that.

We were married at Doc's house. Louise had a friend, Aurélio, who came by and sang, with an accompanist. It was the first time I had ever heard that grand piano played. I didn't know Aurélio and I was expecting some fat little man in frilly white shirt and tiny black plastic shoes with a Mexican night club *quiverando* delivery, some fellow sobbing out that Granada would live again. Not at all. I couldn't have been more wrong. Aurélio was a young college student with a crystal-pure tenor voice and no tricks. He sang "Because God Made Me Thine," first in Spanish and then in English.

Because—you come to me with naught save love ...

Aurélio brought tears to my eyes, and to everybody's eyes. We took the Mobile Star down to Costa Rica, stopping uneasily in Guatemala only for gasoline, where they sell it not by the liter but by the gringo gallon. We were getting the hang of trailer life. It was like towing a barge. It was like living on a small boat, or in a bank vault. We went to the Pacific side of Costa Rica, to the Nicoya Gulf, and set up camp near a village called Lepanto. Here in the bay water Louise went fishing for the first time in her life. She took up fishing with my little freshwater rod and spinning reel, and I couldn't get her to stop. We had the place pretty much to ourselves. Some kids came over from the village now and then to look at us. At night the crabs dragged themselves about over the sand and fought over our potato peelings. One afternoon a motorcycle came roaring in through the palm grove. A young American couple dismounted and took off their helmets and set up a tent on the sand. They wanted to know where they were. They borrowed a funnel and then a bar of soap. Then a towel. Then a crescent wrench.

We had them over for supper. They had been to Panama, to the end of the road in the Darién jungle, and were now making their way back to Denver. Louise asked if they meant to stay on for a while.

The girl, offended, said, "What? Here? No, we're not beach people."

Snubbed on our honeymoon by a female biker. We fed them anyway and fed them well on boiled lobster tails and melted butter. Their plan, when they left home, was to go to a place called the City of Dawn—in Mexico, they thought it was—but they had no map and couldn't figure out how to get there. They had asked questions along the way, but that was unsatisfactory too, as most of the answers they got were in a foreign tongue. Once started, though, rolling on was the thing, inertial forces at play, and so they had continued south down the isthmus until they came up against a forest wall deep in Panama, where the road stopped dead in their faces, at the Darién gap. Their pilgrimage had turned into a brainless endurance run. The boy, who had some name like Rusty or Lucky, said he had learned about the City of Dawn from a very interesting report in a magazine I would never have heard of, called *Gamma Bulletin*. I asked if he had a copy.

"No, I don't keep things."

Not even a map. Too programmed and stifling for their taste. He still wasn't quite sure where he was. He was much surprised that we had heard of the City and the UFO magazine, and a little doubtful that we actually knew the writer of the article.

"The same Wade Watson?" he said. "There are probably a lot of people going around claiming to be him. I sure would like to talk to that guy sometime, the real Wade Watson, just me and him rapping together. That contact of his is already one of the most famous in all the literature."

The girl said she no longer believed there was such a place as the City of Dawn, or that there was a real person named Wade Watson. She said she had learned how to sleep on a moving motorcycle, with her heels hooked on the foot pegs, or how to go into a restful trance anyhow. She was homesick and weary of straddling the noisy bike day after day. Their appetite was good. They made short work of our tasty *langostinos* and said goodnight. In the morning they were gone. One of them—Louise suspected the girl—stole a jar of grape jelly from us. But there it was, independent confirmation from this Randy or Rocky, or at least evidence enough for me, that Wade Watson and *Gamma Bulletin* were behind the whole business. It was good enough to settle the point for me and put my mind at rest. A kind of rest. Wade had started the thing rolling with his curious pulsing dream, but he wasn't *El Mago*.

We got back to Mérida in March. There were no nasty letters for me. The hate mail had stopped for good, and I rather missed it. Doc and Gail were working away. Mrs. Blaney was still in place, hanging on. Alma was dead and buried in the warm sand of Yucatán. They had put her in on top of Karl's bones, to save the cost of a separate plot, about seven dollars. The Posada Fausto was still for sale. McNeese was living there now, in Alma's old room, and Art and Mike had taken a double room upstairs. They said the rush of events was over. Nothing at all was going on. The sea gathers force and breaks at last on the ninth and greatest wave. Then the ebb. Fausto said there were no such neat cycles in his life. Things never let up, no matter what he did. He said a man would make any bargain, however degrading, to have peace at home, and that the radio people in Mexico City should put the story of his life on the radio for all to hear and call it "Female Complaints."

It was odd seeing Art and Mike without their soft white straw hats. They had taken to sitting around all day like convalescents in their bathrobes and socks. Louise got the impression that they meant to sit there in the lobby like that from now on, not venturing out much anymore. She had a premonition that they would end up there with their pictures on the wall, in Fausto's gallery of the fallen, perhaps dead in a suicide pact. Art and Mike had a dark side, she said, that I was unwilling to see or too dense to see. "You and Fausto don't know what's going on half the time." There was something about them, my friends the Munn brothers, that she didn't care for. "Two smart guys living in smug obscurity," she said of them.

She found us a shady spot under a tree at an older and cheaper trailer park. On the first day there I killed a *cascabel* at our doorstep, a rattlesnake, what Alma called a *Klapperschlange*. Try to save a few pesos on the rent and you end up beating off pit vipers.

She was the one, old Alma, it turned out, who had sent me the poison pen letters. You never really know where you stand with anyone. There I was secretly preening myself over my good deeds and all the time she despised me. My clumsy gestures of help must have been intolerable for her. It was Louise who caught it, not me. She had a good eye and she showed me how the typing from Alma's *máquina* matched that of the letters. She said the spite-ful old woman had too much time on her hands and had probably sent many such letters to any number of people, an old mama spider dropping her venomous eggs here and there in secret places. Alma was Ah Kin and Alvarado and Mr. Rose. She was *El Mago* too. I wasn't too dense to see that. She had written the City of Dawn letter.

Louise said a plastic owl would have frightened the snake away. Why had I not set out a dummy owl, a great horned owl made of plastic? I told her it would have taken a plastic owl nine feet tall to get the attention of that *cascabel,* and I pointed out further that it was an eagle, not an owl, with a writhing snake in his beak, that the Mexicans had adopted as their national symbol. She said I should have picked the snake up on a pole and flung him over into someone else's space. Let someone else deal with him, with his horny tail plates klappering away. Keep the blood off our hands. I had no pole. With anyone else's difficulty Louise always assumed a plastic owl or a handy pole of just the right length. I didn't go out of my way to kill snakes, she knew that, but neither would I have these big fellows gliding around underfoot in my yard.

It was called The Five of May Trailer Park. On the third day Eli Withering showed up in an old Cadillac. Plenty of room in that cruiser to stretch out his long legs. Or rather it was the middle of the third night. He came tapping on the window glass with his thick yellow fingernails, of some layered, hoof-like material, which he could have used for screwdrivers. He made quite a racket. "Hey! In there!" he called out. "About time to warsh this old wore-out truck out here, ain't it?" I turned on the floodlight and went outside shirtless to greet him. He was clean-shaven

and his hair was trimmed. He stood beside a pale green
Coupe de Ville with a white vinyl top.

"Put out the light," he said. "I don't want anybody to
see me. They told me you got Emmett's trailer. Not a bad
deal for you. I didn't know it would roll. Here's something
else you won't mind."

He switched on a flashlight and counted out my
$500 on the hood of the car.

"What, it wasn't enough?"

"A thousand wouldn't have been enough. Sauceda
took it, all right, for all the good it done me. What he didn't
tell me was that the federal *acusador* already had me lined
up for an Article Thirty-three."

"I told you to get Nardo."

"He might have put it off a day or two, that's all. Naw,
they wanted me out bad. I was gone the next morning for
moral turpitude on top of abusing the hospitality of the
Republic and disturbing the national patrimony."

He paused and then counted off two more twenties.
Interest, he called it. "There. Past due but there it is."

"I wasn't worried about it."

"Then you should have been, Budro. I wouldn't be
here except I need to talk some business."

A sleeping woman lay sprawled across the back seat.
"That's Freda." He said he was living with her in Belize
now, it made for a change of air. He was scouting around
and working some ruins, mostly picked over. Lately he had
found one in the hills up from the Sarstún River. It was
small but untouched and he wanted me to help with the
excavation. The fever was on him.

"People down there don't know what they're doing. They missed the causeway. It's just like the ones at Tikál, and I saw what it was right off. At least three temple mounds. They look like spurs off a hill and that's why nobody can see them. We'll have it all to ourselves. We'll cut three quick trenches and see what we've got. Then a month's hard work and we'll skim the cream and be out. I'll split right down the middle with you. One month and we're out clean with a nice haul. I guarantee it. Or two months at the most. We'll move a hundred cubic yards of dirt, just you and me. Look at this. I turned this up in the first hour, just poking around with a machete."

It was a small alabaster figure of a seated fat man. His arms were folded across his belly and his cheeks were puffed out. One hand was missing. He looked like the pink plastic pig on Louise's key chain.

"Not bad. It's old."

"Old? It's pre-classic white goods. How much of that stuff do you see? And that's a surface find. Keep it. Go ahead. You just keep that little booger. For me that's a cull."

No one was better at this work than Eli, snuffling around in the woods like a pine rooter hog. A steady and silent digger, too, from daylight to dark, stopping only now and then to gulp warmish water from a jug, or to eat two or three strips of raw bacon, with his head thrown back in the way of a sword swallower.

"The thing is, I'm out of the business, Eli."

"Yeah, I know you say that. Once you see this place you'll change your mind. It won't hurt you to take a look

at it. I'm telling you, man, I'm on to something here.
Valuable early stuff. We won't even mess with the pots.
My luck is turning. I got me a good car now. The niggers
are right. Buy old Cadillacs and expensive shoes and white
corn meal. I found me a good woman, too. If you're real
lucky you might find you a woman like Freda one of these
days, but I doubt it. What do you say?"

"I'll think it over."

"Don't think too long."

"Why don't you get Rex Tully? He's down there
somewhere, isn't he?"

"Him? Whining all the time? In his two-tone shoes?
You can't get that guy to do any work. Always down with
his risons or his hernia or the pink-eye or something. He
wouldn't last two days." "Risons" (risings) was Eli's word
for boils.

"He's not all that bad. Tyrannosaurus Rex. He's good
company anyway."

"He's bad enough. You can have him. I don't want no
part of him myself. Let me tell you what he's doing. Him
and his pal Fisher, this deserter from the British Navy, have
got this old rotten wooden boat anchored out there behind
the breakwater. Rex says they're going to load it up with
live birds and go to Florida, him and this English wino that
you couldn't trust for one minute out of your sight. Little
silky green birds that sing. Rex says the Cubans in Miami
will pay big money for these birds. But just this certain
kind of bird. They all want one of these birds at home.
They miss their birds. They can't get the kind of birds they
want in Florida."

Louise was stirring inside. She said, "Who is it, Jimmy?"

"An art student."

"Well. Why are you standing around out there in the dark? Bring him in and I'll make some coffee."

"All right."

I passed on the invitation. "Come on. Wake up your friend. We'll have something to eat."

"Who is that you got in there?"

"I don't think you know her. It's a girl I married. Louise Kurle."

"Married. God almighty. They didn't tell me that."

He was hesitant to wake his woman, and then did so in a gentle way, leaning through the car window. He touched her. They spoke. He popped back out and said, "Naw. Freda's not hungry. She's been eating soft cheese all night. We can't stay long. I didn't even stop at Shep's. I ain't got paper one and I got to be back across the Hondo River before sunup. I'm in with a couple of guys there at the border. They work out of the fumigation shack. Here, let me show you something else."

He threw up the big trunk lid and dragged out a wooden box with an open end. Inside the box there was a ramp with riffle bars—narrow wooden strips nailed down in a pattern of broken V's—and at the bottom a swatch of carpeting to trap particles of gold. It was a homemade sluice box.

"See? We can work the fast streams, too, while we're at it. How about it? I found the place and got everything lined out and still I'm giving you half. You won't never get a better deal than that and you know it."

The woman was fully awake now. She got out of the car and stretched her long arms, then got back in—the front seat this time.

I said, "You might take her with you."

"Who? Freda? What makes you think I would take a nice lady out in them stinking woods?"

"She could help around the camp while you dig."

"I wouldn't never let her live like that. We got us a nice little apartment in Belize City with a balcony and a kitchenette and a propane cookstove. Up in the front room is where we have our couch and our record player and our magazines. That's where we sit at night when we want to listen to our music or look through our magazines. That's our place on Euphrates Avenue that I got fixed up real nice for her. The mattress on the bed is all hogged down and wallered out in the middle but we're going to get a new one. What makes you think I would let her live like a pig out in them woods? Freda don't even drink. She knows how to keep books and that's a good trade to know. Bookkeepers can go anywhere and get work any time they want it, like sign painters."

He gave me his address on Euphrates Avenue and said he would wait two weeks for me and no longer. I was to bring all my tools and a roll of coarse-mesh screen wire for sifting boxes and my three-burner Coleman stove and a can of white gasoline.

"But you ain't coming, are you, Budro?"

"No, I'm not."

I said I probably wouldn't be venturing out much anymore, into the *selva*. He opened the car door, and a pomegranate rolled out. Neither of us made a move to pick it up. A sour and messy fruit. Somebody gives you one and you haul it around until it turns black or rolls away out of your life. He introduced me to Freda. In the light of the dome lamp, I saw her face for the first time tonight. It was Beany Girl, all cleaned up and looking pretty good in a white shirt with faint blue stripes. Her hair was tied up with a blue ribbon, and there was some more blue on her eyelids. She was coordinating her colors these days. She was brushing her hair and washing her face and even painting it. But still jumping into cars, it seemed, like LaJoye Mishell Teeter. She had put on a pound or two. Beany Girl was getting regular meals now out of the kitchenette, and perhaps snacking a bit on that couch. Eli and Beany Girl at home with their magazines. An evening at home with the Witherings.

"Glad to meet you, Freda."

"Hi."

"You doing all right tonight?"

"Yeah, I'm okay."

A spark there of the old defiance. She recognized me, all right. I had some questions for her but I couldn't think of how to put them, with Eli standing there. He showed me some of the advanced features of the Cadillac radio, how in the scanning mode the needle would glide across the dial and stop for a bit on the stronger signals. I told him I wouldn't be needing my three-burner stove and he could take the thing along if he wanted it. He went to get it out of the back of my truck.

Beany Girl spoke to me without looking at me. "All right, it's me. So what? What have you got to say to that? I knew I would run into you again somewhere. I told Dan we weren't through with you."

"I heard you left him at Flores."

"You heard right, Curtis."

"Good move. What happened there?"

"That's my business. I suppose now you'll go running off to tell him where I am."

"No, we won't be seeing Dan anymore. Dan is right where he ought to be."

"That's how much you know."

"I know he's gone."

"That's what you think. You don't know him. There was a girl in Seattle who refused to dance with him. It stayed on his mind real bad and he came back two years later and smothered her with a pillow. You don't know his powers. He'll find me if he takes a notion to."

"Not this time. He's dead."

"Where? What happened? I don't believe it. How do you know? He hasn't completed his mission yet. Dan has a glorious destiny."

"He's gone, don't worry. The mission didn't work out."

"Who told you about Flores?"

"That's my business."

"Do you know for a fact that he's dead?"

"Wild pigs are feeding on Dan. You can take my word for it, Beany Girl."

"I still don't believe it. Are you going to tell Eli about me? Well, go ahead and see if I care."

"Why would I do that?"

"Do you know what happened to Little Red? I keep thinking about her. Do you remember that little skinny girl?"

"She's okay. The Mexican boy, too, if you're interested. It's a little late in the day for you to be worrying about them, isn't it?"

If there had been a hatchet on the seat, she would have split my skull with it. "I wish Eli would tear your head off. He could do it too."

"You think so? He's certainly got the reach on me. I think he might want to quit before I did. Hard to say. But you may be right. I better not start anything."

"All right, I should have taken those kids with me but I was afraid of Dan. You don't know how it was. I had to slip away in the night. You don't know anything at all about his powers. He was a beautiful man five years ago. You don't know anything about me either. You think I'm just some old trashy bag but you don't know the first thing about me. I don't suppose you ever made any bad mistakes in your life, Curtis. You think you're a just man too, just like Dan does."

I asked her about the Gulf of Molo. Where was it? What was it? She was going to give me some kind of answer, too, but then the trunk lid came down with a thud and here was Eli again. Anything in the way of a door *El Zopilote* shut with decisive force. The stove was packed away in the trunk—and so was my Coleman lantern, I learned later, with a box of spare mantles. He gave me his hand.

"We got to get on the road. You give it some hard thought now. If I don't see you in two weeks, I'll catch you sometime on the go-around. I'll holler at you one of these days. Tell everybody at Shep's to kiss my ass. Don't let your plow get caught in a root, Budro."

He drove away at a creep, lights out, down the lane of darkened trailers, and when he reached the highway his headlights blazed up and he honked once.

The only lighted box in the park was our Mobile Star. The coffee was made and so Louise and I sat up in our own kitchenette and had coffee and broken cookies from the Hoolywood bakery. She wanted the names of my visitors for her diary, to get it up to date, right up to the minute, the last event of the day duly recorded. *Some people named Eli and Beany Girl came to call from Belize in an old Cadillac*. Rudy sometimes made false entries in his diary, she said, and he saw nothing wrong in the practice. We talked some about going home, or I talked about it, going back to Shreveport. Louise thought we should stay on here for a while.

"It's early in the year. Let's give Mérida another year."

She knew she could count on me to put things off. She had a plan, too, and nothing to do with sitting on a rock and watching milk goats this time. If we could get loans from Beth and Dr. Flandin, she said, we could make a down payment on Fausto's hotel. My good friend Refugio Bautista could be a partner and serve as the owner of record. Fausto himself might be persuaded to carry the note. We could have our own hotel on Calle 55. Neither of us had ever learned a useful trade, but we weren't dumb.

We were quite capable of managing a narrow hotel. After all, we weren't genuine drifters, not by nature. We weren't really beach people. You had to commit to something. You finally had to plant a tree somewhere.

"What do you think?"

It wasn't a bad idea, if we could put together the down money and get some long-term credit. She had thought it all out. A mom-and-pop hotel, with mom no doubt perched behind the cash register all day. There was no telling what innovations she had in mind for the old Posada. I feared debt and already I missed going out at night and putting my light in people's faces but it was a better plan than any plan of mine and I said we would see. I said we would talk some more about it. It comes to me now, late, as I wind this up, what it was those hippies were singing on the hilltop above the river. It was "My Darling Clementine," a good song.